Giddy Moment

Giddy Moment

ERNESTINE GILBRETH CAREY

Little, Brown and Company · *Boston* · *Toronto*

Published simultaneously in Canada
by Little, Brown & Company (Canada) Limited

PRINTED IN THE UNITED STATES OF AMERICA

To C. E. C.

I couldn't stand it, sir, at all
But up and kissed her on the spot!
I know — boo-hoo — I ought to not,
But, somehow, from her looks — boo-hoo —
I thought she kind o' wished me to!

— WILLIAM PITT PALMER

Part One

Part One

Chapter 1

AT Mother's insistence, I have agreed to write a sort of kickoff to her book. I confess that I do this now with a sense of duty rather than with genuine pleasure.

Perhaps this attitude in a daughter may seem surprising. Surprising or not, I find it difficult to share the secrets in a most intimate journal. Still, we Dents know that convictions carry fire only if we *live* them unfailingly, day in, day out. Also we are aware that the American public has long demanded and deserved answers to the following questions:

Who is Maybelle Dent?

How did she become involved with a radically new lipstick, panicking the billion-and-a-half-dollar cosmetic industry and her fellow citizens?

Why on Saturday, January 14, 1961, was Alvin Perkin, world-famous newscaster, cut off the air and dismissed by the Continentwide Broadcasting Company?

What justification can newspapers find for continuing to ignore Mrs. Dent and the uproar created by the announcement below:

Excerpt from the *Perk Predicts* program, Station ZDQ, New York, New York, Saturday, January 14, 1961.

"Good morning, friends and listeners across America. Here is Alvin Perkin wishing you and your family the best of the best.

"Today's first news flash is Giddy Moment, the lipstick recently launched in Arlington, Long Island. (Arlington, as you

*read in this morning's newspapers, has been given the Arcturus
Award as the most civic-minded suburb in the entire United
States. If I feel pride in this little community's being singled
out for this great honor, remember that I was born in Arlington
and make my home there still.)*

"But, my friends, did you read in today's newspapers about
Giddy Moment and its unique, irresistibly-kissable-you guaran-
tee? Did you learn about the excitement on Arlington's Main
Boulevard? Or about Mrs. Maybelle Dent, one of our most re-
spected homemakers and mothers, being questioned by Nassau
County Police? No, I assure you that you did not.

"And why was this unalienable right to see and to know
denied . . . yes, denied? Because, ladies and gentlemen, our
town of Arlington, its mayor, Chamber of Commerce and wider,
more powerful interests, succeeded in muffling and squelching
facts on Giddy Moment. Also they have made a last-ditch effort
to muffle and squelch me. But to no avail, I assure you.

"For many months now, I have been subjected to intolerable
pressure and threats. But these cannot and will not intimidate
me. Our press and our citizenry may be throttled by well-
intentioned, self-elected do-gooders. Regardless, Perk Predicts . . ."

"Because of unforeseen operating difficulties, the Perk Predicts program cannot continue as usual this morning. Instead
we present the Cotton-picking Swingsters, in a medley of old-
time favorites."

If today I twinge over that all too familiar "transcription"
and others preceding it, as a daughter I have good reasons.
Regardless, it's time to flick back the calendar to a previous
January so that Maybelle Dent can speak for herself. (Bravo,
Mother dear. Painful as this is, we're proud of you!)

NINA

Maybelle Dent's Journal . . .

Friday, January 15, 1960

PERHAPS every woman at the age of thirty-five asks herself this question: Who am I?

My day of reckoning began this morning under the most unromantic circumstances. The kitchen was warm, cozy, and fragrant with bacon. Nina had hurried off to school, banging the door behind her. And there I was in my favorite blue-sprigged house dress, washing up the breakfast dishes.

For the first time in several years I didn't turn the radio dial to the *Perk Predicts* program. Because by now, I'd seen more than enough of Mr. Perk Predicts. He may be a sensational newscaster and a charmer over the air, but as a next-door neighbor, he's been a zero. Yes, the rudest, coldest, most self-centered broomstick of a man anywhere in Arlington, Long Island. Not that I like being unkind, but what I've said is the truth.

So today, feeling fed up with Mr. Alvin Rat-tat-tattle Perkin, I didn't switch to his station ZDQ. Instead I let one of those uplifting, thought-provoking programs come rolling. There! . . . This would show who was boss here, with a mind of her own.

Now after a spell of organ music, a Mr. Leonard with a deep, deep preacher's voice demanded, "What troubles us more, dear friends? What we have done wrong or what we have lacked the courage to try?" Oh, but his dead serious tone reminded me of my father, and of dear Joe, who passed on last year.

Right away I jumped to attention, since Papa and my husband were the dignified type, inspiring obedience. Goodness, did those two have such a hold on me still? What had happened to the gumption demonstrated a moment ago? Why was

I at a loss, for pity sakes? Didn't those radio-box, brain-teasing questions deserve a prompt retort?

But somehow answering back took effort. After a long breath, I managed to ask, "Why bring up troubles, Mr. Leonard?" (Ah, there I was, off and running, with my voice pert as could be.) "We have them here now and again of course, like when Nina has one of her sniffling colds. Or Pluto refuses to touch his platter of beef heart. Or the washing machine breaks down. But is this worth mentioning, really?"

That's off my chest, I thought. Now maybe I can wash dishes in peace.

Yet, as Mr. Leonard continued, I began to see that he was talking good sense. "Very well, sir," I conceded, mopping a plate, "I'll admit that I've had my share of failures and broken resolutions. For example, I've postponed writing in this journal for over six months. I've failed to fuss with more elaborate hairdos, to cut down on sweets, to correct *my birdlike way of accumulating and storing worthless trivia.*"

Hadn't Nina confirmed this in a recent criticism? "Mother, you're like a satisfied robin, forever squatting on its nest. Here a big exciting world erupts from minute to minute . . . and you couldn't care less." But seventeen-year-olds are critical, of course, especially when they've matured early.

I might be discouraged by my shortcomings, I suppose, if I took them more seriously. Or if I didn't know that I do well in the domestic areas closest to my heart.

Yet I am sorry to say that I tend to be timid and lazy. Much as I hate to admit it, dear journal, we know that this is a fact. For example, right now there is every reason for me to seek first prize in the Tasty-Flour National Baking Contest. (Haven't friends said repeatedly that my angel cake supreme and fig macaroon recipes are stupendous?) However, I have not had the fortitude to *make* myself list the ingredients and pop them into the post-box.

Also, I have continued to decline invitations to speak at my church and Woman's Club. I cannot say why, since I take pains to live my belief in gracious homemaking. Surely no one sets a nicer table, entertains more hospitably, or fixes more charming flower arrangements. But do you suppose that I wouldn't die twenty million deaths at the thought of stepping up and facing an audience?

This morning as Mr. Leonard kept repeating that we human beings must dare and bear regardless, I recalled that this was Fay Hick's philosophy too. Hadn't my best friend given a similar sermon at our last coffee session together? "You're so naïve, Maybelle," she had said, tossing her tiny head with its clusters of black curls. "But why wouldn't you be, protected first by your parents, next by your husband and now by your daughter? Honestly, until I came to Arlington last year, I wouldn't have believed it was possible. Grow up, dear. Do! You'll find it's lots of fun."

Through Fay's and my close association together, I am beginning to see that living in one house and one town since birth may present handicaps. Also, marrying after freshman year at college and having a baby nine months later would not help to make me worldly and sophisticated.

In contrast, dear Fay has had a brilliant career as a chemist for a top beauty-preparation concern. After becoming Jack's second wife, she retired from business and moved into his mansion on Rollandale Road. The romance, of course, had developed *within* the Amyrillis Company, where he is vice-president, specializing in merchandising and promotion.

It is hard for me to understand why two individuals as unlike as the Hicks were attracted toward each other. Jack is the solid-citizen type, with a jaw of steel, and Fay is a sort of sizzling firefly, forever in motion. There is love, respect and admiration between them, I'm sure. But unfortunately each is a go-getter, willful, dynamic and overcompetitive. Perhaps one knock-down-drag-out battle, or the coming of a child, or both, will teach that marriage requires sacrifice and give and take. Anyway, I long to see them work out their problems if they can.

Fay and I might never have met last year if I hadn't been collecting for the Heart Fund as usual. I shall never forget how frail and woebegone she looked when I blew into her gigantic, overstuffed living room. Dainty as a Dresden doll, I thought, as she twinkled toward me on her spike heels.

Then I suppose I must have begun to bubble some news about Nina and Pluto. Anyhow, in no time we were sitting side by side, enjoying a cup of tea and chattering like schoolgirls.

Within a few minutes each of us sensed that the other was lonely. Yet I remember taking pains not to mention Nina's resenting my "fuss-budget ways," now she's a high school junior. Further, I held back the statement that with her attitude what it is, Pluto's companionship has been a godsend.

Since the beginning of our acquaintance, I've known that Fay would never welcome domesticity and leisure time. When she's not complaining about being bored or childless, she says that she dislikes Arlington and almost everyone who lives here.

Also, she has resented Jack's hectic travel schedule and the fact that he has been detained repeatedly by New York City business engagements. "He's so stimulating . . . so smart, such fun. In the years when we were building new beauty products together at Amyrillis, we had so many wonderful bedeviling sessions, day after day and night after night. But look at me, stagnating and drubbing my fingers, while Jack . . ."

Other people might seem dismal crying the blues this way, but Fay never! In the midst of histrionics she lets you know somehow that she is half laughing at herself, enjoying a sense of tragedy. Even when tears are in her eyes, she is sort of smiling too, as if to say, "I'm a ninny, of course. But isn't this too wonderfully heart-rending?"

The more violently she carries on sometimes, the more she demonstrates exhilarating, capricious pleasure. Perhaps she likes to fancy herself as a miniature Eleonora Duse, in addition to being a scientist.

It is hard for me to pin down this quality in Fay, especially since I tend to overlook it. Whenever she throws herself about or weeps, I think, Dear oh dear, where's the first-aid book? What should I do now? Then, when I offer a handkerchief or make some bungling gesture, she's apt to say, "Ho, don't panic, Maybelle. I'm just getting this out of my system. What's the harm?"

Regardless, I have been able to ease Fay's loneliness as I did again *tonight,* by inviting her to dinner. It is warming always, to hear her say that such attention keeps her from going "stark, raving mad."

But now Mr. Leonard brought me back to the present and dismissed these thoughts with a roar. "Remember, my friends, nothing but our own intentional evil can injure us today or in the future. We must have faith to do whatever we are called upon to do."

My, but those words, out of a radio box or not, hit like a tremendous clap on the back. So once I'd finished the dishes, straightened the bedrooms and dressed, I sat right down with my pen. After listing the two receipes, I tucked them into an envelope addressed to the Tasty-Flour Company. Anyone can do anything if he tries, I told myself.

Yet in the midst of this satisfaction, my conscience began to twinge. By now, surely I should have been making the rounds for this year's Heart Fund drive. Instead, I had been dallying, resisting the need to step out into wind and ice.

Oh dear, why had I listened so attentively to that live-a-better-life program this morning? Already it was making me see myself in the sharpest, most revealing and unflattering light. No more nonsense, I told myself. Collect your Heart Fund paraphernalia and off we go!

Once I was in my beaver coat and little blue hat, Pluto began to moan protests, of course. "Stop crying, dear," I soothed, putting my cheek next to his. "If you're a good boy, I'll bring you a lovely new chocolate bone."

After I had marched down the porch steps, we followed our custom, he pressing his taffy-colored face against the glass while I threw kisses. "Good-by. Good-by. Guard our home well."

Glancing next door, I observed the thick tracks of Alvin's car. Ah, but he was far braver than me, driving into New York City today, regardless of the weather. Neither snow nor ice, wind nor hail could keep him from his studio. His job owned him body and soul; it always would.

Remembering his name at the bottom of my list, I couldn't help wincing. If only it were possible to avoid him once he returned home promptly as usual. But would this be neighborly or decent? Also, in spite of his ripping tongue, wasn't he unfailingly generous in his contributions?

Ha, I thought, I wonder how he'd like me to greet him this way: "Hello, I didn't listen to your horrid program this morning." Probably he wouldn't give a hoot or show any sign of emotion. Still, didn't his mother Lucretia used to say that her only child was sensitive? "Underneath, Maybelle, he's a kind, considerate boy. I wouldn't be alive now if it weren't for his care."

Well, Lucretia Perkin had been gone for over a year by now, her death following Joe's by less than a week. Strange that such a bossy little woman had raised this six-foot newscaster son, whose laconic smile, horn-rimmed eyeglasses and carrot-colored hair were beloved across America.

Rooted in your tracks and nowhere, I scolded, catching myself. One . . . two . . . three . . . forward march.

As I made my way down the block, I felt happiness come flooding like sunshine. What could compare with the joy of living here in Arlington? Again and again every sidewalk crack, lamppost, gate and tree seemed to shout its welcome.

Oh, if only everything could stay *exactly* as it was, with no further improvement or building. From the beginning, we had been a town dedicated to the best in raising children, with emphasis on family life, schools, churches and innumerable civic activities. No houses were handsomer than ours, with their early American architecture, hedged lawns and towering beech trees.

As I made my calls in sequence, I noticed that the interiors of home after home seemed very similar. I mean they carried substantial dimensions, green or Wedgwood blue walls, plenty of ruffled flowered chintz, shelves of bric-a-brac, African violet plants . . . and an air of being lived in.

In a way I suppose that we suburban housewives tend to be alike too. Unfailingly we welcome visitors, urging them to stay for a cup of coffee or tea. Once any business at hand has been settled, the sociable time begins with a discussion of hors d'oeuvre recipes, TV programs, teen-age problems or the latest Spock theories. Sooner or later we make a point of sharing bits of inspiration clipped from a magazine or a newspaper. Today, for example, Edith Baxter, our mayor's wife, read an Edgar Guest poem winding up this way:

> *'Tis not within ourselves alone*
> *Lie merit and success,*
> *But in the thoughtfulness we've shown*
> *To others in distress.*

But one neighbor, next to last on my list, stood out in contrast to the others. Oh dear, what an ordeal, I thought, walk-

ing up the Thorpe sidewalk. Once I get inside here I'll never
be able to get away. I wish Grace would increase her interests
and repertoire of conversation.

"Come in, Maybelle," she cried a moment later, pulling me
through the doorway. "Heart Fund, is it? Here's my check,
signed and ready." She stood like a weary college girl, tall,
slim, with close-cropped hair. Then, as her handsome black
poodle sniffed at my skirt, "Ah, Spike longs to see Pluto as
usual. We must get our babies together more often."

After we had settled ourselves with some coffee, she asked,
"You take cream and three lumps of sugar still?"

"Yes. And no one's going to talk me out of it."

"With your figure what it is, why worry?" Then, after discussing diets interminably, "How's your friend Fay Hick coming
along? Is she still aching for the Amyrillis Co. and her cold-
cream mixing pots?"

"Not at the moment. She's hoping to work out a compromise
with Jack . . . a laboratory built in that barn of a cellar.
What's more, she may have some good news *tonight*, when she
comes to my house for dinner."

"Three cheers. I wish her luck." In spite of her pepped-up
tone, Grace sat looking mournful in her flannel shirt, English
shoes and beautifully tailored slacks. "What wouldn't I give to
put my experience to work again! Somehow, lately, I feel
smothered."

Oh dear, must I listen to this tale of woe? It grinds on and
on like a language-lesson record. If only she were as vital, as
dynamic as Fay . . .

"How I long, Maybelle, to return to Thorpe's Warehouse
and Storage Company as Steve's assistant. I've told him that I'll
never become a carbon copy of his mother, skilled at cooking
and sewing." Her face brightened unexpectedly. "But good luck
to Mrs. Hick, anyway. And tell her if she needs someone with
my talents eventually . . ."

"Maybe the three of us should go into business together," I quipped. "With Fay manufacturing some pharmaceutical, me selling it and you warehousing and delivering it, we could be quite a team."

"Ho . . . that's the truth. Oh, you're such a tonic. I wish you'd come more often."

Having settled this topic, she brought up the fact that Arlington residents tend to fall into four main categories: celebrities, millionaires, college deans and air captains. "But do you know, I've never once met that Alvin Perkin?" Then, chuckling, "I hear that besides being a bit of a zany, he's never married."

Somehow this comment didn't seem amusing. Though I was annoyed with Alvin, I must have felt some wisp of loyalty to him. Zany or not, hadn't he been an unusually fine son always? "Well," I said, "with his father deserting his mother years ago, Alvin's had heavy responsibilities."

"That should make him all the more interesting. So *please* try to introduce us some day."

Why did Grace remind me of Fay as she clung to this subject? Perhaps it was the eloquent use of hands and body. But wasn't Fay the last person to speak of celebrities or to wish to meet them? Perhaps she knew too much about their bursts of temperament and passion for perfection. With her scientific accomplishments filling a page and a half of *Who's Who*, would she have chosen me as a friend otherwise?

Though Grace kept urging "Stay, stay," I made my departure at last. Retired business women remind me of banked fires, I thought, as I stepped out into the ice and wind. What a load of energy lies packed away, seething inside them. No wonder they seem so restless.

Now, with all but one canvassing call finished, I remembered my agreement with Pluto. Oh dear, that cussed hardware store was blocks away. Why had I been so impulsive? Yet a promise was a promise . . . to man or to dog. Besides, if I paused for a hot chocolate en route, the ordeal could be made quite palatable.

Half an hour later, with Pluto's toy in my pocket, I turned back into my own familiar block. Ah, but it was a temptation to scuttle home, to start a fire in the hearth and to settle down enjoying the coziness. Why shouldn't I do this immediately, with my lips chapped, with fingers and toes throbbing from the cold?

"Since you started this Heart Fund circuit, finish it," my conscience seemed to cry. "Stop stalling."

Nuts, I thought, walking toward the Perkin house. Can't I call my soul my own any more? Alvin, please, for once, don't be sarcastic today.

Now I had come upon him busily scattering salt crystals on his steps. Yes, there he stood in a dilapidated army jacket with his crew cut blazing against the whiteness beyond. "Hello," I said, forcing politeness.

"What is it this time, Maybelle?" he asked with no pleasure. "Retarded children? Or defective adults?"

Oh, but I disliked this greeting. Why hadn't his mother taught him better manners?

While I was struggling to hide my irritation, he escorted me into the living room. Then, after writing a check twice the expected amount, he murmured, "This year I feel less stingy than usual."

Meanwhile I found myself waiting for his mother's step, the tap-tap-tap of her cane. Indeed her presence seemed to be disturbingly alive here among the handsome Victorian furniture, antimacassars, gilt-corded fringe, oil paintings and musty, leatherish odor. At any moment wouldn't she grip my fingers in her clawlike hand?

"What's the matter?" Alvin asked, as I stood transfixed.

"Just thinking." Then, putting his check into my pocket, "Many, many thanks."

"It's nothing," he murmured, flushing.

With our transaction completed, I hurried outdoors again. "Good-by, Alvin," I cried, skittering down the walk.

"Watch that ice. It's treacherous as hell."

Ah, but there was a surprising boyishness in his tone, the rosy cheeks, spiky hair and lean shoulders.

"Watch it," he yelped again.

My feet veered off into comically opposite directions. As I fought for balance, snow and sky seemed to meet, separate and swing together again. No use, I thought, clutching the air desperately. Down we go. Then I was lost in a surge of roaring blackness.

Next I seemed to be lying in a field of daisies with gnats swarming down my throat. And someone overhead was demanding, "Maybelle, Maybelle, are you hurt?"

"Go away. Leave me alone."

Deep, sonorous, beautiful voice. Could it be Papa's or dear Joe's? Oh, how my head twinged.

"Easy, now." Someone was dragging me up into a sitting position.

"Who . . . are . . . you?" Now I identified the lightish blue eyes behind the horn rims, the flaming hair and the deep dimple in his chin.

"Bravo for us," Alvin wheezed after hoisting me into his arms. "Thank God you've kept down your weight, else we'd never manage this." As he spoke, I caught a whiff of tobacco. "Here we are. One step at a time. And don't you dare sue me, dear neighbor."

Then we were bumping along with my arms locked about his neck.

After navigating the steps we were on the porch, then in the living room approaching the sofa. Next Pluto was leaping, barking and licking my face.

Chapter 2

Dent Journal . . .

Friday, January 15, 1960 (*continued*)

ONCE Alvin had placed me on the sofa, he was surprisingly kind. "Put this over you," he said, ripping off his jacket and tucking it around my neck. Then, as my teeth kept chattering, he hurried off to the kitchen.

After examining myself, I was relieved to find no signs of broken bones. You'll be lame and bruised tomorrow, I thought, but you're fine really. Maybe there are compensations in landing on your head. But what in the world is Alvin doing, making such a clatter? And who would have expected him to be whistling "Mother Machree," of all tunes?

Eventually he returned with a cup of ink-black coffee which made my head and lips throb more than before. "Does it taste that fierce?" he asked as I choked. "You act as though you've been poisoned."

While he settled himself close by, I debated making some witty answer. Surely a man who enraptured women listeners morning after morning with commercials on "America's favorite, most delicious, most delectable breakfast brew" should be able to serve a less noxious mixture. Yet I was too weary to remind him of this fact.

Now I must have dozed for a spell. Jerking back to consciousness, I found myself in a haze of shadows and pinkness with no sign of a visitor. Only that jacket with its worn spot near the collar indicated that my imagination hadn't been playing tricks.

Of course, late afternoon is the time which I love best. At sunset the walls of our living room turn rosy beige with our curtains resembling clouds. Consequently, I like to stretch out on the sofa, waiting until Nina returns from after-school activities.

But now, curled in my favorite spot with Pluto beside me, I couldn't find the usual serenity. The tobacco fragrance of Alvin's jacket and its khaki masculine texture carried a new disturbing tang. Ah, but I'd missed having a man about this past year.

Running my finger over the lapel, I remembered how Mrs. Perkin used to cry, "My son will never return *alive* from overseas. Why did they take him from me? Why?"

Still, it seemed hard to picture casual, diffident Alvin as a soldier. With that acid personality, how had he succeeded in rising from private to colonel? Perhaps he had been placed in public relations. But wouldn't he have been sadly unsuited to this field? Even back in our high school days together, he'd been the cat-that-walks-by-himself type. Especially during sophomore year, when he wore the wrong sort of stringy ties and socks, with his complexion anything but nice.

At graduation, however, in his white flannels and overtight navy coat, he had proved to be an eloquent valedictorian. Overnight, it seemed, he had become a stunner, with his gleaming, greased pompadour, his skin right again, his body and voice magnificently dominating.

After he got his Ph.D., his voice unquestionably led him into radio announcing. But neither Arlington nor Midwestern schooling could be blamed for the annoying, bulletlike speed of the *Perk Predicts* delivery. Was it, I wondered, an Alvin affectation or the result of severe nervous strain?

Pulling the jacket closer, I had to smile at giving so much thought to my neighbor. Imagine . . . when earlier today I wouldn't even give his program house room!

With my lips chapped as they were, smiling proved to be the worst possible torture. I must hunt up a remedy very soon. Years ago hadn't I stored one away somewhere, my birdlike habits being what they were?

But cozy as I was, I couldn't make myself move yet. Instead I kept pondering how Alvin and I had remained strangers since childhood. From eighth grade onward my interests had been dating, dancing and sociability, though teachers said I had a knack for writing. "If she has a brain she takes pains to conceal it," I heard Alvin tell a friend in study hall. "What a fluff-head."

Fluff-head or not, I always got along well with men and boys, enjoying their hearty ways. Then one night after freshman year at college, Papa brought his law partner home for dinner. Though Joe was a widower in his forties, my parents made every effort to promote our marriage. After the wedding they gave us this house, moving to a bigger one down the street.

Naturally my husband and Alvin were never congenial. "That insolent boy next door," Joe used to say. "He's an upstart if ever I saw one . . . with no respect for law and order."

Enough of these reveries, I told myself, aware of the surrounding darkness. It's time you dressed and began to think about dinner, with Fay Hick due within an hour or so. Though chicken will broil quickly and she's always easy to entertain, Fay's sure to expect full attention, especially since she may be full of news of herself, Jack, Amyrillis and the home laboratory she hopes to build.

After switching on a light, I dragged up to my feet. By now I was aware of no pain, *except* for the smarting of my lips, which had grown worse. (Some people may be particularly sensitive in areas such as scalp or teeth, but my delicate zone has always been mouth and face. Once this part of me has become chapped or sunburned, the agony grows, demanding a soothing remedy.) Only a camphor stick can bring relief, I thought, concentrating on the ache and thus scarcely able to endure it. Oh dear, dear, I'm in no mood to start searching for medication now.

Climbing the stairs I felt dizzy again. Why had I let myself take such a beating today? Why hadn't I found the courage to use the Lincoln, regardless of the treacherous streets? Oh my lips, my cracked, throbbing lips.

As I arrived in the bedroom, I forgot pain in pleasure momentarily. Ah, surely the rose-garlanded wallpaper here was a perfect background for precious antiques, white-tufted bedspread, chaise longue and mirrors. But how could I have been so forgetful in straightening up this morning? Pale blue satin mules lay scattered near the bathroom and my monogrammed nightgown hung over a chair. Also I had failed to replace the stopper of my favorite bottle of Crepe de Chine. No wonder a heavenly fragrance permeated everything here.

Now, as the ache grew intolerably, I glanced into the bathroom closet with a sigh. Returning to the bedroom again, I opened one bureau drawer after another, digging through gloves, handkerchiefs, scarves and innumerable fripperies. How right I had been this morning in confessing failures and broken resolutions. Indeed there was every evidence of them in the accumulation here.

Continuing to seek relief stubbornly, I turned to the closets. Oh, but I grew increasingly chagrined as I poked into old cartons in sequence. Even a "satisfied robin" (to use Nina's phrase) would know better than to store away old spools, fragments of knitting yarn, unmatched stockings and such. Tomorrow I'll clean out this nest of junk, I told myself. It's a disgrace . . . Ow, my face!

At last I came upon a battered humidor which brought Joe painfully close. "How this makes me miss you, dear," I whispered. "No man ever loved his wife and child more. Or provided for them better."

Prying open the lid, I expected to find a good cedary smell and remnants of tobacco. Instead there was a musky, sweet-grass odor rising from a collection of riffraff. In turn I identified dried-up vials of perfume, odds and ends of soap, sachet, face powder. Indian essences and a locket encasing a four-leaf clover. Then I came upon a tiny metal cylinder, bent and rusted. Success.

After opening and sniffing the cream it contained, I applied some to my lips. Then I stood for a moment or two feeling thankful. The pain had gone completely. What a blessing.

Examining the camphor stick more closely, I found that its texture seemed slightly dry. Also there was a gentle peach-petal scent instead of the expected camphor pungency. That's odd, I thought.

Now I realized that my spirits seemed to have soared up, up, *up* to mountain height. Also I felt full of zing, fire and new determination. Beginning now, I told myself, I'll take pains to dress for dinner and pretty my face. Nina's right. With effort I could look far more attractive than I do.

Without bothering to repile the cartons in the closet, I jumped out of my clothes and into the shower. Under the needling spray I kept caroling my favorite song, "Beautiful Dreamer." Ah, but I'd forgotten how firm, smooth and white my skin was. Or that I was so shapely from throat to toe.

After drying myself vigorously, I put on my sheerest, daintiest underwear. Next I hurried into a new crimson dress and matching pumps. When I had fussed with my corn-colored curls and complexion, I applied more of the camphor stick. My, it felt good.

Soon I stood before the full-length mirror preening like a bride. Even on my wedding day, I couldn't remember feeling lovelier. Examining myself with increasing wonder, I caught new luster in my china-blue eyes. And my five-feet-two height seemed to carry more stature. Oh, but it was hard to believe that this radiant, smiling vision was a widow with an almost grown daughter.

Now, for no reason, my thoughts went galloping back to Alvin Perkin. What darling, funny little creases he had at the corners of his mouth. Weren't those lightish blue eyes, behind their horn rims, clear as an April sky? How long, how awfully long it had been since I had felt the warmth of a man's arms or smelled tobacco on a breath. Yet why should such details make me ready to swoon? Why did I hope desperately that he might return for his jacket soon?

"Hello, Mother." After banging the door behind her, Nina had come striding up the stairs. "Lord, what a grind at school today . . . My lead in *Bernadette* is coming fine, though some of the lines sound soupy." Still in her camel's-hair coat, with her nose pink from the wind, she threw herself down on the bed. "Say, you look good, dressed to the ears. But isn't Mrs. Hick our only dinner guest?"

As Pluto gave a horrid growl from his position on my pillow, she told him, "All right, bossy, if you insist." Then, rising and speaking in a tone exactly like her father's, "I'll never know why you let him lie *wherever* he pleases."

In the past we have had so many arguments over our pet that I try to avoid the subject. But since it had come up again now, I pleaded, "Try to be patient, dear, won't you?" Then, as she stood with that serious scholarly look in her wide-set brown eyes, "Why stop beast or man from enjoying harmless pleasure?"

"I know I'm licked here before I begin," she said, using an expression picked up from Larry Drake, her steady beau. "But spoiling Pluto is no kindness and you know it." Then, with a sharp look, "Say, whose army jacket is downstairs on the sofa? Don't tell me a man's come into your life."

"Alvin Perkin was here this afternoon."

"He was?" Her jaw dropped. "Oh dear . . . and I missed

him." Rolling her eyes, she groaned. Then, after I had explained the situation, she said, "If King Saud had come to your rescue today, it couldn't be more tantalizing . . . Say, while I think of it, Larry will be here after dinner tonight. I hope you have a cake baked and ready for his usual late-evening snack. When he comes from Harvard, he's always starved for home cooking."

"Don't worry about my preparing for a man's appetite," I glowed.

Normally I would have proceeded to pump Nina about Larry, since she and her "steady" seem too serious in their relationship. But tonight I held back my questions about this sensitive-featured, milk-complexioned young man. At least these two young people aren't discussing marriage yet, I thought. And they seem happy in their mutual interests, such as the defense of civil liberties, higher mathematics, travel and vocabulary-building.

"Good. Larry'll be tickled pink," she cried, hugging me. "You know, Mother, in your way you're nice."

"I try to be," I said, patting her shoulder. Then, as she stepped away, "Dear, you know Mrs. Hick should be here any minute. Will you be kind enough to set the table while I get busy in the kitchen?"

But she was staring with dreadful intensity. "Aha . . . I see you wearing blue eye shadow tonight. Why?"

"Is it a crime to improve my appearance? Haven't you said repeatedly that every woman has the right, in fact the duty, to make the most of herself?" Oh dear, here we were as usual, all set for an argument.

"You know perfectly well that I was talking about the intellect mainly . . . Besides, at your age vanity isn't so hot."

Then, thank goodness, the doorbell rang. "Heavens," I cried, making a dash for the staircase. "Don't tell me Fay's here already."

"She's never put you into such a swivet before," Nina called after me.

That's true enough, I thought, running toward the vestibule. (Ah, surely, I did feel in a very special partyish mood tonight. But why?)

Even before opening the door I sensed deep in my bones that our visitor was a man. What could be better? "Come in, whoever you are," I caroled, twirling on my toes.

"I'm here for my jacket," Alvin said, bowing as he stepped forward. "Mind if I pick it up?"

"No-o-o-o . . . I don't mind . . ." Leading the way into the living room, I wondered why his eyes continued to avoid mine. "We've been expecting you, Alvin . . . truly . . ." Ah, but he must have noticed how my words trilled like a birdcall.

"Have you?" He was still staring at his feet.

"Ye-e-e-es," I said, smiling and getting his attention at last, while Pluto barked his displeasure.

"Mother, I'll be down in a minute," Nina cried from upstairs. "Hi there, Mrs. Hick. Wait till you see my nose and chin. They're responding beautifully to your skin treatment."

Stopping in his tracks, Alvin had turned deathly pale. Mercy, what was wrong with the man? Was he having a stroke or a heart attack?

Now he seemed to be beginning the gymnastics of a champion swan-diver. After bouncing on his toes several times and lurching his head and body back into position, he stretched his arms up and outward into an enormous V. Then, moaning, he plunged toward me.

My, I thought dizzily, what's going on here? I've charmed men in my day never, never, *never* like this. Why, he's gone overboard heart and soul. Whee!

As Alvin's dimpled chin came closer, his arms tightened about my waist. Then his lips were on mine, hot as a flame.

Chapter 3

Friday, January 15, 1960 (*continued*)

"WHY, *Mother!*" The rest of Nina's exclamation was lost in a terrible gasp as she entered the living room. Now, while Pluto continued to bark wildly, she choked, "Uh-uh . . . Uh-uhhh . . . Uh-uu-u-uhh."

In normal circumstances I would have extricated myself from Alvin's arms and rushed to save my only child. But today I simply couldn't.

Yet I knew in a sort of dream that Nina was leaping like a jack-in-the-box while she kept pounding herself on the back. "For shame, Mother," she cried, after collecting her breath. "Imagine making out this way at your age."

Meantime Alvin and I stayed as we were in our searing embrace.

"Mother, Mother, Mother," she squealed, flying toward us and shaking my shoulders. "Are you out of your mind? Have you taken a drug or something? Oh dear, how can I help you?" After wrenching Alvin and me apart, she scolded, "Look what big idiots you've made of yourselves. Honestly."

"I dare . . . say . . ." poor Alvin stammered.

"Dare indeed! Don't use that word here, Jack the Ripper. I'll dare you, so you won't forget it. Suppose Larry or our minister or Mrs. Hick had witnessed that scene a minute ago? What would they think, do you suppose?"

"They'd think we'd lost our senses. And they'd damn well be right."

"Mr. Perkin, I've always known that you were unfriendly and rude," Nina said, showing a woeful lack of manners herself. "But I never guessed that you were so brassy and bold. For years you've taken pains, haven't you, to avoid my mother, father and me? Then suddenly you march into this house and . . . and . . ." She stamped her foot.

"Please control yourself, dear," I said, ignoring Pluto, who was whining and rubbing against my legs. "When a guest comes to call we must remember our breeding."

"Breeding? Ho . . . was what I saw a minute ago your idea of hospitality? How would Emily Post like that clinch?"

It was a little cruel, I thought, for Nina to taunt me with Mrs. Post's name at such a moment. Surely she knew perfectly well that this woman has always seemed to me like a sort of goddess.

Finally I stammered, "Well, dear, we Dents like to be neighborly, don't we?" Ah, but a second later, I wished I had bitten my tongue . . . stupid, stupid!

"Neighborly, Mother? For Pete's sake, do you call what I saw a minute ago . . . ? If the kids at school got half as cozy on their dates, what would happen to the birth rate?"

Truly I was horrified. "Why, Nina!"

"Face facts, Mother."

"Stop such talk," I cried, stamping my foot.

"You inspired it, didn't you?"

"Oh dear . . . dear . . . dear . . ."

By now Alvin was very red in the face. "I . . . I . . . can't understand what happened. I've never encountered such a situation before . . . I . . ." Backed away in a corner, he had become his shy, unhappy self again.

"My heart bleeds for you, sir," Nina said tartly.

As I kept watching our guest with sorrow, he said, "Maybelle, you know very well that I came here tonight for *only* one reason, to pick up my jacket." Then, turning to Nina, "Everything was on the up and up until your mother greeted me."

"Then the sky was the limit, was it? . . . Don't start explaining what happened. Didn't I see it myself?"

"Please," he protested. "Look, Nina. Listen, Maybelle . . ."

He seemed so much like a youngster caught stealing cookies that I couldn't help saying, "Maybe we're taking all this too seriously."

"Thank you, Maybelle. Honestly, I'll never know what got into me. Once you came close tonight, dear neighbor, I was a goner . . ."

"Stop!" Nina shouted. "What drivel."

Not being able to silence my daughter, I decided to ignore her. "Something hit me hard too, Alvin," I confessed. "It was like being spun in a loop-the-loop."

"Oh, Mother, Mother, I'm surprised at you."

"I'm surprised at myself."

"Bah."

I have loved Nina intensely from the moment she was born. But now I was ready to slap her.

"What got into me?" Alvin asked thoughtfully. "What?"

"You think you're smarter than the next person," Nina howled. "You used that jacket as an excuse for coming here, sir. You *planned* to catch my mother off guard, didn't you?"

"No indeed . . . Indeed no. You're off base by twenty miles. Has anything in my behavior ever been reminiscent of a Casanova? Don't you know that I'm always ill at ease with women?"

"Ho . . . After tonight you expect us to believe *that?*"

Having heard more than enough, he stepped toward us. "Listen, my friends. Is the average dame anything to shout about?

A delectable dish in her twenties has her good points perhaps . . ."

Well, you may be sure that I didn't like this remark. Rushing at him, I shouted, "So now you dare to add insults to the rest, do you?" Then, gripping his shoulders and looking up into his eyes, "Aren't you ashamed of yourself . . . ? Aren't . . . you . . . Are . . . . n't . . . . . you?"

Again, his lips rocketed down on mine.

"Murder," Nina bellowed. "Oh Pluto, Pluto, what can we do?" Then, as he continued to bay dolefully, "Something is wrong here. Really, really wrong." After tackling Alvin on a run, she managed to yank him away from me.

"Strange . . . very, very, very strange," he said, as I staggered over to the sofa. "The moment you got near me again, Maybelle . . ."

"My," I said, leaning back and taking a deep breath. "I never."

"Hm-mm-m. More and more, Maybelle, I can't understand this. When you sit there twelve yards or so away . . . I feel no spark, no flash, nothing. But if you should come close again, I suppose . . ." Then, with his blue eyes alight with interest, "Very well, my dear. Get to your feet please and we'll try this once more."

"Once more?" Nina almost screamed.

"Certainly. How else can we find out?"

"Find out? Find out *what?* Haven't we seen more than enough?"

"It's this way," he said patiently, as I continued to lean back where I was, quite exhausted. "Let's grant that the circumstances today are unusual. Here two innocent individuals, your mother and I, suddenly find ourselves tossed about like zombies. While she keeps her distance, everything is O.K. But the minute she doesn't, all hell breaks loose. So please, can't we try this once more?"

"No."

"But a harmless little tête-à-tête may shed some light."

"I tell you no. No. No. *No.*"

He stood observing her silently, while some plan seemed to hatch. Then leaping forward, he grabbed her with all his strength. "Hang on now, baby. If we can't use your mother in my experiment, we'll use you. Let's see, are you irresistible? Or aren't you?"

"Eee-ee-eeh, Mr. Perkin. Stop being so fresh."

"Just a harmless little test, my dear," he soothed, tilting her chin expertly toward his. "Hm-mm, she's seventeen or so, pretty, appealing in her way, vivacious . . . Hm-mm. Does she make any impression? Does her chemistry raise hob with mine?"

"Stop. Stop. Stop." Nina was fighting and kicking savagely.

Confronted with such bedlam, what mother could sit by helplessly? It was bad enough, wasn't it, for this rogue to have toyed with me? But now here he was abusing my daughter. "Remember that you were born and bred a gentleman, Alvin," I cried, hurrying to my feet. "Unhand her or I'll call the police."

Ignoring me and Nina's fists hammering against his chest, he said thoughtfully, "She's a nice little armful . . . Yes, tranquilizing as a tumbler of warm milk. But beyond this, she's nothing. Nothing." Then, cocking his head toward me and grinning, "Does this shed any light, dearest Maybelle? Are you following my thinking?"

"What *thinking*? Would any upstanding American woman allow her child to be manhandled this way? Release her immediately."

His lightish blue eyes deepened with concentration. "Let's see . . . Hm-mm . . . Maybelle, you must have something which Nina has *not*. Interesting. Very interesting. We're this far at least, aren't we?"

"Right now we're no place," I said, tugging at his coatsleeve. "Now I'd like your attention, Alvin, please."

"You've approached me at your own risk, my dear." Then, as our glances met like arrows twanging together, he yelled, "Owee-eee-ee. Here we go again." As one hand thrust Nina aside, the other gripped the back of my neck.

For a fraction of a second I wondered if my lips might be magnetizing Alvin's somehow today. Then I wasn't the least bit concerned by the whats, whys and wherefores. Because having that dear man where he was, tall, warm and filled with love, seemed right. In fact, it was heavenly.

"Enough. Break it up," Nina called out. "Class is dismissed."

Pluto had begun to howl again. But do you think I cared?

"Blast it," Nina said in a voice that seemed to be miles and miles away. "What clucks. They're completely unconscious."

I was dimly aware that our doorbell was ringing and that Fay must be arriving for dinner. No matter, I thought, she's an old friend who expects informality.

Now I could hear the door scrape open as our visitor cried, "Hello, Nina. What a relief to be out of that miserable wind." A pleasing, teasing, spicy fragrance seems to accompany Fay always. It was here already as she said, "Pet, you look a little washed out. What's the matter?"

"Plenty's the matter, Mrs. Hick. Plenty."

"Where's your mother?"

"Over near the piano . . . See?"

Fay's pattering footsteps paused. "Why, Maybelle Dent," she murmured. "Here you have a serious beau and I never even guessed it . . . Don't tell me he's Alvin Perkin, of all people!" Then, as this produced no response, "What's going on here, Nina, a charade or something?"

"A charade, Mrs. Hick? Look. These two have lost their wits."

After a moment of silence, Fay spoke again, her voice jarringly close. "Maybelle, imagine you of all people casting convention to the wind . . . I hate to spoil your fun, but I *must*."

"Thank goodness you're here with your smelling salts," Nina cried, as I began to gasp in a wave of ammonia.

"Sorry, folksies," Fay cried, waving her deadly dose under Alvin's and my noses. "But let's come alive a little, shall we?"

"Thank goodness you're here, Mrs. Hick," Nina said again.

Chapter 4

Friday, January 15, 1960 (continued)

SITTING here on my chaise longue tonight, I realize that Mr. Leonard's uplifting words have produced two results already: They ootzed me into a getting those recipes off to the Tasty-Flour Baking Contest, and now, after months of delay, I am bringing this journal up to date.

Truly, if Joe could see me in my apricot negligee, busily engaged with my pen, he'd be pleased and proud. "All you need, Maybelle," he used to say, "is more follow-through. Then keeping our family diary will become a pleasure."

When I used to protest that the work involved was a chore, he was unfailingly patient. He explained that in reading his mother's journal after her death, he had gathered many surprising insights. Until then, he had never guessed that Granny Dent retained all the curiosity and delight of a child.

I can understand why this discovery continued to overwhelm him. Because Granny at ninety was very much the bejeweled *grande dame*, looking fearfully grim and ancient.

Also, I am ready to go along with Joe's insistence that Nina may gather similar rewards from my entries. Yet I know very well that I could not express myself freely at the moment if she were looking over my shoulder. Of course she has every right to read this chronicle whenever she wishes. But I hope that she may decide to postpone the impluse until she has gained more tolerance and understanding.

I am willing to admit that I have taken the long way round tonight before returning to a painful subject. But since I am committed to "daring and bearing," there must be no further dallying.

I realize, too, that I should have welcomed Fay Hick's coming when she did a few hours ago. But of course I was far from pleased. Surely she could have used a more thoughtful greeting than that "Folksies, let's come alive a little." Also, if there is a more frightful odor than ammonia, I have never encountered it.

It seemed particularly tactless to tell Alvin, "Go home and sleep it off, my friend. Tomorrow you're sure to feel better." Imagine daring to hint that he was intoxicated!

Still, I suppose that his actions suggested this possibility. And mine must have too. Because after Alvin's departure, I continued to feel awfully lightheaded. I remember waving my arms and singing "Beautiful Dreamer" while Nina pleaded, "Mother, try to calm down. Do."

At last Fay got me upstairs and into my negligee. Then, once I was settled in bed, she must have given instructions to call the doctor. Because I recall Nina's flying off to the telephone before she began to dress for her after-dinner date.

Soon I became my calm cheerful self again. "You're a good friend," I said, as Fay hopped up on the chaise and stretched out her tiny legs.

"You too, Maybelle — one of the best." She sat with that look of intensity, of depth and sadness which scientists must carry. How frail she seemed, how almost transparent with her yellow-green eyes fringed by long black lashes.

I could see that she was wearing a sleek purple suit, another of those which she has custom-made at Bergdorf's. After noting a new exquisite strand of pearls, I asked, "Isn't this another gift from Jack?"

"Yes. But I'd trade it and everything else for more of his

companionship. Those dratted after-hour business sessions. But we've been through all this a hundred times before."

"You worked at Amyrillis long enough to know its demands on time," I said, forgetting my problems in the joy of helping Fay with hers.

"I know, but if I have to eat dinner alone one more night, I'll scream. Oh I'm so bored, so utterly, miserably sick of myself."

"You're not the only Arlingtonite who feels this way," I said. "Today Grace Thorpe was crying the exact same tune." Then, as this comment produced no comfort, "But I know the past year hasn't seemed easy."

"Easy?" An extraordinary brightness flamed out of her, emphasizing the ebony crown of head, the delicate lines of cheekbones and throat. "I tell, you, Maybelle, it's been hell. *Hell.* Jack's been sure that I'd find myself. But let's face it, I haven't. Who *could* . . . loving work as I love mine? If I'd been older or incapacitated, perhaps I'd welcome retirement. But here I am, scarcely thirty, with the best years of life ahead."

"I know."

"Obviously, though, Jack wouldn't let me continue at Amyrillis, now he's second in command there. Even though Mr. Huggin, the president, kept urging it . . . And my working for a competitor is out of the question, damn it."

"I know," I said again, though I didn't understand really.

"Jack's the most generous, sweet man in the world. I'm smart enough to know it. But he's been blind about my hating Arlington and that monstrous hulk of a house. He hasn't been willing to believe that all the love and luxury he offers can't compensate" — she tapped her forehead — "for daily exercise here."

Bending forward, she added hoarsely, "However, last night, when we discussed this problem for the thousandth time, he made a concession. So Monday . . . yes, just three days from

now, we're starting to build a laboratory in our basement
. . . What do you think of that?"

"Oh, Fay, I know how you've wanted this." I couldn't resist
jumping from my bed and giving her a hug.

"I knew you'd be tickled too," she said, as I climbed back
under my afghan. "Can you imagine the thrill of getting back
to creative work again? Isn't it stupendous?"

"Bless that John Calhoun Hick. I've been praying that he'd
see the light."

She rocked back and forth in a tizzy of delight. "Before
long, believe me, I intend to perfect another new formula,
revolutionizing the cosmetic industry."

"Once you set your mind on it, I'm sure you will," Nina
said, joining us now. Then, turning to me, "How are you
feeling, Mother? Better?"

"Oh, yes," I said, noting how handsome my daughter was,
although overself-assured for her seventeen years. Then, glancing
at her mouth, I couldn't help saying, "Must you wear that
extra-dark shade, dear? Truly, I don't like it."

After observing herself in the mirror, she tossed her smoothly
combed head.

"Why not blot your lips a bit?" Fay soothed. "Then they'll
look as lovely as your skin does now. Ah, I see you've been
using my Aphid-Milk Lotion faithfully, haven't you?"

"Uh-huh. Just as you instructed, every morning and every
night." Nina ran a finger across her chin. "All my friends have
noticed the improvement."

"I can see it myself," Fay said, squinting professionally. "I
was sure that Aphid-Milk Lotion would contribute just the
right amount of stimulus, moisture and lubrication. You look
charming, dear. Who's coming tonight? Larry?"

"Always and forever Larry," Nina said, as though repeating
her marriage vows. "He's taking me to the movies." Then,
after a concerned glance at me, "Or so I hope."

"If you had a child of your own, Fay," I said heatedly, "I'm sure you wouldn't encourage all these fancy complexion treatments."

She trembled as though she had been struck. "Child? Did you say child, Maybelle? How can you mention this lack, when you know we've been disappointed month after month?" Tears welled from her eyes in slow, steady drops.

"Forgive me, dear. Forgive me." Throwing off the afghan again, I hurried to her side. "It was a slip of the tongue. I didn't mean it."

"Oh. Oh. Oh," she moaned, peeking through the fingers clapped to her temples. (Minx, I thought. Overdramatizing everything and enjoying it!)

As the doorbell rang, Nina continued to watch us quizzically. Then, after grumping, "Dr. Baxter would come now, wouldn't he?" she hurried off.

Soon a familiar voice boomed from the stairway. "How well I remember bringing you into the world, young lady . . . What a fine specimen of womanhood you've become."

I may as well say now that Dr. Baxter is proud of the number of babies he has delivered in forty years of general practice. His brother Horace, our Arlington mayor, keeps predicting that "Dr. Lucius" will be honored for his outstanding achievements within the year. If this should happen, the story will be shouted by newspapers across the country. (Is there any doubt of this, with Mayor Baxter being the chief stockholder of Transworld Press? Remember the space given to his daughter Anna's debut, as well as her graduation from Bennington last June? And isn't it a fact that any bits of news reflecting glory on our town and its administration are publicized day after day, far beyond their importance?)

As Dr. Lucius approached, Fay was sobbing still, her shoulders heaving desperately. Instead of being concerned for her, I found myself scrambling from bed, powdering my nose and adding more of the camphor stick. Then, after climbing back under the afghan, I settled myself fetchingly.

While Nina went off to her room, the doctor appeared in the doorway. "Good evening, Maybelle," he rumbled, standing in a sort of Winston Churchill pose, cheeks pink, eyes benignly gray. Then, as Fay continued to moan, he marched toward her. "There, there, my dear."

After hauling out his watch and thrusting a thermometer under her tongue, he began to feel her pulse. "One hundred and one," he said after a couple of minutes. "You belong in bed, young woman."

"These attacks keep coming," she gulped. "My husband insists they're psychosomatic, but I know better."

Of course it is true that Fay has been subject to crying spells in recent weeks. Soon after Jack left on that trip to Los Angeles she kept weeping hopelessly. "What will I do with all those servants underfoot and life so deadly dull? I can't bear it. I can't."

Another time the rosy-cheeked baby on a magazine cover sent her into hysterics. "Sometimes I think people go out of their way to hurt me," she cried, throwing it across the room with a Duse gesture. "Because other wives accomplish what I can't, must they remind me of it again and again?" Also she has kept insisting that neighbors take pleasure in snubbing her. "I wouldn't join the Woman's Club even if they asked me. What a horrid, highhanded town this is."

In spite of her flair for the dramatic, I had felt deeply sympathetic. Tonight, though, I became chagrined at her attention-getting antics. What a selfish little prima donna, I thought, as Dr. Baxter's broad back continued to hide her completely.

"We've wanted children so badly," she told him. "If anyone makes even the slightest reference I fall apart."

"Don't let yourself, my dear. You must keep busy with

other thoughts and activities. Then you'll discover that nine months to the day . . ."

As they continued to talk together, I croaked, "Yoo-hoo. Isn't anyone the least bit interested in me?"

Our man of healing continued to concentrate on Fay. "Worries accomplish nothing. The things we agitate over seldom happen."

"You're right," she sighed. "In my years as a chemist, I never used to agonize like this."

"Chemist, you say?"

Bah, I thought, as she mentioned something about her professional name being Dr. Fay B. Amelia . . . Also how she had been playing with Bunsen burners and beakers when other youngsters were busy with their blocks.

"Well, well, well . . ." His voice rang with admiration. "So we can thank you, can we, for those remarkable epidermic and glandular studies? Unquestionably, Doctor, they're a work of genius."

Unable to endure this a moment more, I groaned piteously. And now Dr. Lucius swung about on his heel.

"You seem a little flushed, Maybelle." His tone as always was kind and fatherly. "How's that forehead? Hot?"

"Ye-es . . . Terribly."

Clutching the thermometer and full of dignity, he trod across the room toward my bed. "Let's identify the trouble, my dear, if we can."

Now, while my body tingled with expectancy, he came close. After peering into my face closer and closer, he threw back his head with a ridiculous braying noise. Next he half slid, half tumbled down over me.

"Glory be," Fay cried, jumping to her feet. "Where are my smelling salts?" Soon she was applying them and dragging our visitor to his feet.

"Why *must* you keep interfering?" I squealed from the depths of my pillow.

"I'll come back to you in a minute," she said briskly, as she led Dr. Baxter toward the chaise longue.

"I recommend . . . a . . . little . . . rest and quiet . . ." he muttered, leaning against her like an avalanche. "Yes . . . rest and quiet . . . rest . . . and . . . quiet . . ."

"You're so right, my friend," she said, glancing at her watch as she placed her fingers on his wrist. Then, before he could protest, she popped the thermometer into place.

"What are you doing?" I scolded. "Can't you leave well enough alone, Miss Fix-it?"

"Ssssh." She put her tiny, red-enameled finger to her lips. "Calm down and lie still, Maybelle. You're next."

Chapter 5

Dent Journal . . .

Friday, January 15, 1960 (*continued*)

TONIGHT, as I write, I realize that I have never known anyone with one tenth of Fay's capabilities. From the moment we met months ago, I have been impressed by her nimbleness of thought and action . . . especially in emergencies.

We might never have encountered trouble as we did during our very first get-acquainted session, if Greta, the Hicks' new German waitress, hadn't made a grievous mistake. Being unacquainted with their prize-winning Dalmatian, she had let him plunge off outdoors.

Almost immediately afterwards, Fay and I heard Duke screeching for help at the top of his lungs. Though details are hazy in my mind by now, I recall that the weather was much as it is today — frigid, windy, with occasional flurries of snow. Surely no average woman would have chosen to run outdoors without a coat. Or to intervene in a dangerous dog fight. Yet, unmindful of herself, Fay rushed into that snarling pack of animals.

Soon she returned smilingly with that great bleeding animal in her arms.

I guessed at once that she must have grown up among doctors, hospitals and laboratories. How else could she have bathed and bandaged the wounds so swiftly, sewing the worst of them with a surgeon's needle? Meanwhile, she took all this for granted in the most charming way. And once she finished, she clapped Duke on the flank affectionately. "There now, you big lug. Next time tackle something you can lick."

I suppose that Greta's devotion to her mistress — and Duke's too — may have begun then and there. Anyhow, I've noticed that everyone in Fay's household worships her, sensing qualities which she takes pain to hide.

Again, in my bedroom tonight, Fay showed skill in coping with the unexpected. After examining Dr. Baxter, she led him downstairs. "We keep warning my dad not to overdo," she said with wonderful tact. "But like all doctors, he's never learned to safeguard his strength."

After returning and making a second examination, she gave a long, probing look. "All right, Maybelle. Is this your idea of fun?"

Before I could answer, Nina joined us again. After learning that I felt far better than before, she pointed toward her watch. "Mother, are you sure you're well enough to get dinner? Good . . ." Then, smiling at herself in the mirror, "Larry's coming at seven-thirty, folks. So let's hurry."

It pleased me to see that her attention was glued on the sociability ahead, with no sign of disgruntlement toward the past. But Nina has always been one to accept what she calls my "Maybellish ways and fancies."

"Please use your own cosmetics, dear," I said as she reached for some perfume. "I've asked you hundreds of times to leave mine alone."

"If you need anything, pet, just say so," Fay said generously. "I have enough jars and bottles at home to outfit an army."

"Well, I suppose I'd better dig up some leftovers for supper," I said, hauling myself up. "It's too late to cook chicken by now."

"I'll start setting the table," Nina said, hurrying off.

"Maybelle, I don't understand you," Fay said, after I had scrubbed my face and lips carefully. "Tonight I've seen two men take a tailspin the minute they came close. If only Alvin Perkin had jackassed about, I would have accepted it. But when Dr. Baxter joined the fraternity . . ."

By now I had zipped into my crimson dress again. Sweeping a brush through my curls, I giggled, "Who would have thought that Dr. Lucius of all people . . . Tsk . . . Tsk . . ."

Her catlike eyes glowed. "Tell me about him, Maybelle. Isn't he married, with six grown children?"

"Oh yes."

"Has he ever shown any weakness for women?"

The question was so ridiculous that I yipped with delight. "Dr. Baxter? Certainly not. Are you crazy?" Reaching for the little camphor stick, I started to apply it.

"Don't," Fay commanded.

Whenever she gets unusually bossy, I could shake her. But I managed to hide my annoyance as I asked, "Why?"

"Because thus far I haven't been able to find one thing wrong with you. Or with the doctor either, except for a slightly rapid heartbeat. Therefore we must seek other causes for your condition."

"What condition?" Oh, but I was more annoyed than ever. "Is it strange for two men . . . ?"

"Let's say it's challenging. Very challenging," she soothed, her yellow-green eyes drilling into me.

"All right. Fair enough." But I felt ruffled still.

"Come on, Mother," Nina called from downstairs. "Please get going, will you?"

"Just take that ham out of the icebox, if you will, dear. And that bowl of boiled potatoes too. I'll be along in a minute."

"Ham? Must we? Phooey."

Fay had come close, reaching for the little lipstick. "I've never seen this brand before. What is it . . . an antique?"

"Well, yes . . . in a way."

After smoothing a bit of the cream on her wrist, she kept sniffing it. "Hm-mm. Strange. I expected this to be one of those old-fashioned camphor remedies. What a delightful texture and fragrance!"

Now there she was, poking into my possessions exactly like Nina. Oh dear, if only some objects and phases of life were my very, very own.

"Yes, Maybelle, I see this has its points," she continued. "What's its history?"

How I wished that we could postpone this subject. "It began as a camphor stick," I said a little coldly. "But being stored away for three years must have changed it somehow."

"I see. Given the right combination of circumstances, anything is possible. Anything." A brilliant gleam had come into her eyes. "May I try a bit of this on my lips?" Then, when I had nodded without enthusiasm, she began a series of deft strokes back and forth, up and down. "Mm-m-mm. Delicious."

Her voice seemed to carry a new lilting quality as her body began to tremble. But I couldn't think twice about this, because Nina was calling more loudly than before. "All right," I cried back. "We're coming."

As we started downstairs, I saw Fay take a last approving glance at herself. Though her mouth has never been her most striking feature, it seemed so tonight, with its moist, cherry-red, velvety sheen. Perhaps whatever elements were in that mixture had caught fire in her blood.

"Jack should be here by nine o'clock, shouldn't he?" she asked, following me into the kitchen. "Ah . . . only two hours from now. I simply can't wait."

"You're nuts about him, aren't you?" I asked, as she began to prance over the linoleum.

"Uh-huh. Crazy, wi-ild."

While I was preparing supper, I tried to put our recent ex-

periences into some sort of order. Granted that our two visitors'
reactions had been less than gentlemanly, had I, Maybelle
Dent, behaved like a lady? Mixing the salad, I pondered the
fact that I had been really eager for overtures. What could explain this and my disregard for the proprieties?

Could some female weakness, one which I had never sus-
pected, have shown itself today? Might it have gathered secretly, silently, in the years of Papa's and Joe's dominance?
Or was it the outcome of my striking my head on the ice today? Regardless, as a respectable woman I would have to guard
my conduct in the future. Otherwise Nina and I would become
the butt of endless gossip and jokes.

Yes, I thought, adding mayonnaise, mustard and paprika
to my mixture, we cannot dismiss this lightly. Then, glancing
across at the kitchen mirror, I tightened my lips. Since I had forgotten my manners twice, it seemed right to be paying penance
now with my face scoured and unblessed even by camphor
remedies. Yet it would have been pleasant to feel more like a
siren this evening.

Meanwhile Fay kept doing little cha-cha steps, her fingers
snapping in rhythm. She has always had a mischievous, elflike
quality which is delightful. But now she seemed to boil with
a new torrid beauty. Jack should have let her build that laboratory months ago, I thought, bending over the salad again.
Look at the difference it's made already.

As we settled ourselves in the dining room, I breathed
in its Old World, dignified atmosphere. Surely the authentic
Hepplewhite furniture, scrolled gilt-edged mirrors and crystal
chandelier typified the best in tasteful suburban living. (Several
years ago Joe had given permission for me to do as I pleased
here, with no limitation on expense. But afterwards he never
let me forget that our local decorator had charged three times
what he should. Still, I have never believed that lack of business shrewdness should affect aesthetic pleasures.)

"You have wonderful balance, Maybelle," Fay said, as I sighed with satisfaction. "Nothing gets you down for more than two seconds, does it?"

"So far it hasn't," I said, smiling across the candlelit expanse of mahogany and china. "I hope it never will."

Nina fought back a disapproving choke.

Though I was proud of our surroundings here, I knew that I must apologize for our simple menu. "Please forgive these odds and ends," I said, after serving the sliced meat, potato salad, rolls and coffee.

"Odds and ends aren't the half of it," Nina said, pushing a bit of watercress to the side of her plate. "I've never cared for ham, Mother. And why didn't you warn me about onions in this salad? Can you imagine how Larry will be thrown to-night?"

"Well, dear, just try to keep your face away from his."

She was too chagrined to answer.

"Never mind," I said cheerily. "Thank goodness there's a remedy for everything these days. Just try a bit of that new Tasty-Foam Toothpaste I bought yesterday. It's been highly recommended on the radio."

"Not Tasty-Foam, Maybelle," Fay said sharply. "Why must you be so gullible and trusting?"

"But Alvin Perkin keeps pushing this brand on his radio program."

"Humph. Don't be sold down the river so easily."

"But over and over he insists . . ."

"Of course he does. I've heard that spiel so often I could repeat it word for word. From the standpoint of the *Perk Predicts* sponsors and Alvin's salary, it's a bang-up job." She shook with irritation. "Yet what has that dentrifice to recommend it beyond a sassafras essence and that soapy froth? Nothing. Absolutely nothing. Recently I tested it to convince Jack the formula was idiotic. What's more, I collected a ten-dollar bet.

Ho . . . ho . . . you should have seen his face when I won that round, hands down."

"Now see, Mother, how you put me behind the eight ball?" Nina cried. "Here Larry comes all the way from Cambridge and right off you ruin me."

"Stop being so tempestuous, pet," Fay soothed, unconscious of her own similar trait. "Once you finish here, get some old-fashioned clove from the kitchen. There's nothing more effective still."

"Now, isn't that a splendid idea?" I asked, enormously relieved. "You'll find a half box there on the second to bottom pantry shelf. I saw it this morning."

"All right," she said glumly.

"Cheer up. You'll live," Fay teased.

But Nina was far from pleasant during the remainder of our meal. "I'll never, never know, Mother, why you make such starchy desserts," she said, after I served thick slabs of cake. "Do you want to wreck our complexions and make us fat as blimps?"

"For pity sakes, dear, what's wrong with sweets winding up a meal?" By now I was ready to cry. "Your father always said that no one's baking could compare with mine. Besides, a woman's meant to carry a bit of flesh."

"Well, I intend to watch my figure. And you should too."

"That's enough, miss. I'll thank you to avoid personal remarks, please."

"Here, here," Fay cried. "Stop this commotion, you two." Then, with a reassuring nod toward me, "This tastes marvelous, Maybelle. See? I've polished off my plate."

"I'm glad somebody appreciates me," I said mournfully. "But I fear that the lightness this time isn't up to usual standards."

"Ho. You're overmodest always," she chided, as I rose and made my way to the pantry, where Pluto was waiting. "I wish you wouldn't be."

"Come in, dear," I cried. "It's time for your treat at last."

As he galloped yelping at my heels, Nina glanced at her watch. Satisfied with the time situation, she groaned, "Now Mother's ritual begins."

Once I had seated myself again, I crumbled the remaining cake on my plate. While Pluto's eyes turned to velvet and his nostrils quivered, I told him, "Yes. Yes. You've been very patient. Very sweet and good." Then, holding an enticing fragment aloft, "Now *sit*, sir. *Sit*."

Scrambling wildly, he rolled over on his back, his belly exposed, his stub of a tail beating a tattoo. "No. No. No," I pleaded. "*Sit*. Now we'll have to begin again. But you may have this mouthful anyway."

"Mother, when you spoil him so, he'll never learn."

Truly, Nina is Miss Jangled Nerves tonight, I thought, continuing to instruct my pet. "Sit, Pluto . . . Lie down . . . Roll over . . . Turn in a circle."

As he bumbled, barked and wolfed down his handouts, Fay became impatient too. "Ahem," she coughed. "Please, could we turn our attention to another matter now? What I have in mind is important. It may pain you, Maybelle, but . . ."

Since she was so intent on changing the subject, I set down my dish for Pluto to lick. "There," I told him. "Entertain yourself. Mommy must get back to business."

Clearing her throat again, Fay drummed her fingers on the table. "Girls, it's time we put our heads together. I've waited until now to discuss a most important subject."

"Oh dear," I cried. "Please don't. I'm not ready to think about that nonsense again."

"No matter. We must figure out why two men did a double flip today. I don't need to remind you, Maybelle, that Dr. Baxter . . ."

"Dr. Baxter?" Nina screamed. "Are you saying that when he came to examine Mother, he . . ."

"Yes. And you're old enough to know it."

"But it's impossible!" Nina exclaimed, after hearing details. "He's such a nice, grandfatherly man, everything that Alvin Perkin isn't. Oh no. *No.* This is unbelievable." She turned to me. "What's got into you? Can't a man come into this house without such dreadful things happening? If people in Arlington should hear about this, they'll say we're balmy."

"I'm beginning to think we may be," I said, running my fingers across my forehead. "It's like a silly dream, isn't it?"

"Silly? Don't you know, Mother, that a woman your age, especially when she's a decent widow . . ."

"I don't know what I know," I said, perspiring. "Truly I don't."

"Emotion won't help us think clearly," Fay said, every inch a chemist now. "We must determine the *why* here before we can weigh and evaluate results. Before Jack picks me up tonight, I intend to gather some facts. The explanation may be simpler than we guess. Now, Maybelle, tell us about your day, please, from the moment you woke up."

"Well, let's see . . ." I blinked. "So much has happened that it's awfully hard to start."

"As you come to anything different from your usual routine, please say so. Even if it's as bleak as trying a new soap or breakfast food. To a chemist like me, details are essential, even the most minor ones."

After I had told about listening to Mr. Leonard instead of *Perk Predicts,* Nina pushed back her chair. "Must I stay, Mrs. Hick?" she exploded. "Could anything be more boring than this rehash?" Then . . . "All right. But for Pete's sake, Mother, speed it up. Larry's due in a few minutes and I want to be ready."

"Larry will be coming into our picture soon," Fay said. "That's another reason why we need your attention now."

"All right, darn it."

Finally I came to my rounds for the Heart Fund. Winding up with the call on Alvin Perkin, I described my tumble on the ice. "You know, girls, for a minute, I thought I heard Papa or Joe asking, 'Maybelle, Maybelle, are you hurt?' "

Fay was taut with interest. "What were your first words in return? Do you recall?"

"Oh yes. Once I realized that it wasn't either of those dear men, I cried, 'Leave me alone.' "

Her face fell. "While Alvin was helping you home, how did you feel?"

"Awful. But wonderful too. And very, very dizzy."

"Nothing else?"

"Isn't that enough?"

"I suppose it has to be," she sighed.

"Then, Fay, when I woke up on the sofa it was twilightish and Alvin had gone. My lips were painfully chapped, I remember. So I hunted up a remedy." Then, clapping my hands, "Aha, here's something interesting maybe."

"Go on," she muttered, with eyes smoldering.

"I'm sorry, Mother," Nina said, getting to her feet. "I've got to run on upstairs. You'll excuse me, won't you, Mrs. Hick?"

"Please don't touch anything on my bureau," I called after her.

"All right. But your room's always much handier than mine."

"I'm sorry Nina's been so uppity tonight," I said a moment later. "But you know how teen-agers are, especially when they're going steady."

If Fay had heard, she showed no signs of it. With her eyes half closed and her tiny arms crossed over her breast, she sat silent as an Egyptian princess. "Now let's come back to that camphor stick," she said, her throat palpitating. "By the way, it has real staying power. I can feel it on my lips still."

"Can you?"

"Oh yes. Remarkably so."

Now, as the doorbell rang, Nina raced to answer it. "Oh Larry, come in," she crooned. "How nice to see you."

"Believe me, I'm glad to be here," he said, as though on a public platform delivering a carefully rehearsed speech. "What a dismal drive. For a time I thought we'd never make it. The ice was stinking."

"Lord, is this their usual lingo?" Fay snickered. "How endearments have changed since I was a girl."

"Larry's too proper for my taste," I whispered. "If Harvard is helping him, I haven't seen it yet. But Nina adores him."

"I was afraid you men might have a bad skid or something," she was saying in wifely tones.

"Clean up the lenses of your eyeglasses, sweet. Then you'll see we didn't."

"Heavy weather meets heavy weather," Fay said, shaking her head. "I feel like an octogenarian."

"Mother'll be out in a minute, Larry . . . with a friend she wants you to meet."

"Great."

Once I had caught this signal, of course I jumped to my feet. "Come on, Fay. Forget camphor sticks for a minute and try to be sociable."

"Why not?" she cried, clapping her hands and beginning little dance steps again.

As I led the way into the living room, I realized how quickly and devastatingly our children grow up. I had first become acquainted with Larry as a chubby Sunday school pupil. In fact I had almost lost patience as he roared his displeasure for a solid hour. In time, though, he grew better adjusted, loving to memorize songs, passages from the Scriptures and the spelling of classmates' names.

A few years later, he began to deliver our evening paper as a means of earning spending money. "Dad doesn't want me to coast, just because he owns the Star-Drake chain of de-

partment stores," he explained in that serious way of his, "and
with my allowance small as it is . . ."

As a high school sophomore he began inviting Nina everywhere, though she was two years younger. And now . . . .here
he stood directly ahead of us, looking like a young Italian priest
in his dark suit, dark tie and immaculately polished shoes.
"Good evening, dear," I said, shaking hands. "It's always nice
to see you."

While Nina beamed, he bowed, his eyes friendly as a
spaniel's. "Charmed as always, Mrs. Dent."

"It's hard to believe you're such a big boy," I said, forgetting
Fay for the minute. "Remember how you kept howling that
first day at Sunday school?"

"Please, Mother," Nina winced. "No one likes to hear about
when he was little. Don't you know that?"

Larry patted her shoulder. "Once you attend a big university,
you don't mind so much. It's just before that it hurts."

"Excuse me, Fay," I said. "This is Nina's friend, Lawrence
Drake . . . Larry, you haven't met Mrs. Hick until now, have
you?"

"Your husband and my dad — Stanley Drake — play golf together, don't they?" Stepping forward, he placed his hand in
hers.

Nina and I stood enjoying this happy scene.

Now, as Fay started to answer, Larry teetered, gave a gasp-
ing sort of croak and gripped her violently.

"What happened?" I demanded, as she flashed out of sight.
"Wasn't she here a minute ago?"

"Look! Look! Look!" Nina screamed. "They're kissing and
making out like fools."

"But they can't be. Fay's a married woman."

"Look at them! Look at them! Oh, Mother, Mother, isn't
this the *last thing* you would have expected?"

"Indeed it is," I said, beginning to believe my eyes at last.

Oh dear, I thought. Fay's been alone far too much lately. It's not like her to make passes at a college freshman.

"It's Mrs. Hick's fault," Nina shrieked. "She's old enough to know better."

"I'm not sure that it's anyone's fault, dear, human nature being human nature. You'd better run upstairs and fetch Fay's salts. They're on my bureau, I believe."

"But Mother . . ."

"Let's talk about this later . . . Just do as I say."

"Larry Drake, of all people," Nina moaned, dabbing at her eyes. "When I think of the letters he's written, how he's said again and again that we're meant for each other . . . that he wants to marry me . . . Men are awful meanies, aren't they?"

"I wouldn't say so. Run along, please."

As she dragged herself toward the stairs, she called back. "This is the saddest moment of my life. I'll never forget it. Never."

I must stay calm, I thought. Plenty of people have kissed before now . . . and will in the future. Besides, as Mr. Leonard said this morning, "There can never be too much love and ecstasy in our misguided world."

"Did you say the smelling salts were on your bureau?" Nina called from above. "Oh yes. I see them."

Glancing at the spot where Fay had disappeared, I waggled my finger. "Now, Miss Fix-it. Suppose you add *this* to your collection of facts."

Chapter 6

Dent Journal . . .

Friday, January 15, 1960 (continued)

"GLORY be, what an evening," Fay said, after the young people had gone off to the movies. She was lying in a huddle on my bed, while Pluto kept sniffing jealously.

Observing her with no pleasure, I pondered the reversal in our positions. Here I was in the chaise longue, sitting as erect as possible and looking a bit smug too, I'll admit. My, it had been a satisfaction to wave those salts under her nose and to cry, "Let's come alive, folksies, shall we?" Yet who could forget how deeply she had disturbed Nina? Or how, as a consequence, she had prevented my tidying up the dinner dishes promptly?

While Fay continued to speak in a disconnected singsong, I recalled how she had ogled herself a moment before. Standing in my negligee, she had asked her swaying reflection:

> *Was this the face that launched a thousand ships*
> *And burnt the topless towers of Ilium?*
> *Sweet Helen, make me immortal with a kiss!*
> *Her lips suck forth my soul: see, where it flies!*

"Sweet Helen, climb yourself under that afghan," I commanded, shoving her. "One, two, three, heave-ho."

"Martinet, sadist," she hissed.

"Names can never hurt me, Fay. Goodness knows I like to

think the best of people. But when you set y‹
did, for a mere boy . . ."

"Larry was sweet," she said, thrashing abou‹
Sweet. Sweet."

When she had become more rational, I said, ‹
Tonight's happenings may prove to be a blessing.‹

"No clichés, if you please. I can't endure them."‹

"But haven't we every reason to be thankful? Those two young people have needed a good shaking-up. They're taking themselves much too seriously."

"So as usual every cloud has its silver lining?" Oh, her tone was biting.

"Certainly." Then, remembering how Nina had blazed at Larry once he came out of his coma, I couldn't help laughing. "Oh ho ho . . ."

"There's that cussed resilience again," Fay groaned. "I'll never get used to it."

"Won't you? How I wish Jack could have popped in on us tonight. Can you imagine his surprise at seeing his golfing partner's son entangled with his wife? Oh ho ho!"

After picturing this possibility she tittered weakly. Then, half eager, half smiling, she asked, "Do you suppose that I'm on the verge of a nervous crack-up?"

"Of course not. Remember what Dr. Baxter said: 'Keep busy. . . . Try to accept things as they are.' "

"If only Jack and I could have a child one of these days — then maybe we wouldn't fuss with toothpaste bets and such. I hope once I begin work in my laboratory . . ." Tears had come to her eyes.

"There, there. When Jack comes you don't want to look upset, do you?"

Her mood began to brighten. "I adore him. I do. I do, even though I've been a trial to him lately . . . Marrying impulsively as we did means that we have so much to learn still, so many adjustments to make. We're both so willful . . . each of us trying to demonstrate superiority to the other like a couple of spoiled kids."

"But, Fay, is it wise for a woman to try to prove to her husband that she's smarter than he is? Whenever she wins an argument, isn't she apt to lose some of her charm for him?"

"Where did you get that crazy idea?"

"I don't know. But doesn't it make sense? Of course Jack is proud of you and he should be. But can't you concentrate on making him all the more sure that *he's* wonderful? Isn't this a wife's main job?"

"But he knows he's wonderful already. We all know it to the point where it makes me cross sometimes. Besides, in business he hated anyone, man or woman, to kowtow, flatter him or lack the courage of his own convictions."

"You're no longer at Amyrillis, Fay Hick. When will you begin to realize it?"

"I don't know," she said again, shrugging her shoulders. "But I've admitted already shortcomings as a wife. And all my life, I've insisted on learning things the hard way."

After we had chatted some more, she jumped to her feet, washed and dressed. Soon she stood twirling in her tiny strapless pumps. Ah, but she seemed all lightness, femininity and anticipation. Imperfect or not, there's only one Fay, I thought.

As she began prettying her face, I remembered my cluttered dinner table again. "If you'll excuse me for a minute, dear."

"No you don't," she yelped, forcing me back into the chaise. "Stay *put* until we finish some business here."

"But," I began, while Pluto growled a warning.

"Shush. Do as I say, Maybelle."

I love you, Fay Amelia Hick, I thought. But when you're this way, you're unspeakable.

After combing and patting her black ringlets, she said, "I'm sure this little camphor stick is mystifying you too. Mind if I

try a bit more?" Without waiting for an answer she picked up
the tube and applied it. "Nice. Very nice."

"Now you're finished, toss it in the watebasket and good
riddance." While I was speaking, I saw her become more
flushed, radiant and energetic. Imagine!

"Notice what's happening here? Whee, I feel wonderful!"

Truly all this seemed increasingly strange. But I wasn't ready
to admit it yet.

After giving herself another approving look, Fay whipped
out a notebook and fountain pen. When she had settled herself on the bed again, she began to write. "Let's see, this is
Friday, January 15, 1960, isn't it? The temperature here must be
seventy-eight or so . . . Now, you say you found this camphor
stick stored away in Joe's old humidor? Hm-mm."

What will power, I thought, as her tiny body, legs and feet
continued to quiver. But why must we review all these dull
details now, for goodness' sakes?

"Point out the closet and the carton in question," she
ordered.

"Oh dear, must I? This is boring."

"No matter. We have a duty toward science."

"I couldn't care less."

"You're too big a girl to look petulant. Come on!"

Ah, but I disliked confessing and demonstrating my foolish
hoarding habits. Why did Fay have to be so insistent and nosy?

Once I had hauled out the humidor, she grabbed it in a
flash. "What, oh what have we here?" she caroled, removing
each item in sequence. "Oddments of soap, sachet, perfume
and face powder dried up and stale . . . Aha, and look at this
cunning old locket." Then, after fingering the packet of Indian
essences, "Thank Heavens these attars are available in the
market still. Oh, but we're lucky."

"Are we?"

"It's stupendous, Maybelle. Stupendous. Listen . . . once

we've tested the silver in this trinket, we'll learn whether its
interaction carries significance." By now she had become every
inch a chemist. "There's not a single element here which can't
be duplicated one way or another. Yes, with a bit of patience
and skill, we'll match this formula exactly."

"Now may I put my possessions back where they belong?"

"Yes. But of course I plan to take this humidor and its contents home with me tonight. And once my laboratory is
built . . ."

Oh dear, I thought, observing her blazing eyes, the luminos-
ity of skin and hair, Fay's far from normal still. Imagine this
goofy idea.

"Think of it! Think of it!" she shouted. "Do you know that
every cosmetic manufacturer is *aching* for a new lipstick
formula? In the past ten years, what superlatively unique item
has our industry developed? Has there been anything since
that smudgeproof lanolin-base product became famous?"
Then, as I looked baffled, "Surely you remember its marvelous
advertising blurb: 'Won't smear off, eat off, drink off or kiss
off . . .' "

Of course this rang a familiar bell. In fact I knew those
words as well as my own name.

"Yes, there's been no progress made on lipsticks in the past
decade. Absolutely none. Oh, what an opportunity lies ahead.
This will be the most cussedly challenging project *ever*. In no
time I'll show Jack, Bernard Huggin and everyone else at
Amyrillis that I'm Dr. Fay B. Amelia still."

"But isn't this common knowledge?"

"You forget that retirement for a year hasn't been good.
There's always the danger of losing one's skill or getting care-
less." Then, throwing back her head, she yodeled, "But before long, I'll make the industry sit up and take notice."

By now I had begun to enjoy the picture of Fay in a white

coat surrounded by bubbling test tubes. "Once you're in your laboratory I'm sure you'll have a picnic."

"Picnic? Do you think that tracking down and duplicating this formula will be easy?"

"No. But I'll bet you have fun."

"Fun? *Fun?*" She tossed with anger. "Do you suppose that we're discussing paper dolls, dear girl? Aren't you aware that if I achieve this lipstick it will be a scientific phenomenon? If we're able to harness and share this potential with humanity, won't it open vistas beyond comprehension?"

"Now, now, Fay . . ."

"Good Lord, Maybelle. Here we're faced with the challenge of the ages and you babble about picnics and fun." Reaching for the camphor stick, she held it reverently. "After witnessing drama on three occasions today, won't you grant that amazing chemical changes have taken place here?" As I sat silent and hurt, she added, "Once this mixture was on your lips and mine, what happened?"

Oho . . . so in her unsettled state of mind, she thought this bit of a stick could induce sex emotion and kissing? Imagine a scientist sailing off on such a notion!

"Concentrate, dear," she said more gently. "Won't you admit that my theory makes sense?"

"No . . . not yet." Still, I knew that I had worn the pomade before dinner. And afterwards Fay . . .

"Aha!" she cried, reading my thoughts as she does frequently. "So light dawns at last, does it?"

"Maybe so."

"In time you'll agree with me," she promised. "As I said before, I don't anticipate too many difficulties in duplicating this formula. And once we succeed, we'll take our findings to Amyrillis. As usual, top executives there will hem and haw about anything radically new. But in time, Bernard Huggin should sway conservative Jack with the usual pitch: how we must continue to be courageous leaders and years ahead of competitors. Yes, I'll bet my life on it."

"You sound like a smart business woman, Fay."

"Ho, I've never been a business woman. Basically I'm a chemist and a damn good one. I've never taken credit for my formulas proving to be such money-makers. How could I, with Jack's merchandising and advertising astuteness what it is?" Her face glowed with pride. "But I know this. He and I have been a one-in-a-million team together from the very beginning."

How I envied her her knowledge and worldliness. Why, in contrast, was I so naïve? Then I heard myself asking like a schoolgirl, "Say, what goes on in that lovely Fifth Avenue Amyrillis building? On shopping trips I've always wondered."

"Nothing exciting." She shrugged her shoulders. "Mainly window dressing, showrooms, beauty salons, executive offices and stuff. The real eye-openers, of course, are over in Jersey. Some day you must see our floors of laboratories . . ." Her eyes misted. "Ah, they're fabulous."

"But it's the Fifth Avenue place that entrances me . . . You know, with its glass exterior, canopy and beautiful doorman."

"Just stuff and window dressing," she repeated. Then, with a sharp glance, "Incidentally, if we should get a turn-down from Amyrillis, some day you'll find yourself learning plenty. Because then we'll be forced to take on manufacture and distribution ourselves."

"You mean you and I might go into business *together?*" She nodded. "Wonderful. I'm a whiz-bang at selling. You should see me every year at our church bazaar, getting rid of more bric-a-brac and hideous white elephants . . ."

"Really?" she asked, unimpressed.

"Oh yes."

Now again she had slipped back into that Egyptian pose, her eyes somber, her expression drawn and intent. Poor dear girl, why was she so subject to delight one minute, pain the next? Why did fire seem to kindle and consume her from head to toe?

During the next hour or so we sat building air castles. Increasingly I began to feel that we might be on the verge of many exciting new experiences. What's more, we might be able to include Grace Thorpe in our setup, forming a trio one of these days, for better or worse.

When Nina and Larry returned at last, Fay jumped to attention. "False alarm, damn it," she said, after identifying their voices. "For a minute I thought it was Jack." Then, with a sigh, "Tell me, Maybelle. This is personal, but I must get it off my chest . . . Is it normal for a man in his fifties, a married man, I mean, to be tired night after night?"

Since I love subjects like these I couldn't have shown more delight. "Oh deary me, yes. I'll never forget how Joe used to sit in the den yawning over his newspaper."

"Was he increasingly vain too?"

I couldn't help smiling to myself. Joe vain? Heavens no . . . just the contrary, in his comfortable brown smoking jacket with his shirt loosened at the throat. But before I could answer Fay bent closer.

"Jack's become Beau Brummell the Second. Yes, he has! I understand his wishing to look like the best-dressed-man-of-the-year, in business. But you should see the gentleman-at-ease outfits he's begun to wear at home — English lounging slacks, a maroon velvet jacket and bowed slippers, if you please. Maybe all these magazine write-ups about tycoon John Calhoun Hick the Third have gone to his head. Anyhow he's a sketch."

"He's always been handsome. How could he help but know it?"

"Maybe he's trying to look snappier than he feels," she added thoughtfully. "Or maybe my dressed-up, dozing darling needs vitamins and pep-up injections. I'm positive that there's no other woman in his life. Still, lately . . . as a husband . . ."

"A man's work demands every ounce of energy these days, Fay. And with a man of Jack's age, marriage means accepting whatever is left, doesn't it?"

"I suppose so. Well, this phase should pass in time. And who knows but this merry little lipstick may start us on a second honeymoon soon?"

Then we both had to throw back our heads and laugh. Ah, how we enjoyed feeling like teen-agers dabbling into the more serious problems of life.

"Well, we'd better see how our young people are faring," I said, getting up and stretching. "By now they must have settled their grievances. And Larry, you know, always expects his evening snack."

"All right," Fay said, placing the little camphor stick on my bureau. "I'd love some cake and milk myself. I feel eternally starved these days somehow . . ."

After greeting Nina and Larry I was glad to see their renewed happiness together. Ah, but we older people should learn from our children, I thought. Unfailingly they make up quickly, never carrying a grudge.

Once we were in the living room enjoying our refreshments, I remembered the clutter of dinner dishes. "Please don't think I'm a neglectful housekeeper," I told Larry blushingly, "but tonight was . . . most . . . unsettling, of course."

"Oh dear, Mother," Nina scolded. "Don't bring up that subject again, for Pete's sake. We've agreed to forget it. Besides, with world conditions what they are, what do a few unwashed plates matter?"

"Mm-mm," Larry said between mouthfuls. "Mrs. Dent, if your daughter could cook this way, I'd marry her tomorrow."

While I was trying to phrase some sort of answer, Nina jumped to her feet. "Excuse me, everyone. I need to primp a bit. I'll be back in a flash."

"There's no satisfaction like watching a man enjoy his food," I said, after bringing in second helpings of cake.

Now, as the doorbell clanged, Fay cried, "Aha, here comes Jack at last."

"I'll answer it. I'll answer it," Nina crowed from upstairs in my bedroom. Oh dear, was she *there*, using my cosmetics and mirror again as usual? Yes, I was sure she was. What could a mother do with such a headstrong miss?

As the bell rang again, she came bolting downward two steps at a time. Seventeen years old, I told myself, but stubborn as seventy, darn it.

"Good evening, Nina." Jack's voice was heavy with fatigue as he stepped into the vestibule. "My wife's here still, isn't she?"

From the corner of my eye I saw his impeccably trimmed gray hair, square cheekbones and velvet-collared coat. Poor man, how worn and weary he seemed after his overlong day. No wonder businessmen bearing his responsibilities kept dropping like flies from heart attacks.

But at Nina's approach, magic new vigor seemed to transform him bit by bit into Atlas the Strong Man. After rearing back on his heels with muscles flaring, he stood joyfully intent. Me oh my, had he entertained his customers tonight with overstrong liquids? . . . No, Fay had often spoken of his capacities and unfailing clearheadedness.

While I was pondering this question, Fay had leaped up with a happy little yip. "Ah, here you are, honey. I thought you'd *never* come." She ran toward him, arms outstretched and eyes glowing.

For a moment his glance stayed glued on Nina. That child *is* wearing some of that camphor-stick mixture, I thought. Yes, I'm sure of it. But Fay is wearing some too. Now what?

Tripping over a rug in her haste, Fay hurtled toward Jack's chest. "Help, darling, help." In a flash he had reached out,

caught and swept her into a passionate embrace. Too much
happening too fast, I thought, and complicated as a basketball game.

"Wow," Nina blinked. "A double wow. You'd never guess
they'd been married a year, would you?"

Fay was right, I told myself. She and Jack *are* on the verge
of a second honeymoon, with problems solved and forgotten.

Pluto dragged himself out from under the piano, baying
mournfully.

"Far better a kiss between man and wife than ugly arguments," I told him. "So let's be patient."

"Even at college parties, I've never seen such a clinch,"
Larry marveled. "Yippee!" My, it seemed good to hear him
relaxing boyishly at last.

"The Hicks are in love . . . in love . . . in love . . ." Nina
sang out, stepping toward him. As she smiled enchantingly,
she revealed her white, even schoolgirl teeth.

"I'm in love too . . . and you're very, very, very . . ." Larry
yodeled as she came closer and closer. (Evidently he too was
responding to the camphor stick. Wasn't there every sign of
it?)

As Larry wrenched Nina's body toward his, I swallowed again
and again. No wonder Pluto continued to howl with ever-
growing intensity. Truly the goings-on here were far from right.

After turning from one couple to the next, I said aloud,
"Lackaday, what, oh what should we do next?"

As our boxer dragged back under the piano, I stood where I
was, alone and completely forgotten. It had been a strenuous
day. I was in no shape to separate one pair of lovers, much less
two. We need a man's strength and determination here, I
thought, hurrying to the telephone. I dialed the Perkin number.
"Hello, Alvin, hello."

"I'll come immediately," he said, sensing trouble.

Soon he was following me into the living room. "Moonstruck, Maybelle," he muttered, after glancing about and whistling. "Poor beezers." Then, looking more and more mystified, "What the devil's going on here? And why?"

"Fay says it's the effect of a new beauty product."

"*What?*" His agonized look indicated that he was sure my mind had given way. Why did he seem so sensitive to any form of illness, letting pity affect him deeply?

"Well . . ." I heard myself saying. "We've discovered a lipstick with an irresistibly kissable feature. What's more, we plan to have it manufactured and marketed."

"Is that so?" His tone couldn't have been more compassionate or patient. "Here. Let me get you some cracked ice? How's that poor banged-up head?" His horn-rimmed blue eyes were bright with concern as though he were tending his invalid mother.

"I'm serious, Alvin. Watch while I do a demonstration." I began to dance and clap my hands. "Do they hear me? Do they?" I was flying this way and that, with my blond hair bobbing and my dignity forgotten completely.

He stood drinking in this picture.

"Watch again." Now I clapped four pairs of shoulders in turn smartly. "Do they *feel* me? Or respond in any way?"

"Do they? Do they? Do they?" He mocked joyfully. "No, Maybelle. No."

Then, instead of stepping into action, he spoke with reverence. "Aha. This is interesting. Looks like a natural for *Perk Predicts* some day . . . When will this item be on the market?"

After taking a long breath, I said, "*Never*, I hope."

Part Two

Chapter 7

EXCERPT from the *Perk Predicts* program, Station ZDQ, New York, New York, Friday, July 1, 1960.

"*Good morning, friends and listeners across America. Here is Alvin Perkin wishing you and your family the best of the best.*

"*. . . I am ready to state now,* unequivocally, *that a new lipstick formula has been discovered. This formula is so new, so completely daring and different, that it will replace and throw into the discard every other lipstick on the market.*

"*Unfortunately, ladies, you cannot rush to your nearest store to demand this beauty marvel. No. Not yet. Giddy Moment, for such is its name, has just been newly born, newly baptized. Today it is cradled still in the laboratory where scientific skill and a dedicated woman's ingenuity brought it into being.*

"*Because of a promise made to my informant, it is impossible to tell you now what feature makes Giddy Moment the sensational item which it is. Also I am unable to state under what label it will be manufactured or what retail price it will carry. However, it is a fact that top business negotiations involving the possible purchase of this product by a nationally famous beauty concern are scheduled for this morning.*

"So Perk Predicts *that within six months, Giddy Moment will begin to change your life and the thinking of the billion-and-a-half-dollar cosmetic and toiletries industry.*

"*If and when there are new developments to report, I promise that you will hear them first as always on this program.*"

Dent Journal . . . . *Friday, July 1, 1960*

IN spite of resolutions, I see that six months have passed since my last entry. Oh dear, why do I continue to be so lax?

Lax or not, I feel ready to burst over recent happenings. Without question today has been completely unlike any before. Consequently, whenever I pass a handsome Fifth Avenue building in the future, I won't wonder what's buzzing inside there. Instead I'll *know*. And when men start discussing sales, demonstration and advertising techniques, I'll add my five cents' worth with gusto.

It is unlike me, I'll admit, to be writing such statements in the late afternoon, of all times. But with Pluto asleep close by and Nina busy with her summer selling job, I find I must confide in someone. So, dear journal, here we are together on the chaise, with me in my best business clothes still.

Since duty remains duty, I shall cover family news before describing more recent personal events. But this routine, which Joe insisted upon, has never and will never appeal to me. Who really cares about yesterday or the day before, please? It's *today* that matters, isn't it, with tomorrow important only when it comes?

However, here we go, beginning with Nina. Of course she finished her junior year with A grades and every sign of being valedictorian of her class. At this rate there is no doubt that she will be accepted at Radcliffe.

She continues to have positive ideas on civil rights, every phase of sociology and world politics. Also she shows a baffling flair for the dramatic . . . Why must she wear her dark hair slicked back into a schoolteacherish little bun these days? Haven't I protested innumerable times that it is unflattering?

But Fay insists that this simplicity accentuates Nina's smooth babylike skin. Also she approves her passion for bracelets and earrings, the bigger, the more bizarre, the better.

In contrast, it has been a joy to see Nina build leadership in our church youth group. Recently she wrote and delivered a sermon on the Beatitudes, stressing my favorite: "Blessed are the pure in heart." I shall never forget how radiant she looked in that deep blue robe, with the spotlight accentuating the tip of her nose and eyeglasses. Or how modestly she accepted praise for her poise, amazing vocabulary and delivery.

Increasingly, she shows every sign of being an eighteen-year-old with unusually fine ideals. This year again, she refused to join a sorority because of concern for nonmembers. Though she tends to be slightly flat-chested, she will not buy or wear garments to correct this situation. (When I raised this subject for the dozenth time the other day, she said, "Other girls may resort to such deceit, Mother, but I *can't*. Besides, Larry likes me as I am, doesn't he?")

So far, I regret to say, she has shown no zeal for housekeeping or cooking. She has continued to suggest that we use quick-frozen foods, prepared mixes and other time-savers. Also that we eliminate heavy cream, homemade breads and desserts of every type. But I have been adamant in maintaining standards begun by my mother years ago.

Though she insists that love of good food will make me overweight, the fact remains that it hasn't. Perhaps the new girdle which Fay helped me to select at Saks Fifth Avenue recently helps to make a size fourteen fit nicely. In any case I don't know anyone, woman or girl, whose hips, waistline and legs look more trim.

The biggest bone of contention between Nina and me is the fact that she respects neither my breadth of experience nor judgment. "You're so trusting, Mother, it hurts," she's said repeatedly.

This comment came particularly strongly after I had paid

cash for several magazine subscriptions without getting a receipt. But since the young man selling them had a pair of crutches and a shabby naval uniform, who could doubt his character? It is a fact, though, that we have as yet received no issues of *Beautiful Surroundings* and of *More Glorious Living*. Also our sailor has not been seen anywhere in Arlington since.

Surely I have failed to give my daughter abiding faith in people. Yet whenever I express grief over the situation, she seems ready to both laugh and cry. "Come off it," she said no more than a day or two ago. "When you give a sermon like this, you're positively funny."

Until now I have postponed saying that Nina and Larry are engaged. I find it hard to believe that they will be married next June, even though she is wearing her beautiful sapphire-and-diamond ring already. Of course youthful weddings are commonplace these days, but the prospect of this one makes me twinge. Especially since our bride and groom intend to live in separate dormitories next year.

With special permission I am sure that they could arrange to live together in an apartment. But Nina says that day-to-day association with other girls is an important part of education. "Besides, Mother, Larry and I will make the most of week ends, you can bet." Oh, dear, how can one argue with such non-sensical stubbornness?

The more I see our engaged pair, the more convinced I am that they are too alike. Why does their main joy in life center on the first, second and fifth Constitutional Amendments and incessant vocabulary improvement?

Last week as usual they teased me with jawbreakers such as *ratiocination* and *etiology*. "Something as out of your field, Mother dear, as the moon." Of course I haven't bothered to learn the meaning of these words yet. But in an effort at politeness, I made inquiries on the spelling.

Who leads whom in this team, I would not know. But

Larry being the son of the president of Star-Drake landed Nina her summer job in Papa's Arlington store. Yet he himself preferred to take a fling in Wall Street, where his wealth and high retail connections were unknown. Evidently he believes that business experience is an important part of education for men and women alike.

Naturally I was loath to see a young girl earning money and inevitably hardening herself. But what could I do against my future son-in-law's persuasiveness?

Incidentally, he and Nina are saving every nickel toward a honeymoon in Bermuda. "If we earn it ourselves, we'll enjoy it more," they repeat. I cannot understand why they are blind to the charms of Spain, with its beautiful coastline, balconies and darling little courtyards. But like Pluto in his ecstasy over beef-heart stew — each of us to his taste.

It is a relief to be talking about Pluto by now, since he is far less complex than our lovebirds. As I indicated some months ago, his best friend continues to be Spike, Grace Thorpe's beautiful black poodle. I would not know why he always chooses pals who are far smaller and less lively than himself. Or why, day after day, he howls through the neighborhood, seeking his playmate.

Our pet has been through a couple of horrid experiences lately. Several weeks ago he was picked up by the dog-catcher in front of the Perkin house.

Of course I had forgotten that Arlington had installed Mayor Baxter's new animal-policing system. Also that we townspeople had endorsed it as another means of improving candidacy for next January's Arcturus Award. Therefore, I never guessed that Pluto was in difficulty until I heard his heart-rending yelps.

After rushing outdoors I stood glaring after the patrol wagon and crying, "Come back, dear. Come back. Where are they taking you?"

Soon Alvin was at my side, offering his handkerchief. "Stop putting on such a scene. Wipe your eyes, Maybelle." After phoning the mayor, he arranged to have Pluto returned. Also he said that if I kept him indoors until ten o'clock each morning, there would be no danger of future arrests. "On the other hand, if you're eager for a session with Captain O'Rourke of the Nassau County Police . . ." My, but I shuddered at *that* prospect.

In reviewing this incident, I see that there is every reason for Alvin to carry "pull" with Horace Baxter. Hasn't he praised Arlington again and again on his *Perk Predicts* program? And yesterday didn't he eulogize the success of dog-policing as a "means of protecting private property and little children at play"? "Characteristically," he intoned, "our citizens have given one hundred per cent co-operation, welcoming this development with enthusiasm."

When I teased him on inconsistency, he showed no signs of concern. Instead of trying to justify his action, he changed the subject swiftly. "How come you named your dog Pluto?"

"Oh, don't you know?" I laughed. "Joe was a great one for reading mythology in the original Greek."

"So that's it," he said mockingly. "I thought you'd been paying a spritelike tribute to mineral water advertisements." Now wasn't this like Alvin, saving face with a wheezy little joke?

Pluto's other distracting experience came after contracting a severe case of eczema. Once he had spent twenty-four hours at the veterinarian's, he came home shaking, squealing and smelling most dreadfully. Then for several weeks my poor pet had to wear a sort of snug white-ribbed pajama suit, which made him feel disgraced. But this agony is behind us, thank fortune, and he is again his normal, affectionate self.

Now at last we come to me, a person who is beginning to change, to breathe more deeply, stretch and flutter her wings.

Without question this development is tied in with six months of close association with Fay.

Yet in spite of her demands, I have maintained a life of my own. I mean I've followed the practice of washing dishes immediately after meals and making beds with neatly folded, hospital-type corners. I've continued to visit with friends, to gossip in the shopping center, to enjoy rich food and to spend late afternoons on the sofa, relaxing with my eyes half closed.

In addition, I've become increasingly active in community affairs, serving as piano-accompanist for the choral group, as secretary of the Garden Club and heading the PTA refreshment committee.

These interests have been a godsend in easing disappointment over the Tasty-Flour Baking Contest fiasco. Ah me, I shall never understand why the judges failed to give even a minor award to my angel cake supreme and fig macaroon recipes. How in Heaven's name could they have found superior merit in some Maine housewife's lobster pimento pie? Well, at least I have the satisfaction of having dared to pit my skills against those of other women across the country.

I would not know why one failure has a way of raising other old ghosts of disappointment. Anyway, the polite note of rejection from Tasty-Flour made me recall a similar one from a magazine editor: "Try to gain deeper personal experience, Mrs. Dent, before tackling a love story again."

As I read that terse typewritten note five years ago, dreams of authorship died with a crash. Now I would never see works from my pen heaped on newsstands and in bookstore windows. "Give up, foolish," I told myself. Yet how hard it is to stifle hopes, especially those cherished since girlhood.

On the brighter side, I have found increasing delight in Alvin's company. Where would we *be* if he didn't come to dinner so often? Or if, in spite of Nina's dismay, he didn't bring his old banjo along? What fun we've had, evening after evening, teaming up on "Drifting and Dreaming," "Sweetheart of Sigma Chi" and "Moonlight Bay."

One reason that we love these sessions is that my piano skill has improved remarkably. But why wouldn't it, after long, secret hours of practice?

With Nina at school and Fay supervising the thriving lipstick factory in her cellar, I have found time for private daily calisthenics too. This routine began soon after hearing a Woman's Club speaker say, "Ladies, if you start strenuous gymnastic exercises, following them faithfully, you'll gather rewards beyond number."

But this philosophy, I realize, applies word for word to *every* phase of life. Otherwise, would Fay have been able to *prove* herself as a chemist, inventing a sensational new lip pomade and trademarking it Giddy Moment?

If Nina were not so much like her father, I might admit my piano-practicing sessions, calisthenics and growing interest in Alvin Perkin. But of course I would never dare to confess that Fay and I are partners in a cosmetic enterprise.

How amazed Nina would be, though, to hear that we expect to make millions of dollars, with any number of people pounding on our doors!

Goodness knows, I wouldn't know what to do with oodles of money . . . or how to keep track of it. But it would be nice to feel a little important some day.

Chapter 8

Friday, July 1, 1960 (continued)

WHO would have guessed that I carry a secret hunger for importance? Yet, having made this confession, I suppose that I must accept and face it.

Why, I wonder, does eagerness for recognition carry such elixir? Is this a sort of balm easing new burdens? Will it help in making inevitable decisions? Is it a sign of weakness or of growing strength? These are tantalizing questions, yet I am in no position to answer them.

It's so much easier, isn't it, to see other people's motives? Take Fay, for example, driven month after month by zeal to re-establish prestige with Amyrillis. Yet as always she seems overdramatic in insisting that she would die if necessary to achieve this goal.

In any case, two weeks ago, once she had duplicated the original lipstick formula successfully, she persuaded Jack to arrange an Amyrillis conference.

Naturally I was not in favor of moving so fast. But the more I thought about having my first inside look at a big cosmetic company, the more excited I became.

Meanwhile, Fay had chosen today, Friday, July first, for our wingding. It was important, she said, for us to begin with a leisurely breakfast at her home. "This way, Maybelle, we'll collect ourselves nicely for what lies ahead."

Following instructions to the letter this morning, I came roll-

ing up the Hicks' driveway promptly at eight o'clock. Ah, but
I took particular pleasure in its thick borders of blooming
blue hydrangeas. Still, as the stone mansion loomed ahead, I
couldn't help wondering why Jack had built such a monstrosity.

Soon Greta was opening the door with a cheerful "Goot
morning." At the same moment Duke leaped past us exactly
as he had done months before. But knowing his naughty ways
by now, she gripped him by the collar. "No, *Liebchen*, no.
Inside you come before I spank your bottom."

Though the July heat had been insufferable, the Hicks'
rooms were almost chilly. This, I knew, resulted from Fay's
having stepped up the air-cooling units in spite of Jack's objections. "You forget I'm here all day, dear," she had said in
justification. "And you're in and out, aren't you?"

"Still, we don't need to freeze," he had said, shivering and
quite blue.

Today as the Hicks and I took our seats, the breakfast room
seemed cozy. Yet, glancing about, I realized that the décor
was flamboyant by Arlington standards — highlights of vivid
reds and greens, modernistic lighting and a superabundance
of lush tropical plants.

My host and hostess were unusually quiet as they drank their
orange juice. Then, after Greta had served eggs and bacon,
they continued to eat with no pleasure. Why? I wondered,
knowing that this was a favorite dish usually.

To ease the strain, I kept chatting. "Isn't it lovely for us to
be driving to the city today? Won't we have a lark in that
Fifth Avenue menage! Oh, I simply can't wait."

"I'm glad somebody eats breakfast this morning," Greta
said, as I enjoyed a piece of toast spread with her special cherry
jam. Then, with a concerned glance toward Fay, "Ma'am,
finish those goot hot eggs."

"No thanks. Just another cup of coffee, please."

Being well acquainted with the Hicks' habits, I was happy

to see them listening to station ZDQ music as usual. During breakfast we continued to absorb Strauss waltzes, one of them galloping on the heels of the next. Now, as the "Blue Danube" wound up, Jack pushed back his chair. "Excuse me, girls. I must look over some papers upstairs . . . Let's plan to leave in another twenty minutes."

As he marched off, I noticed that Fay's fingers were trembling. "*Perk Predicts* is due to begin immediately," she said with a wink.

Alvin's voice trumpeted out, drowning hers. "Good morning, friends and listeners across America . . . I am ready to state now, *unequivocally*, that a new lipstick formula has been discovered . . ."

"Nice man, you kept your promise," she cried. "I knew you would."

"Don't tell me you made secret arrangements with Alvin," I said, deeply hurt.

"Yes . . . it so happens that I did."

"But partners should never keep things from each other . . . Also, when I saw Alvin last night, he didn't mention this."

"He promised he wouldn't."

"Why?"

"I was afraid you might spill the beans. Look . . . we've got to have every possible advantage on our side before heading into that conference. Besides" — her eyes sparkled — "I've bet Jack five hundred dollars that we'll walk out of it with a signed contract."

"Fay, you didn't!"

"Of course I did. What's more, now I've made that bet, I want the fun of winning it. Why not? Some people play the horses, others are brains at chess . . . but Jack and I . . ." With a jerk of her wrist, she silenced Alvin's voice rapping out some sports scandal.

"I'm not used to such games," I said, frowning.

"In time you will be. Listen, Maybelle. After jeering at our Giddy Moment project it won't hurt John Calhoun Hick to eat crow."

"But . . ."

"No buts. Have you forgotten how he's fought this lipstick from the beginning? No wonder he's goaded me into fighting with equal persistence. The more we catch Jack off guard today, the better our chances to win." She clapped her hands delightedly.

Oh dear, I said to myself, if we should get a turndown on Giddy Moment, she won't be in this minxlike mood.

"Don't sit there looking gloomy," Fay cried, reading my thoughts as usual. "There's no chance for a fumble here. We're sure to succeed and I'll prove I'm a better chemist than ever." Then, as her eyes grew misty, "Maybe I haven't been able to give Jack a son yet. But in Giddy Moment I've accomplished something taking far more ingenuity."

"Now, now . . . don't upset yourself."

"You're right." After dabbing at her eyes, she asked with forced gaiety, "Do you know what part of Alvin's blurb I liked best today?"

"No. Which?"

"That tribute to scientific skill and a woman's ingenuity. Wasn't it nice?"

"Yes. Perfectly lovely. But what I loved best was that touch about Giddy Moment being newly born, baptized and cradled. It made me remember when Nina was a tiny mite, all cuddly . . ."

"I can see how it would," she cut in. "Well, as I was saying before, if Jack gets his comeuppance at Amyrillis, it will be what he deserves. Remember how he's kept insisting that no lipstick ever would, ever could do what ours does? Even after that eye-opener at your house months ago, was he reasonable?"

"I'll admit he's been hard to convince."

She flushed. "That's the understatement of the century. When a man of fifty makes a dive at a young thing like Nina, wouldn't you suppose he'd ask himself the whys behind such action? And Maybelle, if you could know the difference Giddy Moment has made in our marriage. Jack has never felt better nor more full of pep."

Aha, I thought. So my predictions on that score came through, did they?

"Finally Jack had to concede that our lipstick was capsuled dynamite. But he kept right on insisting that I would never be able to analyze or duplicate its formula. His overbearing attitude beyond everything else drove me into spending nights as well as days in my laboratory. No wonder I went without food and sleep, working there hour after hour."

"Poor Fay. This hasn't been easy, I know."

"Easy?" Her eyes burned. "Not exactly. Every time I think of those incessant, gibing wisecracks . . ." She began to imitate Jack's tenor voice. " 'Aha, Mrs. Ponce de Leon, are you still seeking your Fountain of Foolishness?' Then each time I blew my stack, he'd suggest dismantling the laboratory. Believe me, he's been 'for the birds.' "

"So have you," I said gently. "I don't like to say this . . . but how much prima-donna temperament will a man stand? Even one of Jack's good disposition. Do you want to wreck your marriage?"

"What a question. Jack and I love each other. We always will."

"You won't if you keep on this way. Why take teasing and a husband's stubbornness so seriously? Remember how proud Jack was when he saw that you'd solved the formula, duplicating our original sample exactly? It wasn't so much what he said, I suppose, as how he looked — like a child seeing his very first Christmas tree."

"He was sweet, wasn't he?" Her face glowed fleetingly.

"And can you forget how we celebrated at the Golf Club with pheasant and champagne?"

"But haven't you heard Jack say time and time again that no reliable manufacturer will touch such a harebrained item? Hasn't he urged us repeatedly to dump and burn our findings?" Her expression had become brooding again.

"He gave plenty of reasons."

"Too many, thank you, all dating back to the Neolithic Age. Finally, at my insistence, he made the appointment with Bernard Huggin. But now everything is coming to a head to-day . . . Well, I guess I'm jumpy."

"You of all people, Fay?" Jack asked as he appeared again, carrying himself like a general in his London-tailored suit. "Say, honey, do you like this tie better than the one before? While I was upstairs I . . ."

"It's a credit to Sulka and I've always loved scarlet." She beamed with wifely pride. "You're an unusually attractive man, dear."

"You're all right too," he said, bending and brushing his lips across her cheek. "Once this interlude finishes, let's relax for a week or a month, shall we? Or *try*, anyhow?"

Straightening again, he stood with his rather heavy arms at his sides, his rugged features turned sideways. It was a pose exactly duplicating one in a recent issue of *Fortune*. Underneath the picture of John Calhoun Hick the Third, vice-president of Amyrillis, Inc., had been an article stressing his vision, courage, gift for human relations and good horse sense.

What an odd team they are, I thought, glancing from him to Fay. I've tried to help these two friends in their battle over Giddy Moment. But do they want help really? Mustn't they learn the hard way, ironing out their differences themselves? In some ways they're so smart, in others so blind. Regardless, I'm sure they love each other. Oh dear.

"I'll run and get my hat," Fay said now as Jack bellowed

toward the kitchen for a fresh cup of coffee. "You have on yours, already, Maybelle, haven't you?"

"Mrs. Hick iss not eating fit for a bird lately," Greta said, making the rounds with her steaming pot. "I tempt her with thiss and that, but *ach*, she iss a stubborn one."

"You can say that again," Jack agreed, catching the last words.

"Greta, I must have your delicious jam recipe some time," I said in an effort to cheer her. "Mrs. Hick told me you made this treat from home-grown cherries."

"*Ach*, now, you will see it iss simple enough," she smiled, rattling off the ingredients. "And there iss no sense measuring everything to the last speck like the scientists do." She winked toward the spot where Fay had been standing. "Such care iss needful in the laboratory maybe, but in the kitchen . . ." She made a vulgar little blowing noise.

Throwing back his head, Jack roared with pleasure.

"How iss that coffee, Mr. Hick? Goot?"

"Some days you've done better," he said, squinting one eye at me. "But since that new delivery boy has come into your life . . ."

"You mean old Eddie from the meat market?" She blushed furiously. "Because I gif him a cupcake now and again, you think . . ." Beads of perspiration appeared on her forehead.

What a dreadful tease he is, I thought. Poor decent Greta looks ready to cry.

"Are you sure that's your *only* handout?" Jack was almost bursting with merriment.

"Well . . . a bit of milk or tea sometimes maybe . . ."

"Seems to me I've seen a new tender look in your eyes lately. Are you positive there's no hocus-pocus here?"

As he smiled roguishly, Greta caught his little joke at last. "You are the very limit, Mr. Hick," she scolded. "*Ach*, you should be spanked."

"I'm just having some fun," he said, throwing all his super-charged batteries of charm toward her. "The coffee's never been better. You're one girl in a million, Greta, and we know it."

He means no harm, I thought. But sometimes, like Fay, he's dreadfully clumsy.

"Are you looking forward to your first visit to Amyrillis?" he asked, turning toward me.

"Oh yes. Tremendously."

"Offhand, what do you expect it will be like?"

"Somehow I keep imagining incense, brass gongs, and very sheer waving curtains."

"Ho. You're a sketch."

"I can see Fay right at home in a sort of harem outfit." Though embarrassed, I was convinced I should tell the truth. "But it's harder to fit you into the picture, Jack."

"You mean I'm neither the sultan nor the eunuch type?"

"Well . . . I think of you as an American businessman always. One of the nicest and best."

"Thank you, my dear. I'll try to correct your impressions today, with a look-see worth remembering."

"Excellent," Fay cried, flying past us toward the kitchen. Then, as she disappeared momentarily, Jack said under his breath, "The girls here worship her just as they did in business . . . I'd like more coffee but I guess there isn't time."

"Come on, everyone," Fay cried as she reappeared. "Are you ready, Maybelle?" Then, tucking a small package into her handbag, "Heaven help us if we forgot our lipstick samples today."

She stood in her ice-white suit with a bit of veiling covering the crown of her head. How like a bride doll with everything so miniature, fragile and perfect. But didn't she seem unusually rigid and staring-eyed?

"Come on, girls. Let's go," Jack said, waving us toward the doorway. "On your toes and chests up."

Chapter 9

Friday, July 1, 1960 (*continued*)

SO far this morning, Fay seemed to be overburdened
by the appointment ahead.

Normally she would have made some comment on my appearance: "Ah, Maybelle, your skin looks exquisite," or "Don't
you look darling in that Sally Victor hat." Today, though,
she had no time for pleasantries. If I had come to breakfast in
my petticoat, I'm sure she never would have noticed it.

When we had climbed into Jack's long white custom-built
Cadillac, I hoped that she might relax a bit. Instead, the prospect of renewing business friendships seemed to create increasing tension. Long after we had settled ourselves, she kept
drubbing her fingers on the pale blue upholstery.

Today, as usual, Jack was a skillful driver, concentrating
on the road ahead, with little or no conversation. Sitting up-
right at the wheel, he showed a rocklike quality equal to any
emergency — a car stopping dead ahead, a plunging jaywalker
or a sudden hole in the street. Yet the aftermath pinkness
rising from the back of his neck indicated more sensitiveness
than he like to show. Surely he had taught himself unusual
self-control over the years.

Until we reached the Triborough Bridge, of course my mind
kept leaping about like a cricket. For example, I'd remember
that Nina's new yellow cashmere sweater had shrunk when I

laundered it yesterday. Yet how *could* it, when I'd taken pains
to use warm water with the mildest of soapsuds?

Dismissing this tragedy, I'd remind myself that we'd be
meeting the president of Amyrillis soon. What sort of a person
would he be . . . Tall or short? Fat or thin? Gracious or gruff?
Wasn't Bernard Huggin sure to be as I imagined him, swarthy
and round like the old Aga Khan, dogged by secretaries in
wisps of sandals? Then I'd tell myself that the cosmetic industry was not a harem swarming with turbaned slaves. Oh
dear, why was I subject to such fancies?

Next, as Fay continued to brood, I pondered Greta's cherry
jam. How delicious it had been this morning, with just the
right consistency and sweetness. Repeating the recipe, I enjoyed its rhythm: one quart cherries, pitted; three cups sugar;
one small pineapple; honey to taste. Aha, I'd make a good
batch soon, surprising Alvin next time he came to dinner. "Maybelle, this is good," he'd cry, piling a third helping on his
plate. "In your way, you're extremely able." But wasn't my
eagerness for his approval based on more than I like to admit?

Dodging this question, I began to review highlights of
cosmetic history which Fay had revealed. American Indians,
she said, were the first on this continent to grease themselves
against cold weather and insects. As recently as two centuries
ago, beauty-conscious housewives followed a similar complexion treatment, sleeping with strips of bacon on their faces. Also,
for the first time they began to use powder, made from perfumed
egg shells, and lemons as a means of reddening lips. Just thirty
years ago the first portable lipstick was sold in a tube-shaped
container. Most interesting of all, the mudpack treatments
popular in the twenties indicated that women *love* fads, the
wilder the better.

While I was recalling this nonsense and trying for the hun-
dredth time to believe it, we started rolling across the bridge.
"Ah, what drama," Fay sighed, absorbing the towering skyline

on our left. "New York City always makes me feel like David in the midst of Goliath."

Now Jack boomed from the front seat, "When you aim at this market, you have to aim right. But we know this already, don't we?"

"We should."

"Cat got your tongue?" Jack teased over his shoulder.

"No. Just thinking, thanks."

As we rolled from East Sixtieth Street on to Fifth Avenue, he spoke again. "I hope you girls are wearing walking shoes."

"Why?"

"Because I've promised Maybelle a sight-seeing excursion — one which should help you both."

"Haven't I seen everything at Amyrillis countless times already?"

"I expect you to look with fresh eyes today."

"At what, please?"

"At everything. There's nothing like an open, inquiring mind to build perspective."

"Ho. Hum."

"Remember, dear, your experience has been confined to chemistry and manufacture exclusively." His tone carried a hint of warning.

"That's true enough," she said, as we came to a stop before the white-canopied Amyrillis entrance. "Ah, here we are at last, Maybelle."

But there was no joy in her words as her expression continued to be pitifully tense. Poor dear. Why should this appointment scare her so?

After tipping his cap, the uniformed doorman helped us to the sidewalk. Next a beautiful young man, personifying everything in the Ivy League, sauntered forward. "Good morning, sir," he said, reaching for Jack's keys. "Hello, Dr. Amelia." After bowing toward me and jumping into the Cadillac, he skimmed off.

"That's Paul Lathrop," Fay said in an undertone. "He came here to be groomed for a top job. But because of laziness, he's dwindled to being Jack's Boy Friday. Everyone hopes he'll quit eventually and return to the retail-buying field."

My, I'd love to be fifteen years younger, I thought. That young man looks good enough to eat.

"Paul's a sweetie-pie," Fay continued, a little sadly, "well-intentioned, mannerly, co-operative, but far from thorough, and unblessed with ambition."

"Is anyone perfect?" I asked, ready to defend him with my life.

"Come on, girls," Jack commanded. "Let's postpone the chitchat until later."

After we had entered the gold-trimmed doorway flanked with cosmetic displays, I saw a sleek black marbleized sales counter. From behind it a duchess type of saleswoman eyed her customer severely. "Naughty girl, your neck shows neglect," she intoned. "Now, I want you to be more conscientious with Amyrillis Cleansing Oil." Her fingers swooped like a sea gull deep into her bosom, then up and outward in strong, deft strokes.

"Ah," Fay whispered. "What progress we've made since old Dr. Galen the Greek invented cold cream."

My, was there anything chemists didn't know, for goodness' sakes?

Now a henna-haired siren began her sales pitch in a drawling, well-bred tone. "Madam, please never, *never* use a pencil on those brows. Instead, we apply the merest bit of mascara with our brush." Lifting a tiny, rose-colored implement, she made illustrative motions.

"Sales volume would never support this space," Jack said, guiding us toward an elevator. "But as an advertising setup and builder of good will, it more than justifies itself."

Now the elevator, pausing at floor after floor, gave us glimpses of each. Mercy, I thought, craning forward, imagine hairdressing parlors and other services requiring such fancy space and paraphernalia. What a swarming hive of a place this is, with its new products division, billing departments and Lord knows what.

At last we stepped out on a deep-piled platinum-colored rug. Holy cow! Why hadn't I guessed there'd be so many mirrors, such overpowering radiance and light? It was like awakening suddenly in a huge heavenly boudoir, all pink, sparkling and shining. I had never before felt so choked with the fragrance of rose, jasmine, spice, lavender and nicotiana. Mm-mm-m.

After passing a waxlike coiffured young woman receptionist, I became less blinded. Aha, here were showcases highlighting a single face-powder box or perfume, others featuring lipsticks looped by garlands of forget-me-nots. Now I identified Louis Sixteenth furniture and breathtaking bouquets of American Beauty roses, dewy-fresh still.

Finally we approached several clusters of people who seemed to be speaking in pantomime. "This showroom is effective, of course," Fay said, "but the upkeep is enormous."

Coming closer to the gesticulating twosomes, I caught the words of a woman. "Enchanting. Simply divine," she said, from under her mountainous salmon-colored hat. Lifting her wrist to her nose, she sniffed it appreciatively. "What's the name of this new fragrance, Mike?"

"Breath of Sappho, Miss Clancy . . . Spelled S-a-p-p-h-o."

"Nice." After lifting her wrist again, the hatted one got busy with her fountain pen. "We'll try a dozen in assorted sizes."

Now a man's deep voice boomed from another spot. "All right, Ray. Add five gross of that lipstick to my order. If you say it's good I'll take your word for it. And figure the color breakdown for me, eh?"

"Two typical buyers," Jack said in an undertone, "one the smartest dame in our industry, the other a beginner still. With an eye to economy, retailers are employing the latter increasingly, I'm sorry to say." Then, as we passed a closed veneer door, "My office is here. We'll come back to it later."

"Why wouldn't it be where it always was?" Fay asked petulantly. "I can't see anything worthwhile here. What a bore!"

Ignoring her, he led the way down a corridor formed by glistening bricks of glass. "Next I want you to see how we train department store demonstrators. As you may know, Maybelle, they're the lifeblood of our department store business — selected by us, taught by us and . . ."

"For Pete's sake," Fay cried, "stop teaching school, dear, will you?"

"It's time you began to see this business from the sales angle," he warned. "There's more here than you suspect."

"Nonsense."

On tiptoe we entered the rear of a room where a class of young women was in session. "This training program has been in operation for many years," Jack said, waving toward the rows of smoothly coiffured heads. "But we keep modernizing it."

After inspecting the white-turbaned and besmocked female on the platform, I thought, Teacher looks like a model for a beauty advertisement: so dedicated, pure and serious.

Nodding a welcome, she said crisply, "Girls, this morning we have been quoting Dr. Gilbert Brighouse, the Los Angeles psychologist. Let's review his words again now. Each housewife-customer is three persons — what she actually is, what she thinks she is, and *what she would like to be*. Here at Amyrillis, our goal is to help Milady fulfill her dreams, giving her *more* self-assurance and *less* inhibitions. Also we believe with Mr. A. P. Berryer that 'there are no ugly women; there are only those who do *not* know how to look pretty.'"

It sounded so scholarly that I blinked. Dear, oh dear, you'd think she was a Doctor of Laws or something.

"Miss Baker's tops," Fay whispered approvingly. "As you may have guessed, she's a Phi Beta Kappa from Bryn Mawr."

Nodding back, I wondered how she had gathered and remembered such details. What a shame that neighbors in Arlington had never learned to appreciate Mrs. Hick.

"Now we are ready to attack the *hows* together, please, girls. As I have said repeatedly, beauty always begins with healthy habits, a common-sense diet, and a fresh clear skin and scalp." When "teacher" had removed all make-up with Amyrillis Cleansing Oil, she applied Amyrillis Face and Throat Stimulus, All-purpose Cream, Skin Lotion and other beauty aids.

Standing with one half of her face oozing grease and the other a triumph of artistry, she asked. "Now, why did I select this pinky-pink shade, please? Because, girls, it harmonizes uniquely with me and my color shadings."

After her pupils had absorbed this worshipfully, they repeated the process on themselves, step by step.

"Baker's excellent," Fay told Jack in an undertone. "But why didn't she mention my Aphid-Milk? It's a top seller still, isn't it?"

"Certainly." He whipped a notebook from his pocket. "Thanks. We'll correct this before tonight."

"Another thing, dear," she said after we had tiptoed out together, closing the door behind us. "Today I didn't hear enough stress on *quality.*"

"We'll remedy that too, Dr. Amelia," he said, beaming with pride. "You ought to visit us more often. Sometimes we're in more of a groove than we should be."

"But Amyrillis still leads the industry," she said kindly.

"You bet, honey. It always will."

As we entered Jack's office, I almost wept with disappointment. Because, except for a couple of bars of toilet soap and a bottle of deodorant, there was no sign of glamour. Also, the last object I expected to find was the huge onyx penholder with Jack's name engraved on its base.

"How do you like my hideaway, Maybelle?" he asked, surveying the blond veneer walls, full-length bookshelves and battery of telephones. "Nice and comfortable, eh?"

"Businesslike," I said politely, "and really efficient."

"You'll break my husband's heart if you don't notice his array of framed awards here," Fay said, with a nudge. "If you read Latin, you'll observe that Amyrillis has led the industry in high standards of quality, packaging, promotion and performance. That's right, dear, isn't it?"

Glowing with pleasure, Jack cleared his throat. "It would be news if we *didn't* get these honors year after year, along with others for persistence, price and profit. The day we don't, my employment here could terminate promptly."

"You look safe and secure enough still," Fay said proudly. Then, after patting her handbag with its samples of Giddy Moment, "Further, as long as I continue to come up with new ideas occasionally . . . and force you to consider them . . ."

Ignoring this comment, he glanced at his watch. "We still have fifteen minutes before our appointment with Bernard. In this interval, girls, we hope to give you an up-to-the-minute picture of other important factors in this organization, advertising especially."

"Good!" Fay cried. "We need briefing here." She turned to me. "You'll love meeting Terry Newhall. She's a born promoter, clever as hell."

"Sorry we couldn't ask Rose Pfeiffer to drop by too," Jack said, "what with packaging the exact science it *is*, in this business. But as you know already, Fay, Rose has been increasingly whimsical and blind to company policy" — he gave his wife a steel-gray look — "so we're replacing her Monday with a new designer."

Fay's heels clicked together. "But you're mad. *Mad.* How could you let Rose get away? She's sure to avenge herself with bitter competition."

"So what? We can't coddle people who sail off on tangents."

"But her last lipstick container brought a national fashion award again, didn't it? If I were a manufacturer, I'd grab her fast."

"You're not a manufacturer, my dear," he said, grinning mischievously. "Not yet."

Why must he goad like this? I wondered, as he shook with pleasure. Honestly!

"Very humorous," Fay repeatedly slowly. "I'm dying laughing."

"Ho-ho-ho." Jack was slapping his knee. "You should see your face, honey. What a sketch."

"You're impossible," she almost shrieked. "If your teasing was clever, I'd try to endure it . . ."

"Say not so." A gym-teacher type of woman had come bounding toward us with an enormous roll of papers held like a baseball bat. Throwing one arm around Fay's neck, she squeezed hard. "My, Doctor, it's good to see you here, blasting away! Say, retirement seems to agree with you."

While I was adjusting to this windstorm, Jack did the introductions with his usual aplomb. Meanwhile Mrs. Newhall smiled, gripped hands savagely and boomed, "How do you do."

Winching with pain, I caught sight of heaving breasts and thighs under a bizarre dress, of peaches-and-cream complexion and a tangle of henna-colored hair. My, she looked terrifically young, energetic, brave and full of talent.

Setting down her papers, the advertising director hugged Fay again. "If you could know how we miss you! In the past year Amyrillis hasn't come out with one truly new, thrilling product. Jack may not like my saying this so strongly, *but it's so.*"

"There was only one Dr. Amelia," he said, as though speaking of the "deceased." "But let's get to our briefing now, eh, Terry? Time's running short."

She became businesslike immediately. "At the moment we're working on next January's spreads," she said, flattening her papers with one vigorous stroke. "These layouts are typical." She tapped her pencil at a Romanish female face which might have been reciting poetry. After indicating the merest suggestion of a man's profile close by, she added, "In these sketches, as you can see, we plan to keep our treatment subdued and pristine."

"Nice," I said, while Fay kept silent.

"Isn't it? Notice how we've soft-pedaled the item featured here?" She pointed with her pencil again. "This happens to be a lipstick. Regardless, our purpose is to stress Amyrillis as a top-quality line rather than to harp on individual items or dear old sex. Besides, Doctor, I don't need to tell you that our reputation and consumer-acceptance is such . . ."

". . . that we dare to be different from our competitors," Fay said bitterly.

"Right. Exactly right." Turning to the next exhibit, Mrs. Newhall beamed more broadly. "Note here that our approach again suggests impeccable breeding and emphasis on the spirit. I'll admit that our former thinking was brashish. But by now we've graduated from haymakers, promising the moon."

"Jack, I don't understand this," Fay said, her face pale, her neck palpitating. "Wouldn't a sensationally new item with unique powers be buried in this sonnet approach?"

"Dr. Amelia, don't tell me you're interested in advertising at last," the director shouted. "How the leopard changed spots in a year and a half!"

"Times change, you know, Fay," Jack said in a fatherly tone. "And if Amyrillis is to stay the leader in this industry, obviously we must . . ."

"I see," she gulped.

"I wish I could have spared you this," he continued. "But before seeing Bernard today, you need to understand our position fully. Now maybe you realize what you're up against."

"Now maybe I do," she said, throwing back her tiny shoulders and managing a smile. "Further, I'm not licked yet."

While Mrs. Newhall looked baffled, I thought, Oh, I'm glad I'm not a business woman. In Fay's shoes I'd be worn out already.

"Mr. Huggin will see you in five minutes." An owl-faced American-Gothic type of woman had come treading through the doorway. Then, after Jack had introduced Miss Barberry as the president's secretary, he hurried out. "Come along, girls. Time's afleeting."

"You look thin, Doctor," Mrs. Newhall said, hoisting up her papers again.

"Well, I've been working hard in my home laboratory . . ."

"Ho, I should have guessed it. What work of genius is it this time?"

"A lipstick."

"Really? . . . Is that enough of a challenge?"

"If you'd been working with us for the past six months . . . Also, if you'd happened to catch the *Perk Predicts* program this morning, you'd know very well . . ."

"But I did hear it. Such audacity! What a joker!" she wheezed with mirth.

"This time Alvin meant business. And so do I."

"Aha." Mrs. Newhall licked her lips thoughtfully. "Now I begin to catch his pitch about 'business negotiations being under way . . .' So, that's why you're here, is it?"

"Yes," Fay said, as Jack called us again. "Exactly."

Chapter 10

Friday, July 1, 1960 (continued)

THANK goodness that I was able to write here as I did before Nina returned from work. Because once she came into my bedroom at six o'clock crying, "Hi, Mother," I leaped from Amyrillis fairyland back to being Maybelle Dent, Arlington housewife. In that instant I saw myself as a middle-aged Cinderella surrounded by my chaise, rose-garlanded wallpaper and domestic chores.

"For Pete's sake," she said, observing my rumpled condition. "Don't tell me you've been writing here in your very best new clothes. One of these days I must read our family diary. I bet it's a lulu!"

I didn't express the hope of her postponing this session for a good many years. But I'm sure that she must have observed my cheeks flushing with guilt.

Tonight, looking back, I am glad that Nina came when she did late this afternoon. Otherwise we might have missed our little visit together before she went off to join Larry.

As it was, I was able to enjoy her with new understanding, especially as she described her experiences as a Star-Drake summer salesclerk. Now and again I'd say with a jerk of my head, "Ah, there's more to business than meets the eye." Also I quoted Dr. Gilbert Brighouse's comment on housewives' triple personalities with real assurance.

Consequently Nina's eyes kept bulging. "Honestly, Mother, you're getting sharp these days," she said with admiration. "I knew you could be if you tried."

"Thank you, dear."

After putting her arms about my neck, she hugged hard. "I wish I understood you better. But saintliness has never been one of my ideals."

There was no edge in her voice, no laughter, nothing but the merest suggestion of pity. Saintliness? Was she serious? Ah, but I didn't dare to speak. It was as though she had set a pure white bath mat in front of us — one glistening with a strange, ethereal light. She little knows me, I thought.

Surely Joe would be proud to see Nina's increasing dignity and resemblance to him. Tonight she looked particularly handsome in a tangerine Shantung dress. Yet the effect was spoiled a bit by her slicked-back hair and atrocious earrings. Why must she try to be the Queen of Sheba type instead of stressing what she should: femininity, grace and genuine sweetness?

Now that she has rushed off to the city and I have had a bite of supper, it is good to stretch out here again. How happy and relaxed I feel in nightclothes, with restricting undergarments discarded for the time being, thank goodness.

Whatever guilt was evident an hour ago has disappeared completely. Oh, there is nothing, *nothing* to compare with activities which are strictly one's own! Yes, whether they involve writing in a journal or being partner in an exciting business venture.

Here in the coziness of my room with its quiet familiarity, it seems a tremendous jump back to Amyrillis, Inc., and New York City. In so many ways it seems as though today *couldn't* have happened. Yet, as Fay would say, facts speak for themselves.

Again, this morning after she and I left Jack's office, we became a part of that iridescent fairyland — thick carpet, delicious fragrance, mirrors and the rest. Making our way through the showroom, I noticed that the salmon-hatted woman was there, working hard still. Evidently the other buyer had just made his departure, because his salesman was saying to another, "Imagine that jay bird being entrusted with a million dollars' worth of purchasing power!"

As Fay caught this comment, she paused. "Ray, why should you care? Regardless, you get your commission, don't you?"

He stood looking like a graduate from a top business school. "As long as our friend buys from a reliable company like Amyrillis, he won't go wrong. But if he should land in the hands of some unscrupulous outfit . . ."

"He won't," she chuckled. "No industry has finer ethics than ours and you know it. Further, what happens to a buyer who spreads himself too thin? He'll wind up with no co-operation, no well-balanced assortment of goods — in fact with nothing."

"Maybe so, Dr. Amelia," he said diplomatically.

How she knows the ins and outs of this business, I thought. She's jumps ahead of everyone else.

As we approached the presidential suite of offices, Jack demanded, "Where have you girls been?"

"I stopped to talk with Ray," Fay said apologetically. "Is he top salesman nationally still?"

"Sure. Whale of a job . . . unusually sound grasp of the retail picture."

"Dr. Amelia, how *right* to have you here," Miss Barberry said with a crackling smile. "Believe me, Mr. Huggin's been looking forward to seeing you." Then, coming closer and speaking in a whisper, "He'd do anything, he says, to bring you back permanently."

"It's good to be appreciated. But Jack has strong convictions about stay-at-home wives. Don't you, dear?" Turning toward him, she tilted back her head. Then, as he stood grim and lost in thought, she asked again, *"Don't* you, dear?"

"Oh yes," he said automatically. Taking her hand, he drew her several steps away. "Look, honey. Before we see Bernard it's only fair to remind you of this. Today you can't count on any help from me."

"I know."

"I promise not to say anything until you've given your pitch on Giddy Moment. Afterwards, though —"

Interrupting him, she whipped out, "Afterwards you'll aim at my lipstick with both barrels. Is that it?"

"Yes."

"All right. I'll come clean too. I intend to use every possible resource to win my point. As a scientist I must! You're big enough to accept this, aren't you?"

"I have to be."

As the fire went out of her, Fay's chin quivered. "Somehow it seems hard, doesn't it?"

Glancing down at her black ringlets, he managed to smile. "We'll survive. This isn't our first tussle . . . or the last either, I bet. Besides, you're very, very sweet."

"So are you."

Overhearing this, I felt my throat ache. Oh dear, before we finished today, one of them was sure to be hurt. If there was any competitive *relish* or gusto here at the moment, I saw no signs of them. Maybe underneath, though . . .

As some red signal lights flashed overhead, Miss Barberry announced, "Mr. Huggin is ready now."

"Good luck, dear," Jack whispered. "Remember I love you."

"Me too," Fay said, stepping forward resolutely.

Now at last I caught sight of the spacious presidential suite of offices. Instead of carrying any resemblance to a harem, it seemed brittle with the dignity of a London museum. There was an Old World richness in the Persian rugs, massive furniture and betasseled, brocaded draperies. My, but it smelled like a men's club room, though, the staleness of cigar smoke mixed with a piny odor.

After adjusting to the less intense light, I observed a wiry, white-haired little man standing with the decorum of a college professor. As we approached, he was smiling broadly, everything about him very delicate and fine, his brows forming a sort of V. He wore a pince-nez, I remember, and an old-fashioned watch chain. Waving his cigar, he cried out, "Ah, Fay, good to see you. Jack should bring you more often." Then, "And a pleasure to meet you, Mrs. Dent. Friends of the Hicks' are always welcome."

"I've looked forward to this moment," Fay said, her voice and smile particularly appealing.

"Good," he said with a glance which seemed to go right through her clothes. Then, in a tone carrying deep courtesy, "Try these chairs here, friends. The others are deuced uncomfortable."

While he continued to chat with Fay and Jack, I told myself . . . Must be in his late seventies, but wonderfully well preserved. He reminds me of dear Grandpa, with that startled, sleepy expression in his eyes . . . But how can this be, since Grandpa was progressively senile? In contrast, Mr. Huggin looks chirpy and full of ideas still.

But full of what kind of ideas? Remember that glance which seemed to strip Fay naked? Now, now, Maybelle. Stop such unladylike fancies. This isn't like you.

Yet the more I watched Mr. Huggin, the more I could see that he was smitten with Fay. Though his manners stayed impeccable, he kept stealing a lingering look at her bosom, thighs and knees. Still, there was a harmless innocence about him, like a child hungering for a piece of candy.

All this is difficult for me to admit or to describe here. What

I observed was there, nevertheless, and should have prepared me for events later.

As my discomfort over this situation increased, I turned toward the wall on our left. Again I had the feeling that Mr. President had weaknesses, or perhaps strengths, which were surprising. Instead of cherishing original Rembrandts or Millets, he had row upon row of photographs here, all of them featuring atomic bomb explosions, rocket-launchings and experimental missiles. Then I told myself, Maybe this isn't so odd. Fay has often mentioned his passion for science.

"So you admire my collection, do you, Mrs. Dent?" Mr. Huggin asked with a chuckle. I nodded. "It was Enrico Fermi who first drew me into the field of nuclear energy. Since then I've tried to keep abreast of developments. And once I retire from this business, I shall devote full time to them."

"Won't that be nice," I said, although this prospect seemed slightly crack-brained. How could this man bear to leave his beautiful suite of offices for a lot of nasty explosions or winged, whalelike soaring objects? Further, in a world as good as ours, why think so seriously about the future?

He had turned toward Fay with another probing, lingering look. "We still can't lay hands on a chemist with half your fire or imagination." Then, after pausing, with the V of his brows more pronounced than before, "Don't you miss your work here?"

"Well, sir," she said impassively, "I would if I hadn't been keeping my hand in."

"What's that?"

After letting him dance on the griddle, she continued. "Six months ago, Jack built me a little laboratory out in Arlington. Since then I've been working there day and night."

As his eyes narrowed, there was no sign of the previous haze. "Of course you've developed something new. What is it?"

While Jack cleared his throat she said, "It's a lipstick, sir . . . with unusual potency." How relaxed she seemed. Could anyone believe that she had been tense a few minutes before?

"Ha, my dear . . . That reminds me . . ." Mr. Huggin danced the thin wrinkled fingers of one hand against the palm of the other. "You heard the *Perk Predicts* program today, didn't you? Can you imagine any idiot making such crass, unfounded claims? If a lipstick were to replace every other on the market, wouldn't we at Amyrillis be the *first* to know it?"

"I didn't hear that bombshell this morning," Jack said, frowning. "Fay makes a point of listening to Alvin Perkin always. But the man's slam-bang manner has never appealed to me." Straightening in his chair, he sat with his jaw outthrust.

"Sir, my lipstick and the one mentioned on the radio are one and the same," Fay said very gently. "Mr. Perkin happens to live in Arlington. In fact he's Mrs. Dent's next-door neighbor."

"So that's why this lady is here, is it?"

"No. We're partners in the newly formed Amelia-Dent Enterprises, Limited."

"I see." He drubbed his fingers harder than before. "The name of your lipstick is what?"

"Giddy Moment, sir."

"You say it has potency?" His tone had become sharp. "What sort of potency, Fay?"

Glancing toward him appealingly, she crossed one leg over the other. "Before answering, may I ask a question or two? First, what would you say makes a woman kissable?"

"Don't you know? Must I spell it out for you?"

Now really! Who would have expected this explosion from a dear old gentleman.

Sighing deeply, Fay tilted up her chin. Then she said with genuine sweetness, "First, sir, let's agree that Madame drifts into a mood where she wishes to be kissed."

"All right." His manner had become affectionate again. "This sounds reasonable."

She bent toward him. "A compelling urgency zings through her body and soul, doesn't it . . . making her hold herself, every part of herself in a special way . . . Like this." Stretching both arms bit by bit, she fluttered her cherry-colored lips enticingly.

Clearing his throat, Jack started to say something and stopped.

Now why should he object to this? I wondered. Fay's never looked more fetching or cute.

"A most excellent demonstration, my dear," Mr. Huggin said, smiling broadly. "I'll admit I hadn't looked into all this before. But after this . . . er . . . sales talk, it seems to make sense."

"Well, sir, before we go further, a meeting of minds on this point is important. Let's grant that this series of chain reactions may build up unconsciously. Also that in turn, they are broadcast from a woman to a man very subtly, very secretly."

"Aha, you have made a study of kissing, haven't you?"

Jack puffed at his cigarette energetically, while I sat listening and quite forgotten.

"Certainly I've tried, sir. It's been a bit out of my line, of course, but it's been interesting." Jumping up, she began to walk back and forth. Then spinning about on her heel, she faced the president again. "Now suppose that by applying a relatively simple mixture to her lips, a woman can induce the kissing mood immediately? Once her bodily chemistry is changed and the air waves carry their message a limited distance, *what happens?*"

"God knows, my dear."

"God knows, you know, and I know," she said vigorously. "The minute a man comes within a foot of our siren, he melts like wax."

Tipping back his silvery head, Bernard Huggin gazed up into the ceiling. Then he asked very seriously, "Fay, are you saying you have invented a formula making a woman irresistibly kissable?"

"Yes, sir."

"I'll be damned. What an ingenious minx you are!"

"I try to be."

"Oh-ho!" He exploded with mirth. "What mischief idle hands will get into. Oh-ho-ho!"

Of course this hit her like a whip. Turning like a tiger, she cried, "Idle, did you say, sir? Idle? You dare to call one of the most sensational discoveries of this century . . . *mischief?*"

"Watch it, dear. Watch it," Jack warned. "Have you forgotten *where* you are? And why?"

"I don't care," she squealed. "I won't be insulted." Then she went into a fit of coughing.

"Forgive me," Mr. Huggin said, controlling his chortles at last. "I never should have said what I did. Now, my dear, have you a sample of this lipstick handy?"

As she brought the little tube to him, Fay showed every sign of being calm again. But her face grew increasingly pale as she gulped once or twice.

After sniffing the mixture and testing it with his finger, the president asked, "Is this supposed to change my bloodstream and send out signals? Because I tell you it doesn't . . . However, I believe I can identify most of the chemical elements here."

"Ah, but you're right," she cried, as he finished enumerating them. "But there's more here than appears on the surface. Our key problem has been one of *seasoning*, a process which I must continue to study and perfect." Then, while he nodded again and again, she went into a discussion of technicalities. "Now, sir," she wound up, "if I may have my sample, we'll give you a demonstration. And if Miss Barberry could come to take a few notes, please."

While Mr. Huggin buzzed for his secretary, Jack began futile warning signals. Oh dear, I thought, twinging for him. Once Fay makes up her mind this way, all of us are helpless.

"Here, Maybelle, hold these smelling salts, will you?" she whispered, swooping forward and placing the little bejeweled *flacon* in my hand. "Whenever you think it's necessary, get to work with this."

"Must I?"

"Of course. Remember our futures are at stake. One wrong move and we'll be sunk."

"Ah, Miss Barberry," Mr. Huggin said as she marched toward us. "Dr. Amelia is about to demonstrate her newest product. We'd like a detailed record of what ensues."

"Yes, sir." After settling herself a few yards away the secretary opened her notebook briskly. Meantime Fay had been smearing Giddy Moment on her lips.

"Are we set now?" the president asked as she came prancing toward him with arms outstretched. Then, forgetting the stiffness in his old frame, he leaped to his feet.

"Good God," Jack groaned, glaring and clenching his hands. "Are there no sporting rules here? Must I stand by while my wife makes a spectacle of herself? Give me strength and patience!"

Looking from him to the embracing couple and back again, I winced. Poor dear friend and husband, how hard this was for him. Dreadfully hard. But as Fay had said before, in this game of wits and strategy, her future and mine too were at stake. Then, remembering the bottle of salts, I jumped forward, waving it vigorously. "Enough now. Enough."

Meanwhile Miss Barberry had been taking frantic shorthand. "My goodness gracious me," she spluttered. "Truly, I've never seen anything like this."

After our twosome had separated and staggered back to their chairs, they sat quite exhausted. Fay had accepted this situation calmly, with none of her previous Sweet-Helen song-and-dance routine. Still, she seemed to be increasingly pale. This condition is genuine, I thought; it's not play-acting.

"Hot diggety," Mr. Huggin said, when he had regained his breath. "I don't know when I've enjoyed myself more. In business hours, especially. Very nice, Fay. Yes, very, very nice. Congratulations."

"Giddy Moment *is* effective, isn't it," she said with forced enthusiasm. "And once we lick this cussed seasoning problem . . ." Hiccoughing, she tapped her fingers against her lips delicately.

Observing this, I wondered if she might be having a bit of indigestion. If so, she was handling it beautifully.

"Yes, it's a superb accomplishment, my dear," Mr. Huggin repeated, "creditable in every way." Then, glancing at his vice-president, "What's eating you, Jack? You've been sitting silent as an owl."

"I'm fine, sir," he said, flushing. "Fine."

You're a gentleman, John Calhoun Hick, I thought. You could wreck everything on the parcheesi board here. But you won't.

"Now, my friends, we come to demonstration number two," Fay said, getting to her feet again. This time, her gaiety seemed to carry more effort than before. "Everyone watch closely please as I remove every smidge of Giddy Moment from my face . . . and become . . . and become . . . my normal self, unaided by science." After scrubbing her lips with tissue, she sidled toward Mr. Huggin. "Notice I'm wearing no artifices now." She was moving step by step, bosom and thighs swaying alluringly. "There's nothing here now . . . nothing but plain Fay, spelled F-a-y, Fay. As I come nearer . . . and nearer . . . and nearer, sir, does it shake and stir you? *Does* it?"

"Yes, it does. Very much," he croaked, making a frantic grab at her skirts. "You're delicious, my pretty. I can't resist you."

Sakes alive, I thought. What's happening? This isn't right. Down the river we go.

"No! No! No!" she cried, fighting him off. "Stop, sir. You're not supposed to act this way. *Not now.*"

"Who says I'm not, eh?"

"I say so," Jack roared, rising and facing him furiously. "A promise to my wife is a promise. And an experiment is an experiment. And a salestalk is a salestalk. But this has gone too far."

Waggling her finger, Fay made every effort to conceal her dismay. "I'm sorry, Mr. Huggin. This time you didn't play according to the rules. Naughty. Naughty. Naughty." Then, turning toward her husband and fighting back tears, "Look, dear. I'd wiped off every trace of Giddy Moment. That's right, isn't it?" Moving toward him, she paused with her lips almost touching his.

Now what's going to happen, I asked myself, tingling with anticipation. Will Jack take a tailspin too?

But he stood as firmly composed as a slab of granite. "Once an old wolf always an old wolf," he muttered under his breath. "Fay, you should have anticipated this before throwing yourself at Bernard again. A man's entitled to a few lapses as he gets on in life." Then, with a piercing glance at Miss Barberry, "Heavens, woman, you're not including that comment in your notes, are you? Well, strike it out immediately."

After wiping her eyes, Fay turned to me with a smile of pure sunshine. "You know, Maybelle, for a moment I was sure Giddy Moment had kicked us in the teeth. But did you notice how beautifully Jack behaved? What a relief!"

"Relief or not," Mr. Huggin said, catching the last of this, "you've proved nothing to me, Fay, which I didn't know already. With or without lipstick you're a deuced attractive woman."

"Shall I put that statement in my notes too?" Miss Barberry asked.

"No thank you." Fay's tone was ultra-precise and business-like. "But I would like your help on a final experiment, please."

"Must you, Fay?" Jack demanded, scowling. "Haven't we seen enough?"

"After that last fiasco, we need to present more evidence," she said firmly. "Now, Miss Barberry, suppose you stand right here by me. You're not wearing any lipstick today, are you? Very good. Now we're ready."

"Ready for what?" the secretary quavered, glancing behind her frantically. "I'm not sure I like this."

"You will, once you get started," Fay promised as she debated which of the two men to use as her next guinea pig.

"No you don't," they howled in unison. "Not on your life."

"Now, Mr. Huggin, bashfulness isn't like you," Miss Barberry rasped, after grinding on some Giddy Moment at Fay's instruction. "A kinder, more considerate employer I've never, never seen." She approached him with a fixed, Cheshire-cat sort of smile.

Every person reacts differently, I thought, observing this. Maybe I'm no scientist, but I'm blessed with a good pair of eyes.

Now, springing into the air with no warning, she began to click imaginary Cossack boots together. "Oyo-oo-oo-yoy!" she hollered. "Oyo-oo-oo-yoy!"

"Calm down, dear girl, please," the president pleaded, shrinking back in his chair. As she came closer and closer he grew livid. Then, as a lightning bolt seemed to strike between the eyes, he reached up, yanking her down into his lap.

"Oy . . ." The remainder of the chant dwindled off into silence.

"Egad," Jack said, rocking back and forth, with his eyes glazed in shock. "More and more this formula scares the hell out of me."

"Time's almost up," Fay said, reaching for the little *flacon* of salts. "Three cheers for Giddy Moment."

I was right about Mr. Huggin being well-preserved, I thought, watching him with increasing satisfaction. For a man in his seventies, he's truly a wonder!

"Ye gods, Fay," Jack said, mopping his brow with his handkerchief. "How did you dare to pull this stunt today?"

"I was in a tight squeeze," she said with a little gulp. (Was it laughter or indigestion?) "Our revered president will remember this forever."

"He certainly will," Jack moaned. Then, as Fay got busy with her salts, "Dear Lord, why did this woman have to come into my life? Why, oh why?" Then, squaring his shoulders, with his eyes alight, "But if a wild horse can be tamed, she can be too, damn it . . . I'll win this match yet."

Chapter 11

Friday, July 1, 1960 (continued)

UNTIL today I would have supposed that a top-level business conference would be much like a church deacons' meeting. I mean you'd expect important decisions to be made in a very hush-hush, holy atmosphere, with each person speaking with dignity, patience and wisdom.

Perhaps the fact that both dear Papa and Joe were lawyers helped to build my impressions this way. Because truly there was an air of sacredness in their old-fashioned downtown offices. Even the secretaries, such as Miss Agatha Hawkins, tiptoed about on their rubber soles, never daring to speak above a whisper.

Well, it is no secret, dear journal, that I have a great deal to learn still. However, on my next trip up Fifth Avenue past towering buildings, I shall know this much — the best circus acts in the world are right inside there, floor upon floor. With the admission free.

Looking back now at this morning's presidential session, I continue to be tantalized. Also, I am confused by Mr. Huggin himself. Because I've never seen anyone more changeable or subject to impulse. Much of the time he seemed extremely sharp, like when he was discussing the chemical content of Giddy Moment with Fay. Then suddenly he'd get that sleepy, surprised look in his eyes, reminding me of Grandpa. Surely such quirks must throw an enormous burden upon Jack in handling his responsibilities.

I cannot understand why Mr. Huggin was so patient with Fay, allowing himself to be the butt of her tricks. In his place, I surely would not wish to make a spectacle of myself before my vice-president, secretary and a woman guest. Or to sacrifice dignity in eagerness to learn facts. Still, as Fay has said repeatedly, he takes great pride in his company's products being years ahead of competitors'. And in addition to liking Dr. Amelia personally, he knows her importance in making Amyrillis what it is.

I confess that I shared Jack's fears as Fay separated her former employer from his secretary. But soon I could see the foolishness of this. Because once the president had collected himself, he was saying again, "I'll be damned, Fay. You are ingenious." And she was answering with usual modesty, "I try to be."

During this interchange, the look in Jack's eyes was pitiful. Dear good boy, I thought. Your loyalty to your wife has been beyond words today. What a prince!

Surprisingly, it took Miss Barberry quite a time to regain her composure. Perhaps no man had ever before kissed her so violently. Or maybe she needed to release emotions long stifled in her breast. Anyhow, pondering this situation, I began to see Giddy Moment as a boon to mankind, including old maids, the weary, the shy and the aged.

Also I realized that its after-effects, though unsettling, were truly good. Because never once in our experiments to date had any real anger, embarrassment or meanness shown itself. Instead, a cleansing, purifying process resulted in a love-me-love-my-neighbor sort of attitude.

These convictions, piling one upon the other, helped to dispel doubts about our lipstick's power. Gloating with satisfaction, I knew that now, through Giddy Moment, Fay and I would do our share in building a better, happier life for all.

Meanwhile Miss Barberry had managed to get to her feet again. "If you don't need me any more, sir," she said, with beautiful new serenity, "I'll return to my desk. There may be some messages there."

"Very well." Mr. Huggin nodded cordially. "But please don't let anyone disturb us for a few minutes."

Once the secretary had hurried off, Fay turned toward him. Speaking with great restraint, she asked, "Doesn't Giddy Moment do what I said it would?"

Noting the tilt of her jaw, her burning eyes and pallor, he chose his words cautiously. "I'll grant . . . er . . . that Miss Barberry's amazing new appeal . . . and er . . . my response . . . fulfilled all your claims, my dear. It is indisputable, too, that once she removed that lipstick . . . er . . . she became a mere bag of bones again, unfortunately . . ."

"Aha, sir, now we're getting somewhere, aren't we?"

"However," he continued, after clearing his throat, "an item with such impact carries dangers, doesn't it, Jack?"

"I'd like to reserve my opinion for a while, sir."

After making a little gulping sigh of relief, Fay clamped her lips together.

"Fair enough, son. I know this isn't an easy situation for you." Then, turning to Fay, he asked, "Can you imagine what would happen if your lipstick were launched in stores across the country? Think of it." After taking a pull at his cigar, he settled back, blowing out a stream of rich smoke.

"Selling and consumer angles have never been up my alley, sir," she said, with a jerk of her chin. "Once a chemist, always a chemist. Isn't that so?"

"Exactly. Therefore, please listen to me, my dear." As he began stating several objections, Jack forgot himself and nodded vehemently.

"But sir, with every new product before, haven't you been

difficult to convince? Eventually though, without exception, you've come to recognize merits and to proceed full steam with manufacture and distribution. Also, as you've said repeatedly, my record speaks for itself."

"No one would deny this, Fay. I'm ready to admit that we've always come around to your thinking. We may again, in the future. However, at the moment I can't consider this lipstick seriously. Kissing, my dear, is a very er . . . intimate and er . . . provocative gesture . . . between a man and a woman. Could such a . . . er . . . supercharging stimulus to er . . . sex relationships be sold across the counter? That's the key question."

"But haven't you always been circumspect, sir? And haven't you regretted it deeply afterwards? Didn't we miss months of possible business on my Aphid-Milk Lotion and Dorinda? Yet once you recognized and publicized their uniqueness, look at the public response!"

After taking a long, unhappy pull at his cigar, the president said, "That's true. But can't you see that this lipstick is in a field by itself?"

"Of course." Her bosom swelled. "That's why I wish women everywhere to enjoy its gifts. I'm positive that Giddy Moment will benefit humanity, just as nuclear energy does increasingly."

"Nuclear energy has been harnessed and controlled, young lady," he said, glancing toward his rows of photographs thoughtfully. "You raise an interesting comparison, though — one which I promise to keep in mind."

"Suppose, sir, some competitor should beat you to the gun here? Would this be good for Amyrillis?"

"Well." His tone was more patient than ever. "Let's turn to another slant for a minute. Suppose a bartender pushed a super Mickey Finn down his customers' throats. Would this be good?"

Her pale face was impassive.

"Suppose our man advertised his concoction, displayed it prominently, had a beauteous young maiden dishing out tumblerfuls by the gross. How about that?"

Why bring up such nonsense? I wondered. Comparing a lipstick to tumbling Irishmen. Ho!

"But your illustration has nothing to do with Giddy Moment," Fay exploded.

"I'd call it an *exact parallel,* my dear." Then, as her chin began to twitch, "Perhaps, though, if you tried to dilute your product. If you managed to tone it down somehow . . ."

"Sir, you know me better than to suggest such a thing. Have I ever once compromised or lowered standards? No. *Never* . . . I won't now."

"Well," he said kindly. "I repeat, Giddy Moment is a superb accomplishment, without question the most brilliant in your career. In addition it is a most challenging step into the future. Certainly I'd be the last person to underrate such work, especially with my zeal for science what it is." Glancing toward his photographs, his eyes wavered.

There he goes again, I thought. Ah, it's good that Jack is next in command here, with his steady head and strong back.

"Ah, now, Fay, where was I? Let me see. Oh yes . . . In conclusion, I believe that neither the public nor we at Amyrillis are ready for Giddy Moment yet."

Gulping, she tightened her lips and sat debating her next step.

"All right," Mr. Huggin finished. "I've had my say. Now let's hear from our vice-president."

Jack began to speak slowly, with pain, yet with a gleam of satisfaction too. "I've told Fay, sir, that no reliable outfit will touch Giddy Moment. What's more, I hoped during her visit here today that she'd begin to see the reasons behind this. In my opinion, the formula, ingenious as it is, should be tossed out and forgotten."

Fay lurched a little but kept her expression impassive.

"Obviously I agree with your first reaction, son. But as one revering the sciences, I urge Fay to lock away her findings carefully until consumers are ready for them."

There's that haze in his eyes still, I told myself, observing it uncomfortably. Why? I wonder.

Though gray with hurt, Fay managed to keep her tone steady. "Because of my husband's long association with this company, you know I can't take Giddy Moment to a competitor. Also I feel understandable loyalty toward Amyrillis myself."

"If you were to involve yourself elsewhere, my dear," the president's voice rang with displeasure, "you'd be within your rights. But I wouldn't recommend it. Besides . . ." with his glance veering toward the ceiling, "who knows but we might see the merits of this lipstick marketwise sooner than we suspect?"

"No," Jack said loudly. "I'd never involve us with such a zany product."

Old Mr. Granite Stubborn-face, I thought.

"Excuse me, sir," Miss Barberry said, marching toward us with giant strides. "Outside we're being swamped by phone calls. Buyers across the country want immediate information on that lipstick."

"What lipstick? Be more coherent, please."

"You know, sir . . . the one mentioned on today's *Perk Predicts* program. With that special feature and all, retail customers seem to think we . . ."

"Ha." The president danced his fingers together delightedly. "A new beauty fad always begins this way, doesn't it, with demand pounding at our doors. Ha. Interesting!"

"I thought so too, sir. Especially after witnessing the goings-on here a while ago." Miss Barberry's voice became teacherish. "We've told everyone that once we have information, we'll inform them promptly."

Ah, but I could feel myself beam as I thought, What a lovely big audience Alvin has across the country. Imagine his radio announcement creating such a stir!

While the Hicks sat motionless, Miss Barberry continued, "We've had several phone calls from Station ZDQ, including one minutes ago from Mr. Perkin himself. I kept saying that you and Mr. Hick were in conference — couldn't possibly be disturbed. But since Mr. Perkin insisted that Dr. Amelia arranged that Giddy Moment announcement with him this morning, and since he *knows* that she and Mrs. Dent are here now, completing business negotiations . . ."

Jack glared at his wife as he caught this information. Still, there was a flicker of surprise too, mixed somehow with humor and grudging respect.

"In any case . . ." Turning, Miss Barberry started to stride back toward the doorway. "Mr. Perkin is on his way over to Amyrillis now. And when he arrives, I'll bring him right in."

Mr. Huggin seemed delighted with this development. "I've always been curious to meet that man, though I'll concede he's solid brass."

Oh, I thought, what fun it will be to see Alvin in the city for the very first time. Yet isn't it nervy for him to barge in this way, without an invitation?

Meantime Fay had been saying loyally, "He's one of the finest fellows I've ever met. Reserved and unpredictable as can be. But a lamb."

Now the secretary returned with her tall, redheaded, bespectacled prize in tow. "Mr. Huggin, this is Mr. Perkin, whose wonderful program we all know and admire." (Had the Perkin charm produced this enthusiasm already? Or was she still carrying the after-effects of Giddy Moment?)

How lovely Alvin looked, smiling and gripping hands in turn. "Ah yes," he said, with special warmth toward Jack, "so you're vice-president, are you? I should have guessed it."

Instead of answering, Jack seemed to freeze.

Watching closely, I pondered how relaxed and sophisticated my neighbor seemed as he settled back, lighting his pipe. Instead of being the country boy I had known for years, he *belonged* in rich executive surroundings, didn't he? — along with the Persian rugs, museum-type furniture and rows of photographs. He's adaptable after all, I thought. I guess it's only in Arlington that he tends to be ill at ease.

"Well, my boy, you created quite a furor this morning," Mr. Huggin began, measuring him shrewdly. "You must know already that our circuits have been jammed."

"Ours too. We've put on twenty more operators."

Holding herself tensely, Fay stifled another of those little gulps. But no one noticed it.

"Twenty, eh?"

"Yes, sir." Then, after a dramatic pause, "When listeners show such intense interest, it's very gratifying. Also, of course, it's my duty to keep them informed now and in the future with periodic news bulletins."

"Agreed, young man." Mr. Huggin's nostrils quivered. "But isn't it also your duty to double-check information before feeding it to the public?" Then, with his tone growing steadily louder, "You stated very positively this morning that Dr. Amelia's new formula will replace every other lipstick on the market. Am I correct?"

"Yes, sir. Those were my words exactly."

"Hm-mm-m. How were you able to make your forecast with so much conviction?"

"Well, it happens that I've seen Giddy Moment in action. I've tested it personally too." Was Alvin half winking at me, the naughty boy?

"Why did you take pains to conceal the feature making it unique?"

"Who but a buffoon, sir, would shoot all his lightning in one bolt? This first mention was merely a teaser, an incitement to curiosity. I never expected the landslide of inquiries flattening us since — though it's highly gratifying."

The president grunted his annoyance. "Gratifying for you and your Trendex rating perhaps. But not for our cosmetic and toiletries industry. You'll concede this, won't you?"

Alvin exhaled a cloud of smoke. "As the leader in the field, sir, I'm sure you'll admit this truth: When new customer demand rears up shouting, an industry must welcome it. This is the American way, isn't it?"

Both Fay and Jack bent forward.

"Has it occurred to you, young man, that no reliable manufacturer would dare to produce this lipstick at the moment? Will *false promises* increase your popularity? Or your stature with listeners?" Mr. Huggin's eyes glowed with angry satisfaction.

Alvin laughed merrily. "Why should I consider such details? If no manufacturer has the guts to touch Giddy Moment, isn't this newsworthy in itself?" (Watch it, dear, I thought. You're beginning to sound rude. And judging from your rising color, you're losing patience too.)

"Perhaps so, Mr. Perkin, perhaps so . . . But I wish to remind you that the chairman of your Continentwide board and several majority stockholders are close friends of mine. Also our annual advertising appropriation swings sizable influence."

"Sir, suppose we look at this from another angle." Alvin's eyes blazed from behind their tortoise rims as every inch of him became twangingly alert. "If women across this country are denied the God-given right to increase their loveliness and glamour, how will they react? Won't they make themselves heard through their clubs, civic organizations and congressmen? This action, building into a dull, ominous roar as it *will*, again is news, isn't it? And news, sir, *news*, I repeat, is my bread and butter . . . and indeed, my Holy Grail."

Ah me, how could these two men go on this way? Why they were even crueler than wrestlers in television shows. Alvin, oh Alvin, what's made you so selfish?

"I'll admit, young man, that all this is possible." The president's tone seemed flatter. "One offended woman can cause untold trouble for everyone. But there are two points of view here, and both, unfortunately, present dangers."

After stifling a hiccough, Fay asked quietly, "Sir, are you convinced that Amyrillis is big enough, strong enough to slam the door on scientific development? As I said before, that's the key issue, isn't it?"

Mr. Huggin's eyes shifted uneasily. "I repeat, my dear, we must study this thought at leisure." Then, nodding toward Jack, "In matters like this, son, we're agreed that the final decision must be yours. If we were to change this company's policy, you beyond everyone else would have to live with the consequences."

"Well, Mr. Hick, what's your verdict?" Alvin asked gaily, while Fay grew ashen.

"As vice-president I state that if we were to manufacture and sell Dr. Amelia's new lipstick, I would tender my resignation immediately. It's an absolutely impractical, cockeyed item."

Alvin smiled like a cat tasting a tender morsel. "This is for quotation *tomorrow?*"

"Certainly. However, please refer to us as a 'top beauty concern' rather than by name."

After scrawling a memorandum Alvin turned to Fay and me. "Have you ladies any comments to make?"

"Oh no," I cried, with my cheeks blazing. "I just need to sit here and think." Then, as he cackled at this comment, I thought, Why did this miserable man come here today?

Why has he added to our troubles, sacrificing everyone's happiness for the sake of his program? Oh dear, and I like him so much too. Really.

"In time you'll get over this shyness, Maybelle," he jeered. "You're involved here too. What's more, you'll continue to be."

"I'm just trying to help where I can."

"Hide your head if you must, faint heart," he grinned. "But Perk predicts . . ."

"Stop teasing Maybelle," Fay said, her eyes flashing like neon lights against the waxen skin. "I have an official statement to make, Alvin. Here it is: quote, unquote. Within six months Giddy Moment will be available to the American public. I, Dr. Fay B. Amelia, and my associate will manufacture and market it through our newly formed company."

"Now, Mr. Hick," Alvin asked, after whipping off more notes, "have you anything to add?"

But he had jumped to his feet bellowing, "You're nuts, Fay. Nuts."

At the same moment she leaped up, clapped both hands over her nose and bolted off.

Don't tell me she's in the family way, I thought, identifying all the signs at last. Yes, she must be. This time the dramatics are genuine. Dear, oh dear, oh dear.

Now, recalling the final part of Fay's statement, I repeated it dizzily: Dr. Amelia and her associate. Associate. *Associate!* Saints alive, could she mean *me?*

I had hoped to add a bit more here, but Nina and Larry have just returned from the city. Consequently, I must remind them that a nice little late-evening snack is waiting in the icebox. Good night, my journal. Where would I be without you?

P.S. If Fay is pregnant, as I'm positive she is, *what part* did Giddy Moment play in this happy development? And *when?*

Maybe this question is none of my business, but I am tantalized by it, nevertheless.

*   *   *

Excerpt from the *Perk Predicts* program, Station ZDQ, New York, New York, Saturday, July 2, 1960.

"Good morning, friends and listeners across America. Here is Alvin Perkin wishing you and your family the best of the best.

"Yesterday I predicted that a newcomer named Giddy Moment would replace and throw into the discard every other lipstick on the market.

"Immediately many thousands of you responded by wire, phone and personal visits to our Continentwide Studios. 'Tell me more,' you insisted. 'If Giddy Moment is going to change my life and the thinking of the cosmetic and toiletries industry, tell me much, much more.'

"Very well, friends. Listen carefully, please. First, I promise that Giddy Moment will be a sensation because of one uniquely new feature: it is guaranteed upon application to make you, you and you irresistibly kissable. Yes, ladies, within a matter of months, the men and little boys will respond to your charms as never before!

"Secondly, though I could not mention previously the name of Giddy Moment's inventor, I am at liberty to disclose it now. She is none other than Dr. Fay Bernice Amelia (better known to her Arlington, Long Island, friends as Mrs. John Calhoun Hick the Third). Should you wish to know more about this brilliant chemist's achievements, you will find a page-and-a-half listing in Who's Who.

"But now we come to more recent developments involving our new, supercharging, twentieth-century lipstick. After business negotiations reached an impasse in New York City yesterday, a key beauty-aid tycoon made this statement: 'If we were

to manufacture and sell Giddy Moment, I would tender my immediate resignation. It is an absolutely impractical cockeyed item.'

"However, Perk Predicts that within six months, Giddy Moment will be available to the American public. This promise is supported by one which Dr. Amelia gave to me exclusively. Said the good doctor with characteristic vigor: 'I and my associate will manufacture and market Giddy Moment through our newly formed company.'

"To this, the bigee V.I.P. mentioned a minute ago answered, 'You're nuts, Fay. Nuts.'

"But since Dr. Amelia has a record for unmatched performance and success, Perk Predicts that the gentleman in question may have to eat his words.

"If and when there are new developments to report, I promise that you will hear them first as always on this program."

Part Three

Part Three

Chapter 12

DURING the week of October 31 through November 5, Alvin Perkin and his famous program were suspended from the air. However, he and Arlington, Long Island, continued to be in the news.

Excerpts from *Live with Louise* temporarily replacing *Perk Predicts*, Station ZDQ, New York, New York, Friday, November 4, 1960.

"Hello, friends and listeners everywhere. This is Louise Larrabee substituting for Alvin Perkin with a half-hour of news, interesting guests, a dash of this and a dish of that.

"As many of you know already, our one and only Alvin is continuing to rest after a nervous collapse last Saturday. However, I am happy to say that our patient is regaining his health splendidly. As a consequence, the Perk Predicts *program will begin again as usual this coming Monday . . . ha-ha-ha.*

"Alvin has asked me to thank you countless folk who sent get-well greetings and most beautiful gifts. But since your generosity has created a severe jam-up here and at his residence, we would appreciate your calling a halt, please.

"In a moment you will meet some of the very special guests honoring us with their presence today. Meanwhile, Mother — did your family use super-pure, super-cleansing, super-spicy Tasty-Foam Toothpaste as usual this morning?

"Now, friends, since this is National Good Neighbor Week, we are delighted to introduce a delegation of Arlington, Long

Island, citizens . . . ha-ha-hee. First, I am happy to present the
Honorable Horace G. Baxter, mayor, a man who first and last
symbolizes the decency and virtues idealized by fine American
citizens from coast to coast."

"Good morning, Louise."

". . . Also Mrs. Baxter and daughter Anna."

"Good morning, Louise."

"Mr. Mayor, we've heard rumors that Arlington is top candi-
date for the Arcturus Award come January. Would you say, sir,
that your community deserves this honor?"

"Indeed I would. Also I'd like to add that it's a great pleasure
to be here with several close neighbors representing and being
representative of our twenty thousand fellow townspeople."

"Thank you, Mr. Mayor . . . ha-ha. Now, Anna dear, we've
promised to finish with you promptly so that you can rush back
to your job at Star-Drake's. Tell me, do many Arlington girls,
once they finish college, insist on being self-supporting?"

"Oh yes. All of us are hepped on the subject of independence,
making the most of our talents and such."

"Aha. Fine. Fine. Now, Mr. Mayor, we have still another
Baxter here today, don't we? Uh-huh, none other than Dr. Lucius, recently chosen as New York State's General Practitioner
of the Year. Hello, sir, and congratulations."

"Hello, Louise. Just let me say that we in Arlington are plenty
proud of our public health record leading the entire Eastern
seaboard. And of our growing birth rate too."

"Thank you, Dr. Baxter . . . ha-ha-ha. Now, our next guest
is Mr. John Weed, editor of the Arlington Gazette and president of the school board. Greetings, Mr. Weed."

"Greetings to you, Louise. Well, I'll begin by saying that our
little weekly prints only those news items which are fit to print.
That's our policy, pure and simple. Next, I'd like to introduce
one of our outstanding high school seniors, Miss Nina Dent.

Let's hear a bit about our fine public school system, eh, Nina?"

"Very well, Mr. Weed. Good morning, Louise. I'm sure everyone knows already that Arlington ranks number one nationally in educational leadership and performance. Also that our pupils compare academically with the top tenth elsewhere in the United States . . . In summarizing, I'd like to state that we are grateful to our families for supporting high standards. Because these beyond everything else are responsible for our excellent faculty, excellent guidance and absolutely no juvenile delinquency."

"Ha-ha-hee, bravo, Nina . . . Now, isn't this your mother, Mrs. Maybelle Dent, directly behind you?"

"Dear, yes, Louise. That's exactly who I am."

"Ha. Aren't you proud of your handsome fine girl?"

"Yes, oh yes. Especially since she's just been chosen valedictorian of her class. Excuse me, Nina, but I just couldn't resist mentioning this here."

"Then your daughter's still another credit to you and to Arlington, isn't she? Now, Mrs. Dent, I understand that you and the Community Choral Group plan to give us a bit of music . . ."

"Yes, we've chosen a song expressing the true spirit of Arlington: 'March on, march on with hope in your heart and you'll never walk alone . . .' Here we go . . ."

"Beautiful, beautiful. Yes, a real clarion call to building ever-better citizenship. Time's running short, I see, Mr. Mayor, but we'll have time for two final guests."

"Thank you, Louise. On my right here is Mrs. Steven Thorpe, chairman of our student aid and scholarship program. Grace, can you tell us about these activities?"

"Uh-huh. Delighted . . . We've been unusually successful in running a swap shop as a means of helping needy students. Next week we plan to run our annual community rummage sale.

Therefore any Long Island residents with odds and ends available for pickup, please notify the Thorpe Warehouse Company promptly."

"Thank you, Mrs. Thorpe. Now, Captain Timothy O'Rourke of the Nassau County Police, may we hear from you, sir?"

"Sure. Hi, folks. And hi to you, Mrs. O'Rourke, Mike, Kevin, Sheila, Patty and Tim Junior . . . Since most folks know already that our county leads all others in P.A.L. activities, I'll go on to say that I and my force love kids. In return for which, we get their A number one co-operation.

"Now, I'm not saying that everything runs perfectly. Of course it doesn't. Now and again some irresponsible citizen goes hog-wild, causing plenty of trouble. In which case you can bet that I and my boys act hard and fast. But since we live in an up-and-coming part of these United States, by gum, we intend to keep it that way."

"Ha-ha-ha. Thank you, Captain Timothy O'Rourke of the Nassau County Police. And thank you also, Mayor Horace G. Baxter and family, Dr. Lucius Baxter, Mr. John Weed, Miss Nina Dent, Mrs. Maybelle Dent, the Community Choral Group and Mrs. Steven Thorpe.

"It is an inspiration to know that you and your fellow Arlingtonites are committed to building the good and the wise, without sparing effort, sacrifice or dollars.

"Now one final news flash, friends and listeners. The John Calhoun Hicks (he's the beauty preparation tycoon recently upped to president of Amyrillis when Bernard Huggin became chairman of the board) . . . I repeat, the John Calhoun Hicks are expecting their first wee Jack Junior or Jacqueline in late January. This event, repeatedly predicted from this station, was confirmed by Mr. Hick personally less than five minutes ago.

"Again, this is Louise Larrabbee substituting for Alvin Perkin and reminding you to live, live, live! 'By now."

Dent Journal . . .

Friday, November 4, 1960

FOUR months have passed, I see, since my last entry. Oh dear, what wouldn't I give for more persistence? Why must I continue to lapse in buckling down to a day-in-day-out efficient routine?

With Nina tired and off to bed, here I am, nicely settled in my negligee. Again I seem to have been driven to writing here tonight as a means of releasing steam. (How Joe would smile if he could read this statement. "*You* of all people, confessing to tension and nerves?" he'd chide. "Why, for goodness' sakes?" But of course he never guessed that I would become Fay Hick's business partner. Or that my participation would stretch out and deepen as it has.)

It is a temptation to begin an account of Giddy Moment developments without delay. For we have made marvelous progress in spite of Fay's being six months pregnant. Yet I know well that Dent family news must be summarized first as usual.

I am amazed that Nina and Larry have become even more conventional since the announcement of their engagement. Week after week they have been making methodical plans for the wedding, complete with detailed guest lists, budgets and other necessities. "If we didn't know exactly where we were heading, neither of us could sleep," she said in explanation recently. "Besides, there's a satisfaction in handling things *right*."

Her attitude continues to be one of "Hands off, Mother. You go your way, please, and let us go ours." Well, surely these days I am going *my* way very successfully. But I see no need to broadcast this news to the young people, busy as they are with their own affairs.

Though I had imagined that romance might distract Nina from her studies, it has not. Two days ago she brought home another straight A report card and news of being chosen valedictorian. But instead of leaping up and down with satisfaction, she said, "I wish I didn't have to look ahead to that speechmaking hocus-pocus. And planning to wear a cap and gown seems awfully juvenile."

This attitude may be tied in with her recent acceptance at Radcliffe College. Dear Nina! How I hope she will find the rewards she expects there: inspiring teachers, long uninterrupted sessions of study, seminars in the fields of Social Studies and Government, and innumerable insights gained from other women students.

Yet I cannot approve a bride's preferring dormitory housing to close association with her husband. Surely such a choice seems contrary to nature.

Nina has continued to be a Saturday salesclerk at Star-Drake. Consequently, she was the first to discover Anna Baxter there recently. My, how surprised and shocked our mayor would be to know his daughter is dispensing beauty aids. Didn't he say again this morning that she was being indoctrinated into customer service somewhere behind the scenes? Oh-ho, once he becomes aware of *what's what*, I can imagine his blood pressure.

Nina also reported that the new cosmetic-toiletries buyer at Drake's is a handsome young man named Lathrop. Until this afternoon, I did not realize that I had met him months ago during our visit to Amyrillis. But Fay knew, of course, that Paul had resigned as Jack's Boy Friday, after receiving a fine offer in retailing. Also she has said frequently that a person who has had a taste of department store experience tends to hunger for more of it.

Getting back to Nina, I must be sure to mention that she was chairman of a recent PTA program resulting in a code of high school ethics. Without boasting, I'll admit that she made a particularly eloquent speech stressing the responsibilities of parents. "Our mothers' and fathers' examples in daily living," she said, "are far more vital than any list of rules and regulations."

Soon after the Louise Larrabbee program this morning, I was reminded of this incident. Because as we were making our departure the mayor said to Editor Weed, "John, be sure to place Nina's PTA speech on page one, emphasizing her plea against drinking, smoking, profanity and other unmannerly behavior." Then of course the "Yes, sir, certainly, sir" came so fast in return that I had to smile.

Again and again today I have been pondering Miss Larrabbee's introduction of the mayor. She is right in saying that he represents the decency and virtues idolized — or was it idealized? — by American citizens everywhere. But to me Horace Baxter more than anyone else is a reminder of dear Joe's decorum and dignity. (Not that Joe was ever stuffy or sanctimonious; goodness knows he *wasn't*. Still, certain basic qualities surely drew these two men together, years ago, as close friends. This fact may explain why I tend to mention Horace frequently in this journal. Surely I can think of no other reason why he pops up as he does, carrying with him poignant associations.)

But getting back to the present, I wish I could say tonight that Pluto has brought additional honors and joy to this family. The fact remains that he has been difficult since his little chum Spike passed away from a kidney infection. Like Grace Thorpe, Spikey's mistress and my mournful, retired-career-woman neighbor, he refuses to accept this tragedy. Consequently he has vented his spleen by piddling on rugs and nipping at Nina and Larry continually.

Another reason for Pluto's upset may be my increasing absence from home. I would not believe that any animal could resent this as he does, howling night and day. Only yesterday

Alvin said for the fiftieth time, "For God's sake, Maybelle, get rid of that loud-mouthed pest, will you?" But that's Alvin's way, exploding and loving to tease.

In spite of these quirks, how I welcome that dear man's attention and evening visits. Perhaps I am old-fashioned, as Nina insists, in persuading him to bring his socks, shirts and underwear here to be mended. Yet I enjoy serving him in every possible way: sewing, learning to play his favorite tunes, entertaining at dinner with rare roast beef, cheese *soufflé*, crab ravigote and popovers. Poor Alvin. How lonely he must be, living in that big old-fashioned house with all its memories.

Though he continues to warn me about his imperfections, I refuse to take them seriously. Yet it seems unfortunate that underneath Alvin's brass, he likes himself so little. Why, I wonder, must he keep measuring his character against Lucretia Perkin's high standards for her son? Why is he this strange bittersweet mixture? Honestly, I do not know. But I realize that in spite of everything, we depend on each other more and more.

Frequently I wish that Fay and Jack Hick could find similar pleasure together. With conflict between them, of course they can't revel in the coming of their baby. Perhaps this situation is the result of Fay's feeling far from well these past months. Also, Jack has been very touchy about Giddy Moment, making comments such as: "You girls are like children playing with fire. If you had an ounce of sense, you'd quit before you get burned."

But Fay and I aren't quitters or ones to wave the white feather. Having set ourselves up in business, we intend to follow through together. Besides, we have proved to be a fine team, balancing each other well.

This new association, with its resulting strength, began after our visit to Amyrillis last July. At the time, when Fay made her announcement to *Perk Predicts*, I was sure that we were hopelessly ruined. As I was asking, "Associate. Saints alive, can she mean me?" a deep comforting voice seemed to answer, "Yes, Maybelle. Welcome the opportunities ahead. Dare. Bear. And don't evade your duty."

For a moment I thought that Papa or dear Joe was right there beside me. Then I recalled that radio program months ago and Mr. Leonard booming, "We must have faith to do whatever we are called upon to do."

Immediately I felt new surging will power as my headache passed off. Driving back to Arlington, with Fay shaken and ill, I remember being wonderfully cheerful. For the first time since Nina's babyhood, I knew I was *needed*. Now I would develop capabilities and endurance as never before.

Yet tonight, dear journal, four months later, I am ready to confess this to you: If I were free to *choose* an item for my very first business venture, I would not pick Giddy Moment. No, I've learned that this inconsequential lipstick is too demanding, leaving no time for pleasure or thought.

Regardless, as Alvin says with that pixyish smile, I'm "hooked by this cussed beauty aid for sure." I pray that it will be worth all the sacrifices ahead.

Chapter 13

Dent Journal . . .

    Friday, November 4, 1960 (continued)

INCREASINGLY I realize how many people in Arlington tend to think and drive themselves in a single direction.

Right here at home, for example, there's Nina, forever trying to better herself through education and wider personal experience. Next door Alvin keeps weighing every decision in terms of impact on his audience. Down the street Grace Thorpe is using every possible angle to edge back into her husband's warehouse business. Half a mile away, Jack Hick is eternally trying to safeguard Amyrillis, especially now he's president. Finally there's Horace G. Baxter, ever hungry for the Arcturus Award and more personal glory.

Perhaps every American town is buzzing with go-getters like these. Regardless, I believe that an overdose of purposefulness tends to make people less kind than they should be. This could be especially so when a person avenges himself upon another blocking his pet ambition. Look at the punishment our mayor gave Alvin recently.

Surely *Perk Predicts* should have thought twice before criticizing Arlington's most prominent citizen over the air last Saturday. Instead, mocking at his new ten-o'clock curfew for teen-agers, he described it as a "return to medieval cruelty, engineered by a *damned doddering do-gooder.*" Then he wound up shouting, "Are we not agreed, my friends, that such action builds stupid, needless rebellion among our young people?"

Immediately "His Honor" pounded into action, using all his influence with Transworld Press Service and powerful advertisers such as Jack Hick. Waving the banner against profanity contaminating American homes, he brought about Alvin's immediate suspension. Then, at Jack's prodding, he arranged a new Continentwide edict: from this moment onward, *Perk Predicts* announcements could feature *no new, untested-by-consumer products.*

Though Continentwide had no right to bow to such outside influence, Alvin said such action is commonplace. Instead of being browbeaten, he insists that he will mention items such as Giddy Moment in the future. Yes, when the right moment comes, he will show Station ZDQ, Horace Baxter, Jack Hick and listeners across the country that he has convictions of his own.

Meantime it has been interesting to watch our mayor play his cards skillfully. It was he, of course, who arranged this morning's Arlington and National Good Neighbor Week tie-in. "We'll shout the fine features of our town, blotting out that *Perk Predicts* mischief," he told a picked group of us fellow citizens. "Station ZDQ and Miss Larrabbee have promised enthusiastic co-operation."

Though I had no wish to appear on today's radio shindig, Alvin insisted that I must. "Think twice, Maybelle, before you antagonize Horace. Some day you may need that foxy old badger as a friend."

In any case I knew it would be wrong to offend one of my husband's dearest cronies. Still, it is a fact that "His Honor" has taken himself too seriously since he retired from newspaper circles. I mean he overdresses, carries a cane and walks as though bound by an excruciating corset. Also his attitude is far too superior.

This was clear before we went on the air this morning. My,

but I had to smile as he kept rehearsing us like school children. "Maybelle, remember to speak *up* — that gadget won't eat you." And "Tim, be sure to give them the usual blarney, stressing your love of kids."

Though he was right at home in the studio, somehow Miss Larrabbee didn't seem to belong in that atmosphere of dust, time clocks, microphones and dirty floors. Also her white hair, pink cheeks and grandmotherly blue eyes contrasted with her chickadee voice and repeated ha-ha-hees. Yet she seemed to enjoy herself, particularly during the commercials.

Like Alvin, she evidently has a real nose for news flashes. Because when an attendant appeared with Miss Barberry of Amyrillis, she flew into action.

But once I heard those words: "Confirmed by Mr. Hick personally, less than five minutes ago," I felt sick. Imagine such retaliation toward a fellow Arlingtonite! How unneighborly and unjust.

As soon as our performance finished, Nina's one-track mind was clear as usual. Though I had hoped we might do a bit of trousseau shopping, she preferred to go to the public library. "Mother, you know I'll never share your passion for Fifth Avenue stores and frou-frou. Besides, I want to gather more material for my sociology report."

In the past I might have argued or wept with disappointment. But now I was able to say smilingly, "Run along and enjoy yourself, dear." But underneath, I thought, All right, Miss Nina. You continue to go your way and I'll go mine.

After taxiing to the Long Island terminal, I decided to pop into a booth and phone Alvin. "Could you possibly meet the next train? It's leaving right away." Ah, but I wished his delayed "Yes" had shown more courtesy and pleasure. Still, I couldn't wait to see him, to hear him say, "For a novice, you did handsomely this morning."

Once I reached Arlington, I stood waiting at the station

interminably. Oh dear, this was his way of indicating disap-
proval. Hadn't he said many times that unless a person was ill
or indisposed, he saw no need to kowtow?

Now, as I fumed at my stupidity, his lemon-yellow convertible came to a screaming stop. "Hop in, Maybelle. All hell's
breaking loose at home."

Soon we were roaring up the hill. "Gad," he moaned. "We're
up to our ears in trouble. Wait till you see my lawn and yours
too, loaded with junk from listeners."

Ah, but I wished he'd said a word or two about my effective-
ness on the radio.

"Get-well gifts and greetings up to my navel," he uttered
bleakly.

After rounding the corner, we swerved to a halt. "Who
piled those crates on my driveway?" I squealed, observing
them in horror. "And is that a goat, of all things, tied to my
precious dogwood tree?"

"Patience, dear girl. Patience."

"But Alvin, how can I get my car out of the garage? Look
at this mess."

"I am looking. I told you a deluge had hit."

"Lamps, furniture, some Siamese cats and a pink bathtub,"
I said, after climbing out and making an inspection. "Are your
admirers this weak in the head?"

Paying no attention, he wailed, "What am I supposed to do
with that goat? Milk it, for God's sake?"

"No profanity please, sir," I said, using Mayor Baxter's prim
tone and gestures. "Or off the air you go for another week."

By now a large olive-green truck had drawn up behind us.
"Another load for you, Mister," a visor-capped man hollered as
he jumped to the sidewalk. "What are you starting here, a
menagerie?"

Alvin stood in his T shirt and slacks, his red hair bristling.
"No more. No more. We're jammed up. Use your eyes, man."

"Sorry, sir. We have our orders."

"The hell with your orders. Can't you see there's not another inch of space?"

"But this is a load of perishables — turkeys from Maryland, lovebirds from Florida, cheese." Pinching his nose, the man twisted it vigorously.

"No. No. No. I won't accept them."

Returning to his truck, the driver muttered to himself, "You get your orders and they try to take it out on your hide. This Perkin lover-boy is all ha-has and smiles on the radio. But here in Arlington, you see his ugly lip and temper." After hoisting up a noisy, evil-smelling crate, he set it at Alvin's feet.

"For Heaven's sake, man, get that damnable stench out of here. What am I supposed to do — eat those loathsome creatures, feathers and all?" Then, as several gabbling, nonsensical heads poked through the slats, "Jehoshaphat, why are people so infernally stupid?"

"Stupit? If anyone's stupit around here, Mr. Perk Predicts, it sure ain't me."

"Out, I say. Get this garbage out of here."

"Nosirree. It's contrary to orders."

"Who gives a blasted hoot about your orders?" Then, as more heads appeared, nibbling at his trousers, "Oh God almighty, there must be at least a dozen birds here. Peuw!"

"Excuse me, sir." Another uniformed man spoke from behind us now. "Delivery from Fleurette's Greenhouse. Where do they go?"

"They?" Alvin roared, rocking on his heels.

"Yup. The works. Hey, what's happening here — a debutanteee party?"

"If this keeps up, we'll land in a mental hospital," I said under my breath.

"Hospital, you say, Mrs. Dent?"

"Yes, yes, my good man," Alvin cried. "A most excellent idea. Let's relay this load to the sick and needy."

"All right, sir. Glad to oblige." After tipping his cap, our friend went off briskly.

"Dear resourceful Maybelle," Alvin said with pathetic appreciation. "Now where are we?"

"We're here where we was," the first driver sneered. Then, twisting his nose again, "And don't think I like my truck smelling so gamy neither. You take that cage of rabbits back there . . ."

"No. *You* take them," Alvin bellowed. "I won't have them and their infernal droppings within twenty miles of my house."

"Please, young man," I asked in my best manner. "Don't you know some kiddies who might welcome pets?"

"Maybe I do, ma'am. And again, maybe I don't." Then, coughing delicately, "It depends . . . you might say."

Catching the hint, Alvin drew out a crisp bill. "Will this help you to decide?"

"Yep." Pocketing his prize, the man grinned. When he had hoisted and carried off the crate of turkeys, he said with another cough, "If you want, I'll take that there Mrs. Goatikins along too. Out in the country my baby . . ."

"Do take him. And bless you."

"Good riddance," Alvin said as the truck lurched off at last. "In a crisis, Maybelle, you're surprisingly steady."

"I try to be," I said, flushing.

Now a low gray sedan drew up beside us as Grace Thorpe called out, "Maybelle, don't tell me you're moving away or competing with my husband's warehouse." Glancing at the pile-up, she seemed to measure it in her mind, the former mournful air transformed into businesslike alertness.

"Come see what we have here," I urged. "Besides, it's time you met Alvin Perkin."

"That's right. I've been waiting for ten solid months." After leaping to the curb, she gripped his hand firmly. "Believe me, I'm one of your most faithful listeners." She stood looking poised and capable in her lean black slacks, leather jacket and square-toed loafers.

"Your dog and I are well acquainted already," Alvin said, with a rather dreary look at his lawn. "But I haven't seen him digging about lately."

"You won't. Spikey passed away several weeks ago. It was a dreadful loss. But you've confused him with some other puppy, I'm sure. I never let him off his leash."

"Maybe you *think* you didn't," he said vindictively.

Ignoring this rudeness, she turned toward me. "Lord, I've been hustle-bustling ever since I returned from the city. Our pickups for the rummage sale are coming along beautifully. My, it's good to feel *useful*."

"Rummage sale?" Alvin gabbled, changing his tune swiftly. "Beautiful lady, you're the answer to my prayers."

"That's nice to know."

"Can you use lamps, furniture, andirons, a Deepfreeze and a pink bathtub?"

"Certainly. We'll take everything but old shoes. They're too difficult to mate."

"With a full moon it might be different," he said, strumming an imaginary guitar. Then, as she looked baffled, he waved toward his lawn. "Everything is yours. Utterly yours."

"You're too generous," she said, backing away.

"No. No. No. My humble needs include neither turkeys, rabbits, cheese, rubber plants nor bowlegged female goats."

"He's still ill, isn't he?" Grace whispered as he spun about in a circle, pinching his nose. "Shouldn't he go straight back to bed?"

"Aha, bed," he intoned. "And we will all the pleasures prove . . . of peace and plenty . . ." Then, seizing her hand wildly, "Fairest of the fair, how soon can you get a fleet of trucks here? Do you realize that my home is loaded with flotsam and jetsam from forty-eight states?"

"Well," she stalled, with an inquiring glance at me.

"It's this way, Grace," I began. Then, after summarizing, "Now, see why he's welcoming you so ardently?"

But having grasped facts, she had no time for further nonsense. After examining the cartons, she seemed to blueprint their sizes and contents into her memory. "All right, Mr. Perkin. I'm ready to see the balance of merchandise in your house."

Ah, but she carried a new glow and air of efficiency. Good, I thought. This is exactly what she's needed.

Now the Hicks' long lean Cadillac arrived at the curb with frantic horn-blowing. "Maybelle, *where* have you been?" Fay demanded, as she stepped to the sidewalk. "Didn't you get my message at the radio station? I've phoned everywhere again and again."

She stood in her billowing navy-blue ensemble, her fragile head and shoulders contrasting with her waistline. "Listen, dear. The best thing has happened." Then, observing the clutter behind us, "What have we here — the town dump?"

"Come help support worthy Arlington students in their quest for higher education," Alvin chanted, leaping up on a crate with the fire of a rabble-rouser. "Bathtubs, chamber pots and livestock for sale. Ten per cent down with easy monthly payments."

"Balmy," Grace said in an undertone. "I don't envy you, Maybelle, living next door to him."

"But I love it," I cried loyally.

As Alvin continued to prance, Fay roared, "Stop it, you big clown. Don't distract us. I have important business to discuss with my partner."

"So what, Dr. Einstein?" he asked, ducking an imaginary

blow. "You may be boss in your laboratory and factory. But don't pull that little Caesar stuff here."

"Watch that crate," Grace warned, as he kept cavorting. "I won't permit good salable goods to be smashed for the fun of it."

"Ho, a second suffragette ganging up on me. Help. Help!"

"Get down and behave yourself, Alvin," I pleaded. "You know perfectly well Fay is trying to get our attention."

"Is she?" he asked innocently, leaping down among us again. Then, with a bow, "Hello, little mother-to-be."

"Once a jerk always a jerk," she said fondly. "And some day, when we pick a godfather for our son, it *won't* be you."

"Thank you, duck."

"Let's go over to your car and talk," I said, putting my arm around Fay's waist. "Once Alvin gets in this silly mood, he never stops."

"For Pete's sake stop treating me like an invalid," she cried, stamping her foot.

Her sharpness of tone brought tears to my eyes. Nevertheless I made my way to the curb resolutely.

"So you're developing stubbornness, are you?" she asked with surprise. "Never mind. Wait till you hear the good news! Do you remember Paul Lathrop? Well, now he's become cosmetic buyer for Star-Drake's Arlington store . . . And he wants to see us, with Giddy Moment, this afternoon at two-thirty."

"Good."

"So as soon as we finish here, let's stop somewhere for a bite of lunch. Then we can talk over everything and make our plans."

"We'll be through in twenty minutes," I said, opening the car door. "Suppose I pick you up at your house."

"No, I'm staying right here," she said, thrusting out her chin. Then, marching back toward Grace, she asked, "Isn't your husband in the warehouse business? Ah, I thought so. We need to negotiate with him."

After Grace had grasped our needs for Giddy Moment accumulated stock she said, "We have all necessary facilities complete with an experienced woman supervisor — *me*."

"Fine. Once we finish with Alvin today, let's sit down and draw up a contract."

"Come on, girls," he said impatiently. "Enough of this jawing. Let's *go*." Turning on his heel, he led the way toward his house.

After managing to navigate the sidewalk and steps, we reached the broad veranda. "More greetings from loyal fans," Fay mocked as we made our way through a sea of envelopes.

But Alvin was dancing with terror as another truck stopped at the curb. "Help, Mrs. Thorpe, help. Where can I hide?"

Now two men appeared with a mountainous crate on their shoulders. "Air-cooling unit, sir."

After arranging her hands like a megaphone Grace sang out, "Relay it and future loads to Thorpe Warehouse, please."

"Saved from the lions! Thank God for friends and rummage sales!" He kicked a path through the clutter of mail. "Now see what used to be my home."

As we entered the living room I could have wept at its confusion. What would Lucretia Perkin have said, with this cherished spot laden like a freight yard?

"If you walk sideways, you can squeeze through," Alvin called over his shoulder, "though I'm not sure about you, Fay."

"Whatever you can do, I can do."

Now a rasping voice cried, "Don't be frightened, my little deadbeat."

"Stop, Alvin," Fay cried, white as wax. "You scared me."

"Drink her down, toots."

"If that's a bird, I don't care for him," Grace said, jerking her close-cropped gray head. "When we make our pickups later, no noise and feathers, please."

"You're insulting Gerald," Alvin said, glancing toward a corner. "Smartest macaw ever and a gift from Lanky Joe." Then, as we raised our eyebrows, "Hell, you must know that bartender on Third Avenue. Serves the best Irish coffee . . ."

Me oh my, I thought, identifying brilliant green feathers touched with a dash of carmine. Poor Mrs. Perkin would burst if she could see this creature among her antimacassars, rusty-looking coat of arms and old family portraits. Thank Heavens she's been spared this!

As we made our way from room to room, I could have wept at their condition. Surely Alvin's cleaning woman must be very shiftless. The windowpanes were bleary, the floors were a disgrace and the dust everywhere made you choke. Ah, how I longed to get right down on my knees with a pail and scrubbing brush. What a satisfaction it would be to rip off curtains and table linen, returning them neatly laundered.

Of course the kitchen, with its stacks of unwashed dishes, seemed especially depressing. Poor man, I thought, if your mother could see the clutter here, she'd turn in her grave.

It seemed wrong that many of Lucretia's favorite objects were here in their usual places. I mean there was that old silvery brocaded knitting bag hanging on a doorknob, and her eyeglasses lying near some books. Upstairs on her bureau there were silver-scrolled brushes, manicure implements and jars of facial creams. Of course every woman leaves such marks of personality in her home. But it was strange to find them treasured here still.

When we had finished with the upstairs cartons, Fay said to Grace, "Let's go back to the kitchen together for a few minutes. If we're going to get at that contract we'd better start now."

"Maybelle and I will continue to entertain ourselves here,"

Alvin called after them. "So take your time." Then, pushing
me back through the doorway toward his mother's canopied
bed, "Sit down, please."

Imagine such a brain wave . . . *here* of all places, too!

Once I was settled, he began, "I don't need to tell you
that it's been damn lonely this year. God knows, I'm not one
to change my life without thinking it through. But you're a
very comfortable person to be with. Really you are."

This remark may not have been flattering, but it made me
feel good. Flinging back my head, I drank in the sweetness of
him, the crinkles at mouth and eyes, the straight, sensitive features. Just for a minute, though, because he was rattling on:
"Sometimes drastic developments are thrust upon a person. By
now surely it's no secret that I've been penalized by Continentwide. Also, I've been warned to avoid profanity, personal
barbs and subjects such as Giddy Moment in the future. One
more infraction and *out I go* on my neck!"

Now I couldn't resist asking, "But why have you been so interested in Giddy Moment? Are you convinced it will bring
blessings to humanity?"

"Ho. Do you suppose I'm *insane?*"

Surely this was not the response I'd expected, but I managed to conceal my chagrin. "Then why, Alvin, did you rush to
Mr. Huggin's office last July as you did? Why have you kept
urging Fay and me to manufacture and sell it to the public
promptly? Why, once we're set, have you promised to shout our
story from coast to coast?"

Coming closer, he shook my shoulders. "Listen, little ingé-
nue. Haven't you heard me say that Giddy Moment has
enormous news value? Surely you know that it's aroused phe-
nomenal interest — the biggest in network history. Wouldn't I
be a sap not to take advantage of this?"

"But you must have some ideals, haven't you?"

After making a wry face, he hurried on. "Imagine the sensation we'll create when that bonny bit of dynamite lands on the mouths of consumers. Wow!"

There he was, looking ahead into the future, while he missed today's pleasures completely.

"Now, Maybelle, I'll tell you something else. No one at Continentwide or any place else is going to muffle Alvin Perkin. Especially since my Trendex rating is far higher than ever before. Also it happens that the Liberty Broadcasting Chain has made me a fine offer, effective next February. Yes, provided my Trendex continues to soar, I'll switch to a new employer at twice present salary. Not so bad, eh?"

After absorbing all this, I asked, "How can I help you?"

"Well, let's see . . ." Looking into my eyes, he seemed to struggle with some impulse, restraining it with all his strength. Squaring his shoulders he said overloudly, "First, my dear, I want you to keep Fay working in her laboratory day and night. Help her to sell a big deal to Star-Drake's buyer this afternoon. Arrange a rooting-tooting promotion there, backed by plenty of Giddy Moment stock."

"Oh, I promise we'll do this and more."

"Good," he said with a sigh. "Fortunately you have great innocence, faith and gusto, qualities which can be stronger than steel. Also, you're genuinely . . . genuinely . . ."

Oh dear, he was trying to say something important . . . Yet he was fighting himself. Please, Alvin, please don't tease this way!

Then with a choke he burst out, "Maybelle, look. Don't fall flat on your face. I'm sorry . . . I can't find the right words, damn it . . . You see, I never proposed to anyone before . . . But even though it may sound like a soap opera, let's get married." Ah, there he was blushing and stammering like a teen-ager.

Oh, I was ready to sing with amazement and joy.

"Next January, dear, let's plan on a simple justice-of-the-peace ceremony." He bent closer and closer. "Then we'll hop a plane and head for Spain. There's a little villa there by the sea . . . and a sky that's breathless . . . sweet . . . my sweet . . ." Suddenly he had hauled me up into his arms.

"Hey, have you forgotten we're waiting here?" Fay cried from below. "Come along, Maybelle."

After several long kisses, Alvin pushed me away. "A fine thing, madam, enticing me *here* of all places."

"It took courage for us to . . . And it's time you began a life of your own."

"Believe me, I know it." Then, glancing toward the feminine oddments on the bureau, "Incidentally, I'm going to tell Mrs. Thorpe to pack up all these extras and put them to use at last."

"Do whatever seems best, Alvin." Then, pulling his head toward mine again, "I love you. I love you."

"I love you too . . . in my way." There was a suggestion of sadness in his tone. "Once we're married I promise to try to protect you. But until then, with my neck in a noose, it's no secret that I can't."

"Come on, Maybelle," Fay cried again. "Save your talk-talk for our session at Drake's. Let's get going."

Oh dear, would I ever, *ever* be free of her demands? "I'm coming!" I cried back.

Chapter 14

Friday, November 4, 1960 (*continued*)

SEVERAL years ago I watched a Broadway actress romp wildly about the stage as she sang, "I'm in love! I'm in love! I'm in love!" At the time I thought she was far too noisy and emotional. But *now* I know better. Indeed, if I were not afraid of waking Nina tonight, I would shout my happiness from the roof tops. Imagine Alvin selecting me to be his mate . . . at a time in life when so much lies ahead for us both!

Yet, as he warned, we must face and vanquish innumerable difficulties together in the next couple of months. How fortunate that we are in good health, except for my occasional dizzy spells.

Surely I shall try through Giddy Moment to help my darling build a more secure future for himself. Nevertheless, it seems hard to believe that a lipstick is so vital to building audience interest, Trendex rating and a new, better job with Liberty Broadcasting.

Oh, but I'd love to set down my pen for a few minutes, to lean back here on the chaise and dream about our honeymoon in Spain. Instead I must *make* myself list events which belong in this diary, stressing particularly Fay's and my association together.

In recent months she has continued to be a strong influence.

Consequently I move and speak more quickly than before. I fuss with my appearance, indulging in countless new, pretty clothes. I take a weak cocktail before dinner, though I don't enjoy the taste still. Also, I've learned to do some simple laboratory chores without breaking too many beakers.

Best of all, I've begun to walk like a business woman, with my shoulders thrown back and my head aloft. Catching my reflection in a mirror, I keep thinking, What a transformation.

In contrast Fay has changed little, remaining amazingly competent in spite of her condition. For months now, she has been supervising both the laboratory and adjacent factory. Also she has added innumerable employees to our payroll. (How fortunate that Amelia-Dent Enterprises has no financial worries, what with both partners comfortably well off.)

I shall never know how Fay was able to persuade so many former Amyrillis co-workers to join us. First she welcomed two chemists, Dr. Celeste Belle and Dr. Tyrone Surr, both sallow, hollow-eyed and most unlovely. Next she introduced Jim Swanson as factory superintendent, and Tony as stock supervisor.

But her greatest prize is Miss Rose Pfeiffer, whom she describes as the cleverest package consultant anywhere. "It was stupid of Jack to let Rose get away from him," she's said repeatedly. "Without her expert knowledge of consumer psychology, we'd be lost."

Though I would like to admire "Miss Rose," I find her dull, billowy and baby-faced. Also I am tired of her favorite speech: "Cosmetic packaging must mesmerize women into buying on sight. Consequently the industry spends more than one third of the cost of selling at retail in achieving this effect." Very good, Miss Pfeiffer. But who cares, really?

Also I am *not* entranced at seeing Giddy Moment encased, as it is today, in a tiny, white-satinish sort of casket. Yet I have learned to look impassive when our designer says, "I love

the prithtine thimplithity here, don't you, Mitheth Dent?"
(Ho, I'd love it for a funeral parlor maybe . . . but not as a
come-hither hypnotic.)

In the past I have heard Jack speak repeatedly of his fine
team of co-workers. And once many of them were on our payroll, I understood what the word *team* means. Because I've
observed, in Dr. Belle, Dr. Surr and everyone else, pride in
skilled work. Also there is deep, mutual respect which is truly
thrilling.

Fay has continued to be an inspiration to us all. During her
hours at work she has been in consistently fine health and
spirits. Yet once she returns to home responsibilities, she feels
nauseated immediately. Also, in her relationship with Jack she
is touchy as a firecracker.

She would be the first, I believe, to admit her shortcomings
as a wife. Yet when twinged by guilt, she asks defensively,
"Maybelle, why shouldn't I blow up occasionally? If Jack
hadn't bested us last July, would you and I be breaking our
backs now?"

Of course she forgets that Jack is in a most trying situation
himself, these days. Especially since his promotion at Amyrillis
sounds so much better than it is. Didn't he make this clear
yesterday when he said, "Increases in salary and prestige can't
compensate for problems created by my chairman. Gad, it's sad
to see a fine brain deteriorate with age."

As president, he must have every reason to be harried. For
example, a month ago, in spite of Jack's objections, Mr. Huggin bought up all the manufacturing rights to Tasty-Foam
Toothpaste. Last week he created a nonsensical executive job
for a young secretary taking his fancy. Yesterday he insisted
that all Amyrillis labels be widened and flared to duplicate
some aeronautical design. Worst of all, he keeps needling Jack
because of his negative reaction to Giddy Moment. "You were
too hasty, my boy . . . far too hasty. Dr. Amelia may prove

again that she is years ahead of us in her thinking. If lipstick volume suffers as a consequence, I won't let you forget it."

No wonder that Jack returns home night after night looking like a battered warrior. In addition, it must be hard for him to endure the throb of machinery rising from the cellar. Surely he has had more than his share of trials.

Yet he has stopped trying to persuade Fay to halt the manufacture of Giddy Moment. At this point he wishes beyond everything else to give consideration to her and the baby. In spite of his silence his eyes continue to reflect shrewd, cold resolution. And this keeps Fay steamed up and fighting.

How I long to stop this conflict between my two dearest friends. Yet it helps to remember that down deep, they carry the zest of chess players — gloating one minute, brooding the next, moving a key playing piece, then rocking with momentary victory or defeat. Regardless of my fondness for Jack, I realize that he is an ever-present danger to our Giddy Moment success. Why wouldn't he be, battling to protect himself, his family and his business future?

Today it was clear again that once Fay casts aside her role as Mrs. John Calhoun Hick intent on victory, she is her normal high-geared self. Wasn't she in good shape at Alvin's house when we inspected those cartons? Who could miss the bounce in her voice as she called up the stairs, "Come on, Maybelle. Save your talk-talk for our session at Drake's. Let's get going."

Did she guess *what* she was interrupting, I wonder? And if so, did she care, committed to Giddy Moment as she is?

I recall that once we were in her Cadillac, heading for a restaurant, she said briskly, "Thank God our warehousing and delivery problems are solved at last. Further, Grace has promised to supervise our requirements herself."

"Good. She's needed this."

"Believe me, she's needed *more* than this. Did you see how sadly she's neglected her hair and skin? Once we have a min-

ute, I'm going to make her into a *new* person. With a simple
basic daily routine, she'll look at least fifteen years younger."

"Oh dear, why are you always trying to change people?"

Glancing from the roadway, she teased, "I've done pretty
well with you, haven't I?"

"You've tried," I said, catching rising independence in my
voice. Why was it there, for pity sakes?

"Ho. You're lots more attractive lately . . . Today Alvin
showed every sign . . . Why won't you admit it?"

"We'll see," I said gaily, feeling somehow like a puppet
wiggling at its strings. "Come January, when Giddy Moment
is launched, we'll see." Now, why was I being this way? Had
Alvin's declaration gone to my head? Was I annoyed because
I had been hurried away from him? Could I have become
weary of Fay's follow-the-leader game?

Once we arrived at the Clair de Lune, we found it delight-
fully dark and full of Continental atmosphere. It's nice to be
a career woman, I thought as the headwaiter led us toward his
best table. This is the life, heigh-ho.

When we had ordered eggs Benedict and coffee, Fay sipped
her glass of water. How New Yorkish she looked in her ex-
pensive dress and hat. Ah, Jack should see the brilliance in her
cheeks, eyes and hair. What beauty process could compare with
the miracle of motherhood?

"Too bad we can't celebrate with a double martini," she
said, eying me with approval. "Say, isn't that the little green
toque you found at Hattie's . . . ? It's dreamy. But set it
straighter on your head . . . Ah, that's better."

Bossy, I thought. Bossy.

Now she was off into another subject. "In an hour we'll be
seeing Paul Lathrop. That's awfully *soon* . . ."

"It's easier this way. We'll be down to business at Star-Drake
almost before we know it."

Her lips trembled. "That's right . . . Right. But . . . look at me. As president of a super-glamour concern, is my portly appearance any asset?"

"Certainly it is. If Giddy Moment has brought blessings to anyone, you're a walking example, aren't you?" Then, as she pondered this comment, "But I know we can't stress *this* in our sales talk."

"Ha. Sometimes you're a bird . . ." Then, leaning forward and trying to force a smile, "Do you realize that I've never in my life sold an item to a store? How can I be convincing? Surely that appointment at Amyrillis taught us to keep away from shenanigans. I've never been one to be afraid. But . . ."

"Since you know Mr. Lathrop already, he's sure to make everything easy."

"Who says he will? Everyone knows that the most ignorant buyers are the most difficult ones. Jack's said so repeatedly. Oh, oh, oh, why did we ever get into this? Every time I think of setting up a big Giddy Moment promotion, I could die."

"Stop such nonsense. Today's sure to be a lark."

"I wish I could agree. Dear, oh dear. Sometimes I ache because Mrs. John Hick didn't shoot Dr. Amelia fatally, months ago. Why did I let my pride take command in Mr. Huggin's office? Why did I give that foolish statement to *Perk Predicts?* Why have I felt so vindictive toward Amyrillis and my husband?"

"Please, Fay. Don't upset yourself this way."

"If Jack hadn't been so sweet last night, so thoughtful, so thrilled about the baby, maybe I wouldn't blame myself as I do. Why doesn't he *stay* that way instead of goading me to distraction? You know how he's yammered against Fay's folly. Especially since Bernard . . ."

"Now, now. Jack would never hurt you . . . not directly," I said, blundering into the wrong words.

She jerked to attention. "What do you mean, *'not directly'?*"

Ah, but I had been clumsy. "Well . . . let's see. Of course

he's taken a new tack in fighting Giddy Moment. You heard his statement on Miss Larrabbee's program today, didn't you?"

"How could I . . . working in my laboratory? What was it, please?" Then, after I had summarized everything, "Oh ho . . . so those endearments last night came from a twinging conscience, did they . . . or an effort to catch me off guard? Oh-ho-ho. And now my darling fights undercover with Mr. Huggin and Mayor Baxter." Adding drama to her words, she pressed her hands to her waist and groaned.

"I never should have told you this," I said, ready to kick myself.

She continued stubbornly. "I can understand Bernard's tactics . . . and Horace's too . . . But Jack's not going to catch wide-awake little Fay with this grade B ruse. I should think not, the rascal! I'll outsmart him at such strategy."

"How else can he fight Giddy Moment now? Remember he can't clamp down on you directly. Hasn't the doctor said repeatedly that you mustn't be upset?"

"I know. I know." Her chin quivered. "If Jack and I lost our baby, we'd never forgive ourselves."

"So you understand his position?"

"Of course. And I understand mine. This is a showdown between us, his brain and muscle matched against mine." She tossed her head, reminding me somehow of a wild mare — nostrils flaring, eyes on fire. "No matter what, you and I are going to win. Yes, we'll set up a lipstick promotion rocking the United States." Then she laughed.

Overdramatizing as usual, I thought, accepting it philosophically. But my stupid mouth should be sewn up.

As the waiter approached with silver-covered platters, he eyed Fay's glassware mournfully. "So you enjoy your little joke, madame?"

"Yes," she gulped, wiping her eyes. "It's a real killer-diller."

As we rehearsed the conference ahead, she continued to

giggle. But throughout luncheon there was no genuine merriment, no sense of communion together. Ah, but I'll be glad when this pressure is past, I thought, when we had finished and returned to the car.

Once we were rolling along Arlington's Main Boulevard we became truly cheerful. My, the fragrance of November chrysanthemums seemed good, mixed with the tang of oil, gasoline and tires. "I'm getting to like this street and this time of year," Fay said as we reached the department store area. "I wouldn't know why."

Then, as we drew to a stop, she said with a grin, "Lord, I was a weak sister a while back, doubting myself. How could I have underestimated my years of cosmetic experience and lessons learned here and there? We're sure to succeed today."

"We're fifteen minutes early," I said, glancing at my watch.

"I planned it this way. Before talking with a buyer, shouldn't we make the rounds of his department?"

There you go again, Miss Fix-it, I thought as she led the way through a revolving door. Why must you treat me like a child? We're equal partners, aren't we? And it's time I made a decision or two.

"Of course the Amyrillis demonstrator is an old friend, Maybelle. So we'll touch base with her first." Then, as we passed through the lingerie department, "Oh, oh, what a darling nightgown. I must buy it before we leave."

Now we came into an area of blazing lights, dramatic displays and multifloral fragrance. This is a far cry from Amyrillis, I told myself, as Fay paused to spray herself with Arpège. But it's pretty just the same.

"Mmmm," she sighed. "I long to buy everything in sight."

Off to the left, I caught sight of a blue-haired, besmocked matron adjusting a chin strap on a customer. Pausing, I thought, For shame. I'd sooner try on a brassière in public than that thing with its elastic and net.

"Honey, see how comfortable it is?" the indigo-headed one asked, darting forward and fastening a strap under my jaw. "You use this faithfully every night with a mite of Hormone Cream and you won't know yourself."

Glancing into the mirror close by, I stood frozen in shock.

"Come on, Maybelle. Get rid of that horrid thing," Fay commanded, ripping it off expertly. "We didn't come here to play dress-up games." Taking my wrist, she hastened toward the Amyrillis booth. Then, nodding toward a henna-coiffured woman surrounded by listeners, "Ssssh. Watch Madge Reilly carefully. She's a superb saleswoman. Also, she happens to be Bernard's personal barometer on suburban trends."

Though Madge was concentrating on only one customer, her eloquence seemed to hypnotize all. "How lovely you look today," she told a mannish, buck-toothed creature in a mink coat. Then, after a hushed pause, "But have you tried Amyrillis Aphid-Milk Lotion for a more dewy, glowing sheen?" When she had rubbed a bit of the mixture on the back of her hand, she added, "You see how it conceals, yet enriches? Now, once you begin using this in the economy size . . ."

"Isn't she stupendous?" Fay demanded, after a forty-dollar sale had been achieved. "No wonder Bernard jumps whenever she cracks the whip. If Madge demanded grasshopper private parts for her clientele, Amyrillis would produce them overnight. Lord, but she carries influence!"

Then, as I tried to grasp all this, "But don't think she isn't temperamental and difficult. As this department's queen bee, she insists on topping co-workers' daily sales volume . . . Jack says all good demonstrators are this way."

"In selling Giddy Moment, must we use a phony French accent too?"

"Certainly not. The more natural your approach, the better."

Once we get that order from Mr. Lathrop, I thought, my

responsibilities will be tremendous. But being natural, of course, will come easy.

As Madge caught sight of Fay, she gave a generous Irish smile. "Hi there, Dr. Amelia." Then, leaning forward with a chuckling whisper, "Say, I'm happy to hear you're expecting. Also I'm crocheting Junior the cunningest wee cap."

After giving her customers a gesture indicating "Stay put or *else*," Madge came closer. "I'm gunning for a new girl here named Baxter. Ah, the trouble she makes, fresh from college and full of zitz, grabbing sales and the saints know what. Very unethical. Very selfish. So I've asked Mr. Lathrop the buyer to . . . this Saturday night." Her arm rose in a vigorous slicing motion.

Baxter? The minute I caught that name, I jumped to attention. How did this woman dare to speak of dear Anna so slightingly?

Drawing me aside and down the aisle a bit, Fay said in a whisper, "When Madge complains this way, it's a sign of healthy neck-and-neck competition. Hmmm. Let's look up this Baxter person and see her in action."

After making some inquiries, we found Anna busily selling cologne. "Hello, dear," I said, catching her attention. "You look right at home here."

"Thank you, Mrs. Dent." When she had given the friendliest of nods, she returned to her customers. "Now, ladies, you'll enjoy it more if you apply it this way . . ."

My, I thought. If Horace could see his daughter here, he'd explode. But he won't learn the news from me.

"So you two know each other already?" Fay asked with delight. "I tell you, I've never seen a more curvaceous peaches-and-cream little blonde. Any woman would give a mint to look *exactly* like her. As for the impact on men . . . Wow!"

"She's as unspoiled a girl as you'd find anywhere."

"Ssssh. What gestures! What eyes! What a voice! She'll be a perfect demonstrator for Giddy Moment."

"Must we get involved with the mayor's daughter, for goodness' sakes? Can't we find somebody else?"

"Surely you see that Miss Baxter has every requirement — a luscious appearance, charm, aggressiveness, persuasiveness with customers . . ."

"Fay, you know perfectly well that Horace wouldn't like this. If he guessed that Anna was here selling cosmetics —"

"What he doesn't know won't hurt him." Then, more vehemently, "Besides, since he and Jack are playing footsie together, why shouldn't you and I? This way we'll fight fire with fire."

Indeed, I don't like this, I thought. But another little voice seemed to say, Stop being so stuffy. Once our promotion is set for January, Anna can be very helpful.

"What I suggest makes sense, doesn't it?" Fay asked, jerking my arm. Then, without waiting for an answer, "Now let's start up to the buying office. It's almost two-thirty."

All right, I almost cried out, following at her heels. Treat me like the tail on the cat as usual. But at the next opportunity, I'll speak my piece.

Jumping aboard the escalator, she seemed quite flushed and breathless. "Watch it," I warned as she teetered dangerously. "Watch it. Don't take foolish chances."

Steadying herself, she smiled back over her shoulder. "Haven't I taken them all my life?"

As we made our way through the Infants Department, she paused to examine some ointments and talcum. Fay *would* be charmed by this line-up instead of by bassinets, bootees and toys, I thought. Honestly, she's a sketch.

"Maybelle . . . Maybelle . . ." Her yellow-green eyes flashed, emphasizing the transparency of skin. "Have you ever considered the possibilities in baby pharmaceuticals? Do you realize that nothing new, nothing dramatically new has been developed since the Civil War? Diaper rash is still diaper rash in spite of modern science. Lord, but I itch to take a flier in this field."

"First things first," I said, using her favorite expression. "Once the baby comes, you'll have time for a new project. But let's get Giddy Moment launched first."

"O.K.," she groaned. "Fair enough."

Oh dear, I told myself as we proceeded on into the buying office wing. What's hit her lately? Imagine thinking of diaper rash now of all times. Why, when I'm learning to think straight at last, is she starting off on tangents? Then, jerking to attention, Oh heavens, there's the receptionist ahead already. Straighten your shoulders. Remember how Alvin's future is at stake here too. Forward march!

"Stop looking so scared," Fay said, putting her icy hand in mine. "We'll land a nice big order today. I'm sure of it."

"I am too," I said resolutely.

"Mr. Lathrop's two-thirty appointment?" a smiling young woman was asking now. "Down that corridor on your left, please, ladies."

Next Paul Lathrop came sauntering toward us with both hands outstretched. "Hello, Dr. Amelia. I've been looking forward to this reunion."

Chapter 15

Friday, November 4, 1960 (continued)

IF mothers could have the fun of selecting their sons-in-law, I'm sure all of us would make a rush for the Paul Lathrop type of man. Why, I wonder, is there such appeal in clean-cut features, eyes and skin carrying the freshness of youth and an air of supreme self-confidence? Also, why does a lean, loosely slung body look so handsome in Ivy League, impeccably tailored clothes? (Ah, how I wish Nina could be sensitive to these attractions instead of emphasizing intellectual qualities and mutual interests!)

Today as Fay and I shook hands with Star-Drake's cosmetic buyer, he seemed distressingly young for his responsible position. Why, I asked myself, had he wished to leave the security of Amyrillis? Could previous retailing experience somewhere and a year with a manufacturer have prepared him for his duties here? Might he possibly have hidden talents which would reveal themselves now in a burst of glory? Oh, from the bottom of my heart, I hoped so.

But I was hauled back to attention as he said politely, "My office is right here through this doorway, Dr. Amelia. Excuse me while I get some extra folding chairs."

"Lawks," Fay cried, stepping across the threshold. "Imagine trying to work in this airless chicken coop."

At least, I thought, they might have given this place a coat of fresh paint. From the looks you'd imagine this store was on its last legs. The furniture isn't fit for a rummage sale.

"Paul's always been sloppy as a goat," Fay whispered, glancing in turn at a desk piled with papers, and rickety oddments laden with toilet paper, bath salts, jars and bottles. "It will be a miracle if he succeeds here."

"But he's one of the loveliest young men I've ever met."

"The loveliest and the laziest." Her attention fastened on a bulletin board smeared with news pages of cosmetic advertising. "If you want more details, talk to Jack. He'll tell you Paul has a gift for landing jobs but not for keeping them."

Now our host reappeared with two badly battered undertaker-type chairs. After yanking them open, he set them in the remaining space. "As we learned yesterday, these are precarious as hell. So please, Dr. Amelia, sit there at my desk, with Mrs. Dent beside you."

"Stores must spend their money *only* where it impresses the public," Fay said with embarrassing directness. "If I had to try to think in this goat shed, I'd quit."

"Manufacturers such as Amyrillis may squander profits on offices and laboratories," he said airily. "But retailers can't, not with the cost of operation squeezing as it is increasingly. Besides" — he tapped his sandy, smoothly combed head — "where we buyers work doesn't matter, provided our decisions are right."

An excellent answer, young man, I thought. More and more I believe in you.

"You always were a smooth talker, Paul," Fay said, unimpressed.

Now a plump, rusty-haired little woman came panting through the doorway. "Sorry to be late, Mr. Lathrop, but there was a bit of trouble with Madge Reilly. As usual, she hollered until we opened that shipment of Aphid-Milk Lotion and hustled it down to the floor."

"Excuse accepted," he said graciously. "Dr. Amelia and Mrs. Dent, may I introduce my assistant, Mary Stevens, without whose energy we'd be lost." Then, waving toward one of the folding chairs, "Watch it when you sit down, Mary. I'm still black and blue from that accident yesterday."

What an odd team, I thought, as they settled themselves cautiously. Here's Paul, a male fashion-plate, and his co-worker looking like a careworn waitress. I never!

"Yes, in three months Queen Madge has worn me to the nub," Mrs. Stevens said with a sigh. "My, she tries my patience."

"You're new here too?" Fay asked, after a troubled glance at Paul.

"In this department, *yes*, Dr. Amelia, but in the store, *no*. I began from the bottom in handkerchiefs and neckwear. In many ways, though, I've found this job easier than any before. I mean, in this market manufacturers are so kind in sharing responsibility. If a pinky-pink shade doesn't sell, what do they do? Exchange it for peach, carmine or flesh-color . . ."

"We do and we should," Fay agreed. "This way a customer's sure to find what she wants when she wants it, whether a store's buying staff is experienced or not. Besides, our industry is tops in its high standards and ethics."

"That's right," Paul said approvingly. "But as Mrs. Stevens has indicated, our key problem is learning to handle demonstrators diplomatically. Tell me, Dr. Amelia, when Madge, for example, starts screaming like a fishwife, what should I do?"

His assistant broke in. "I say we shouldn't let her walk over us and everybody else. But Mr. Lathrop fears she may jinx us with Amyrillis. He says she has the hex on the top brass there, especially Mr. Huggin."

"Harmony with demonstrators means harmony with our suppliers," Paul said, continuing to look at Fay. "Isn't that right?"

"Jack would certainly say so." She tapped her tiny enameled finger tips on the desk. "We all know that Madge is and will continue to be a consumer sounding-board for Amyrillis. Consequently, she has supreme influence which cannot be discounted."

Oh dear, I thought. Anna Baxter should never make an enemy of such a dangerous woman. I wish I could protect her somehow.

"So," Fay continued, "in the future, Paul, day in, day out, I'd treat Madge like a duchess. I'd act on her suggestions promptly whenever they make good sense. But when she starts histrionics, such as gunning for other demonstrators, ignore them. Yes, take pains to ignore them, because she'll pick as targets only those whose skills match or are superior to her own."

"Good," he said gratefully. Then, turning to his assistant, "Now, this settles our Anna Baxter hassle, doesn't it?"

"It should. Miss Baxter has exceptional talents," Fay said warmly. "We noticed them a few minutes ago."

"Did you indeed? Ah, there's more to that little blonde than meets the eye."

"Plenty meets the eye, Paul. Admit it."

"Well, yes . . . yes . . . I suppose so." Flushing, he stammered to a stop.

My, I thought, he's taken quite a shine to dear Anna. Wouldn't those two make a handsome young couple if they should marry some day?

After glancing from the corner of his eye toward Fay, Paul teetered in his chair. What strategy is he planning? I wondered. He looks like a youngster intent on reaching a candy jar.

"Er . . . Dr. Amelia, could you help us with another problem maybe?" After winking at his assistant, he chuckled in spite of himself. "We're continuing to get hundreds of requests for a lipstick . . . the one mentioned on *Perk Predicts* months ago. As you must know, Giddy Moment has aroused unusually keen customer interest."

Fay fell for this bait beautifully. "Like all products from my laboratory, it has and it *should*." Then, becoming aware of his amusement, she burst into laughter. "Aha, this time you're a jump ahead of us, I see."

"You win, Mr. Lathrop," his assistant cried, rocking back and forth in her chair until it squealed a warning. "My oh my, you solved this puzzle fast."

"Why shouldn't I?" he beamed. "After a year at Amyrillis I knew that one chemist, and only one, could have built this lipstick. So I spread out the welcome mat."

By now Fay had extracted a becoffined gold tube from her handbag. "This sample came from our first run of stock several months ago. Also" — she pointed to the dead-white, pristinely pleated packaging — "as you see, it carries Rose Pfeiffer's unique touch."

"A bit mortuary for my taste," Paul said, after examining the tiny carton. "But who am I to argue with the Da Vinci of our industry? Ithent the thimplithity here juth thweet?"

"Not amusing," Fay scolded.

When he had opened Giddy Moment, he tried a bit of it on his finger. "Seems great." Then, leaning back in his chair, he began to fire questions. "Is this available for immediate order? What is the planned retail price, the cost, the range of sizes and colors? You haven't shown it to other stores yet, have you? Ah, good. Good."

Son, you're handling yourself well, I thought.

"We'll need a volume-getter next January, Dr. Amelia. That's why I called you this morning."

"Yes, we're up against figures from a big hair-treatment fad last year," Mrs. Stevens explained. "If I let myself, I'd stay awake nights worrying."

"I was sure you'd be able to help us, Doctor. In fact, I'm depending on it."

Fay sat expressionless, with her chin in her palms. How smart to bide her time this way, concealing our inexperience.

Paul had become flushed. "We want our store to be the first in the United States to promote Giddy Moment. We want the promise of at least one *Perk Predicts* radio news blast followed by several full pages of newspaper advertising. We want two expert demonstrators working hand-in-glove with our own sales force. Also we ask you to help us figure our stock requirements and to promise deliveries within the hour, as we need them."

Greek gibberish. But, surprisingly, Fay understood it perfectly. "Aha, Paul," she cried, clapping her hands. "I see you've done your homework well. That's a most excellent presentation."

"I intend to succeed here," he said vigorously. "I'll admit that in the past year I didn't apply myself as I should. But . . . well . . ." The words came with effort. "Every man rises to responsibility once he's found a goal."

Me oh my, across from us sat a young man eager to do his best — for himself, for us, and probably for dear Anna Baxter's sake too. Ah, it couldn't be easy to admit faults so frankly. Especially since Fay had been sphinxlike, giving no encouragement. Maybe now, though, she'd unbend and try to be kinder.

"I like you, Paul Lathrop," she said quietly. "I believe in your zeal to do well."

"Thank you."

"In the past," she continued, "I'll admit I've had doubts. But now I'm ready to say yes to your suggestions . . . *except for one*. How can I promise co-operation from *Perk Predicts*?" Then, turning toward me, "Alvin's changeable, isn't he? One minute he's dancing with enthusiasm over something, the next he's cold as a stone. Who would attempt to pin down such temperament? Or to count on any agreement he might make?"

Ah, but I was angry. How had she dared to make that statement? Wasn't it ridiculously untrue? I would have liked to shake her, in the family way or not.

"Don't you agree, Maybelle?"

"No," I said. "Right now I'll give my word, backed by Alvin's, that he'll feature Giddy Moment on *Perk Predicts.* Once we select the date, he'll come through."

After checking his calendar, Mr. Lathrop said, "Then we can count on his co-operation on Thursday, January twelfth, can we, Mrs. Dent?"

"Yes," I said with a triumphant glance at Fay. "I'll bet my life on it."

"Fine," she said, half smiling, "but let's not get overdramatic." Then, turning toward the buyer, "Now, let's settle a couple of details, please. First I'd like to have Mrs. Dent and Miss Baxter handle demonstration together." When this had been agreed upon, she went into a discussion of selling space and Giddy Moment stock requirements.

While the two of them wrote up their agreement, Mrs. Stevens chatted with me. "I'll never learn to stop testing everything I buy," she said, reaching for a sample of our lipstick and examining it closely. "Cosmetic salesmen say this isn't necessary, that it shows I'm a novice in the field. Still, as a woman, I'm bound by this habit. Aren't you, Mrs. Dent?"

"Oh yes indeed," I agreed, as she applied some of the mixture to her finger and smoothed it industriously. "Before purchasing a loaf of bread, I always sniff and pinch it. As for vegetables — lettuce and spinach, especially —"

Looking up from her work, Fay seemed to warn: Cut out this nonsense, for Pete's sake. Can't you forget your years as a housewife?

"I'd be the first to admit," the assistant continued, "that a reliable product from a reliable source means everything. It does and it always will . . . Excuse me, but this chair is so pinchy I can't endure it a minute more." After failing to pull herself to an erect position, she said merrily, "No use. I'm stuck fast. Even a jack rabbit couldn't get loose if he tried."

"I never guessed that stores were so tight behind the scenes," I said, reviewing the jam-up of knees: Mrs. Stevens's, Mr. Lathrop's and mine.

"My goodness, the penny-pinching grows here every day — on space, lights, washroom soap, salaries, everything. It's terrible."

"You live and learn," I sighed, smiling toward this friendly, sensible little woman. What a pleasure it would be to know her better, once I was working side by side with Anna Baxter.

After digging up a pocket mirror, she applied some Giddy Moment to her mouth. "I never wear lipstick or pay much attention to the ads, Mrs. Dent. What's new or different about this or that brand anyway, in spite of their wild promises?"

Before I could answer, the assistant began to squirm violently. "Indeed this does feel nice. Very tasty too." She sat like a squirrel enjoying a particularly choice nut. "Makes me tingle all over."

"It should," I said, as her attention remained completely centered on herself. Gracious, but she's a slow Jane, I thought, aware that this reaction was different from any before. Why is there no glazing of the eyes, no pronounced breathing or Russian Cossack gymnastics? Has something gone wrong with our formula?

Yet, as I sat watching, Mary Stevens became pure woman, radiant and inviting. She had taken her own sweet time, but she was catching fire at last.

"Somehow this lipstick feels better than others," she exclaimed, addressing her buyer directly, with bosom outthrust.

Meanwhile he and Fay had finished writing the last specifications. "Now here's my signature and we're set," he said adding it with a flourish. "This is a moment I shall remember."

"Me too," she cried, folding and pocketing the order. "Here's to our success."

You're a remarkable woman, Fay, I thought. Through sheer courage you win again and again. Then, of course, you have persistence and almost frightening self-discipline. Oh, it's hard to remember that you're a prospective mother. Most of the time you forget it yourself.

By now Mrs. Stevens was showing impatience. "Do I look as good as I feel?" she asked, getting her superior's attention at last. "Do-o-oo I?"

With eyeballs protruding, he shouted, "Do you ever . . . sugar!"

Fay smiled with enormous satisfaction.

Though Mr. Lathrop fought to leap to his feet, he remained glued, his legs flaying helplessly. "Damn the tight squeeze-up here," he bellowed, as the wood beneath him rocketed and shuddered. "Oh, Mary, Mary, dear Mary . . ."

"Hee-hee. So I'm *dear Mary* now, am I? What next?"

"Next I intend to kiss you as you've never, *never* been kissed before!" he cried as his chair collapsed with a crash. "Oh God, why can't those penurious buzzards upstairs provide furniture which hangs together?" After staring from his position on the floor, he grabbed his assistant's knees hungrily. "Bend over here, darling. Do. I ache to feel your lips on mine."

"Come, come, come, Mr. Lathrop," she said, pushing him away. "Stop, sir. Stop this minute. You're wrecking my best nylons."

"But look how you've thrown me head over heels," he wailed.

"For shame, sir." She brought both palms down on his head smartly. "And you a college graduate too."

As their struggle continued, Fay grew gaunt-faced. "Good heavens, Maybelle," she whispered. "Look. Our formula's gone sour. Paul's dying of love, entrapped below there. And Mrs.

Stevens is getting angrier by the minute. Oh dear. Oh dear. Oh dear. I'm sure Giddy Moment has lost its wallop."

"Paul's responding as he should, isn't he?"

"But our lipstick is supposed to affect *both* parties equally." Though Fay kept her tone hushed, she showed signs of panic. "I might have known that storage conditions would raise Cain with seasoning, damn it." Then, turning toward Mrs. Stevens, she said with wonderful self-control, "While you're removing Giddy Moment from your lips, Mrs. Dent and I will try to handle Mr. Lathrop. I'm sure he'll be fine again in a minute."

While we were hauling the buyer back to his feet, the assistant scrubbed her face with a bit of tissue. "I'm sold, Dr. Amelia," she said between swipes. "Women customers will be too."

Ignoring this remark and her own condition, Fay kept tugging away. "Paul, you weigh half a ton," she wheezed when he was on his feet. "What did you eat for breakfast?"

"Breakfast?" he blinked. "When the hell was breakfast?"

"Yes, all in all, Giddy Moment looks very satisfactory," Mrs. Stevens intoned.

Observing her kindly expression, I found myself glowing too. Wasn't the nicest feature of our lipstick the fact that it warmed and lifted the human spirit? If it could be distributed gratis to peoples throughout the world, imagine the lasting peace it might build.

"Good night," Mr. Lathrop groaned, smoothing his thigh. "Mrs. Stevens, we must find ourselves some safer chairs. Two spills in as many days is murdering my constitution. And dignity too, I fear."

Again, absolutely no embarrassment, I observed, as he went on to describe tranquilizing pills "tried lately and producing the exact opposite effect, as you ladies could see. When a woman comes close — well, you get the point already, I'm sure . . ."

First and last you're a gentleman, I thought. Breeding tells every time.

"Now, friends," Fay said, after we had said our good-bys, "if any problems should arise between now and January, Mrs. Dent will come running."

"Just ask for the sales manageress," I cried. "*Me.*"

"Thanks," the buying staff said in unison.

Once we had made our way past the reception desk, Fay continued to brood. But why should she? I asked myself. If Giddy Moment is weaker than it was, we should be thankful.

Approaching the baby department again, she became more and more depressed. As she paused before the rows of pharmaceuticals she moaned, "Drat it. Here I itch to begin something *new* and Giddy Moment does a double flip. I've never had such a poop-out before. Never."

"But everyone seemed more than pleased today."

"Well, I'm chagrined through and through. Having set a goal for performance, I won't permit any slackening, any acceptance of less than the best."

"But wouldn't women prefer a lipstick giving them control of the situation? And from the viewpoint of selling to customers, shouldn't we welcome this development?"

"I won't consider such foolishness," she cried, stamping her foot. "From the beginning Giddy Moment has never been a money-making scheme. Either I live up to our ideals or I admit failure."

"Fay, Fay . . . try to be reasonable."

She paid no attention. "Of course storage conditions are at the bottom of our difficulties. Also we rushed through seasoning requiring several years in a matter of weeks. Obviously newly manufactured stock carries full strength as it should. Then it dwindles bit by bit until eventually we have this."

"Stop worrying, won't you? Mr. Lathrop and Mrs. Stevens were well satisfied. We have their signed order to prove it."

"Nuts. Listen to me, Maybelle. As long as I'm able-bodied and in command of this situation, we'll promote and sell only full-strength Giddy Moment. Yes, even if we have to scrap thousands of lipsticks and run our machines double speed." Then, as I stood crestfallen, "Come along now. What can we accomplish standing here?"

Oh mercy. If she kept acting so headstrong, she'd surely wreck us all.

When she had stepped from the escalator to the lingerie department, I pulled her toward the sales counter. "Here's the little nightgown you planned to buy."

After examining the bit of froth with its bosom of exquisite lace, she cried, "A pox on nightgowns. I haven't time for them now." Then, swaying dizzily, she clutched her waistline.

"All right, dear," I soothed. "We'd better get you home to bed."

"Ho. How ridiculous." Though she was shivering, she took a long breath and squared her shoulders. "I tell you I feel fine. Fine. Besides, we have *work* to do now. First let's drive past Alvin's house and pick him up. Then we'll go to the laboratory and try to correct this debacle."

Had she ever been more trying? No wonder Jack looked as battle-scarred as he did these days.

After we had plowed through the revolving door, she gripped my arm. "Why, oh why is time so pitifully short these days? If only we could postpone our promotion at Star-Drake's, my baby's birth and everything else for a while!"

"Please, can't I carry more of the burden now, Fay? There's every reason why I should." Oh, but I was surprised at the eagerness in my voice. It had sprung out as though released from long imprisonment.

She was silent until we had settled ourselves in her car. Then she said uneasily, "You've asked a fair question, so I'll try to answer it . . . Like all scientists, I'm basically a lone operator. It isn't that I don't trust you, Maybelle. Of course I do . . . But when you've learned as I have to depend on your own skill, ingenuity and strength — when you've had to be this way in order to survive and keep a roof over your head . . ."

"But all this is behind you, isn't it?"

"Why should it be? Have you forgotten that I'm committed to proving an important truth to Jack, to Bernard Huggin and to myself too? Must I repeat all this?" She was shivering again, though she fought to conceal it.

I'm sorry, I said to myself, as a strange new force seemed to rise from my knees to my throat . . . but we've got to reach an understanding here. Otherwise Fay will be sure to start junking stock on hand, bolloxing up production and goodness knows what-all. Then I asked as gently as possible, "Suppose I should take this high and mighty attitude too?"

"What?" She almost leaped up into the steering wheel.

Oh dear, dear. I didn't want this showdown. But . . .

"So I'm high and mighty, am I?" she asked with a little laugh.

"Yes. I think so. Remember, I'm no longer the timid homebody I used to be. You've taught me more than you guess."

"So now you've become a career woman with a mind of your own. Is that it?"

I expected to hear myself say very firmly, "Yes. I also happen to be your partner in Amelia-Dent Enterprises, with equal rights." Ah, the words were right there on the tip of my tongue. Yet the hurt in Fay's voice, soaring up like a violin string, silenced them. How bungling and selfish I had been, adding to her troubles.

"All right," she said sharply. "Go ahead. Speak your piece."

"I can't," I said, aching with the awareness of how fine, how generous she was, in spite of the torments inflicted on herself. "I just don't know what's got into me lately."

Chapter 16

Friday, November 4, 1960 (continued)

FAY may have faults, but she never holds a personal grudge. Of course she blows up whenever she is crossed. Yet once a temper flash has passed, she is the first to smile and try to make amends. Even though Jack and Mr. Huggin may have hurt her pride professionally, I am sure that she continues to love them as people, with strong points, quirks and weaknesses of their own.

This characteristic, I believe, had endeared Fay to me beyond all others. Though she and I are completely unlike each other, we are able to dismiss misunderstandings promptly. Consequently we enjoy a friendship which may be rare between two women.

Today, grievances were forgotten immediately. "Ah there's nothing like fresh air to make you feel right," Fay said, with her eyes glued on the Boulevard ahead. "I could climb mountains now . . . in a pinch."

Observing the feverish color in her cheeks, I wondered, Is this another attempt at bravado?

Now, as we approached the Perkin house, we saw Alvin standing near the curb. Good, I thought, noting the uncluttered lawn, driveway and porch. Grace moved as fast as an express train. I was positive she would.

"Hi, girls," Alvin shouted as we rolled to a stop. "Aha, we're in much better shape here, aren't we? The last pickup was made five minutes ago, thank God."

Ah, but he looked dear in his hound's-tooth jacket, open-neck shirt and slacks. Also he appeared to be freshly washed and shaved, his skin clear as a boy's. Darling, darling, darling, I thought, observing the glow in his eyes, the sun reflecting itself in his hair.

"How was your appointment?" he asked in the most casual way. "Successful?"

"We brought home the bacon," Fay said, using one of the terms which I shall never understand.

"I knew you would."

"So did I," she said, completely forgetful of the doubts expressed at lunch. "It was easy as rolling off a you-know-what." Then, beckoning, "Jump in, will you? We want you to come along home with us."

He eyed her shrewdly. "Has Jack received a shipment of that special sour-mash bourbon?"

"If you're looking for a bribe, dear, the answer is yes."

"Good," he grinned, all six feet of him relaxed. "Get out the glasses and ice. I'll be along in my car."

"So you're too proud to ride with us, are you?"

"Never risk my neck with women drivers. Besides, I need to live a little longer, don't I, Maybelle?" Then, as I continued to drink in the picture of him, he asked, "What's the matter? Was the session at Star-Drake too much of a strain?"

"Oh no. I loved every minute of it. Now I really feel like a sales manageress."

"Certainly you don't look like one," he said gently. "But being in business seems to agree with you."

"Let's stop this small talk," Fay cried, with a toss of her navy-bonneted head. "You may have time to waste, Alvin Perkin. But we haven't."

"It so happens that I have a week to waste," he said wryly. "Remember?"

"Suppose you save such bon mots for your fan correspondence," she scolded, as he stood with his hands in his pockets. "Come along soon. We need you." Before he could answer, she stepped on the accelerator and sailed off down the street.

"Why go so fast?" I asked, as we rocketed around a corner.

"Ho. You should be used to this pace by now . . . especially with your newly discovered independence."

Now why must she bring up this subject again?

"Back at Star-Drake's, I saw, of course, that something was eating you, Maybelle. So, since I don't like mysteries . . ."

"Well," I said, struggling to find the right words, "can't you see yourself that you've changed me?"

She choked back her amusement. "Changed you for the better or for the worse?"

"Time will tell."

"Ha, I'm sure it will. Also, I intend to be around when Mayor Baxter pins a blue ribbon on your bosom, Mrs. American Business Woman of the Year."

"Stop, Fay. You know how I hate to be teased."

She fell into a croaking imitation. "My friends, this lady beyond all others has brought glory, fame and fortune to our beloved community."

I had to smile in spite of myself. "Say, you're quite an expert at speech-making."

Her pleasure vanished. "I'm glad I'm expert at something."

"Why talk that way?"

"For the same reason that we're heading back to the laboratory . . . Because the fruit of my labors has developed a lousy blemish."

Now, as we turned into the Hick driveway, I caught sight of the sweeping lawn broken here and there by birch trees. Behind an edging of newly whitewashed stones, I saw chrysanthemums in a winding parade of bloom. What a perfect play-ground for a child some day, I thought, selecting a spot which seemed perfect for a seesaw, swing and slide. And it will be fine to see a tricycle sprawled there by the front door, though Fay may not guess it yet.

As we came to a stop in the garage, she said, "Tonight Jack will be coming home earlier than usual, darn it. So we'll have to work our heads off now while we can." Reaching for my hand, she squeezed it hard. "Please, please, Maybelle, stay on tonight for cocktails. I need you and Alvin."

"But why? Once those two men see each other again, won't grievances grow stronger?"

"What do I care?"

"You'd better care, Fay. Jack's been unusually patient about Giddy Moment. And you know it."

"Don't mention all this again."

"But I'm sure you have some purpose in mind. What is it?"

"Well . . ." Her eyes half closed. "At the moment I'm work-ing from hunch. Also from curiosity. I told you a while ago that I don't like mysteries. Since Jack seems to be intent on getting Alvin's scalp, let's bring this out into the open. Presto, he'll show his hand!"

"Is that wise? Won't it build unnecessary antagonism? Re-member that Jack is slow to anger and slow to forgive."

"You've pegged him right. The day he explodes, I'm going to head for the hills."

"So you see, Fay . . ."

"I see that I expect you and Alvin to stay here for a while tonight. Besides, I promised him some of his favorite bourbon, didn't I? Though he may have to wait for it longer than he guesses."

"All right," I said, shaking my head. "But I don't like this plan. I'm sure we're going to regret it."

"So what?"

Now, again, that strange new force seemed to come rushing through my throat. "Why can't you be more sensible, Fay?" I cried. "Increasingly you ignore your baby's coming in another ten weeks. Must you continue to gamble with your health?"

"That's my business."

"It's my business too. If you haven't the sense to think of your husband and child, I'll think of them for you."

"You will, will you?" Her tone rasped with anger.

"I must. You know I love Jack . . . Lately you've been treating him abominably. You're so obsessed with winning this Giddy Moment tournament, you can't take time for anybody or anything else."

She sat listening, half indignant, half amused.

"Also, your thinking on Giddy Moment isn't as sound as it should be. You've let your pride as a chemist interfere with common sense. As sales manageress, I intend to sell lipsticks exactly like the sample demonstrated today."

"Oh-ho-ho," she cried, slapping her knee. Then, as I continued to look at her resolutely, "What in the world has come over you, Maybelle?"

"Plenty. I'm fed up with playing your follow-the-leader game. At the beginning I'll admit that this was necessary. But it isn't any more, now I've gathered convictions of my own. Besides, I'm an equal partner in Amelia-Dent Enterprises, though you tend to forget it." Ah, now I had said it at last!

"So this is how I've changed you, is it?"

"As a chemist you've done very well," I said, trying to smile at my little joke.

"Well, we'll know more about skills or my lack of them in another few minutes," she said with surprising quietness. "Let's get into our laboratory now, Madame Equal Partner."

"All right," I said, thankful that our conversation was winding up smoothly. Then, using one of her favorite expressions,

"You go halfway with me and we're sure to hit the big time."

"Like mother, like child," she murmured to herself. Then, turning toward me with probing eyes, "What's developed this drive in you of all people? Aha, I know . . . you're taking this tack because you believe it will help Alvin Perkin. Also you're in love with him, aren't you? . . . I knew it. This explains everything." She squeezed my hand more tightly than before. "But listen, dear. Listen carefully . . . You mustn't trust him. You can't have lived next door all these years without knowing his faults. And surely he's aware of your gullibility, your loneliness . . ."

"Stop, Fay. Stop. I won't listen to this."

"You must. I can't stand by while he twists you about for his own purposes. Why, he'd stop at nothing to *use* you, if it would help to build his Trendex rating. He'd even be crafty enough to suggest marriage, with no intention of going through with it. You must be realistic! Otherwise sooner or later he'll break your heart."

"Please," I wailed. "You mean well, but I can't endure this." Oh dear, but could she be right? Hadn't Alvin tried to warn me himself today?

"Ssssh, here he comes." She glanced toward the approaching yellow convertible. "I'm sorry, Maybelle. Truly I am. But you know why I had to do this."

You did it because of love, Fay, I thought. Being intuitive as you are, you sensed this situation hours ago. That's why you found an excuse to bring Alvin here. Also it explains why you've dawdled instead of rushing pell-mell back to work. But why should you fear for me this way? Am I not well able to look after myself?

"Hello, dolls," Alvin hollered, joining us. "Don't tell me you're still sitting here. Lord, I'll never understand women. One minute you rush off somewhere in a cloud of dust, the

next you sit on your rear ends yack-yacketing. What poor
devil got taken over the coals just now?"

"You," Fay said, as she let him help her out. "Weren't your
ears burning?"

"Of course," he said, winking at me. "The day they don't,
I'll have to change my tailor and my brand of toothpaste."

"Don't tell me you're giving the go-by to dear old tempt-
ing, tantalizing Tasty-Foam," she teased, while I stood frowning.

"No," he said with sudden seriousness. "As of next Monday,
Tasty-Foam will give the go-by to me, now Amyrillis owns it
lock, stock and manufacturing rights."

"Another fond gesture on the part of Jack, Bernard and our
revered mayor," she said, sighing. "Gad, such tactics."

"Once Giddy Moment gets launched, we'll fix that trio,"
he said grinning. "I've promised Maybelle full co-operation
once you settle on a date."

"We've settled on it already." Impulsively Fay reached up,
pulling his head toward hers. "Thursday, January twelfth."
After kissing him soundly she added, "Sometimes I can't help
liking you myself."

"I want you to like me. Also I hope you'll learn to trust
me." (Ah, but he was intuitive too, wasn't he?) Then, clapping his hands together, "Now where is that sour-mash bourbon?"

"Rewards come later, son." Taking his arm, Fay hauled him
along. "After you've finished a chore or two."

Now we opened a door revealing a world of test tubes, laboratory workers in white coats and an atmosphere of purity.
"Mm-m-mm," Fay cried, sniffing approvingly. "Home sweet
home."

In contrast, I was far from enthusiastic. Even after months
of association here, I felt ill at ease with Bunsen burners,
acrid odors and winding glass tubing. All too clearly, I saw

myself as a housewife caught in a web where she didn't belong
. . . and where she never, never would. I would not know
why a woman so adept in her own kitchen should be clumsy in
a related work place. Yet who can fail to be aware of limita-
tions?

Today while Alvin and I grew accustomed to the fluorescent
lights and the throb of machinery close by, Fay hurriedly con-
ferred with her assistants. After this mumbo-jumbo had wound
up, she introduced Dr. Celeste Belle and Dr. Tyrone Surr to
"Perk Predicts . . . our good friend and neighbor, whose
interest means much."

As he shook hands, Alvin accepted this flattery with obvious
suspicion. "She's fattening me for the kill," he said from the
side of his mouth. "When Fay makes speech number seventeen, Maybelle, I've learned to shrink."

"She just plans to run through a couple of experiments today," I soothed.

"She does?" He glanced about for a means of escape.
"With us as guinea pigs? Somebody, quick, get me out of
here."

"We landed a nice order at Star-Drake's," Fay was saying to
her fellow chemists. "But as I mentioned a minute ago, our
sample of Giddy Moment fell woefully short in demonstration."

"Of course we've been on the lookout for reduced potency,"
Dr. Belle drawled, shaking her mop of mud-brown hair. "But
until now I've seen no signs of it."

As Dr. Surr began to squeak out a lot of technical gibberish,
Alvin and I were lost completely. Observing this mousy, waxed-
mustached little man, we longed to burst into laughter. It was
like seeing a living cartoon sporting octagonal spectacles,
beaked red nose and an air of sorrow.

"For the moment I see I'm not needed here," Alvin said,
perching on a stool and crossing his legs. Then, sniffing to-

ward a bubbling jar with its bad-egg odor, he gripped his nose. "Out of this stink comes a lipstick, dear God?"

Now, after Fay had called for our factory superintendent and stock supervisor, they appeared immediately. When she had introduced them, she said, "Jim, would you bring a couple of newly run Giddy Moment samples, please? And Tony, could you dig out some from our very first production? Also, would you see they're identified carefully, the new as A, the old as B?"

Once the men returned, Dr. Surr checked their specimens approvingly. "Very good," he squeaked. "New production is labeled A as it should be, old production is B."

"Sonny-boy catches on fast," Alvin whispered mockingly.

"Maybelle, please come over here," Fay commanded. "Take sample A in your hand and stand there, next to . . ." She deliberated a minute. "Next to Tyrone."

Oh no, I thought, dying at these instructions. Dr. Surr may be an able chemist, but as a man he's positively repulsive. If that mouselike nose comes near me as I'm sure it will . . . Oh no. No. No. No. This goes beyond the call of friendship or my duties as a business partner.

While Alvin winked gleefully, Fay handed sample B to Dr. Belle. "Suppose you line up there next to Jim." She waved toward the shirt-sleeved giant of a superintendent.

"Oh-ho-ho," Alvin howled as I kept writhing. "You should see your face, Maybelle. I wish I had my camera here."

"Shush." Fay gave him a black look. "If you must act like a two-bit burlesque comic, march yourself out." Then, as he jumped up with alacrity, "No you don't. Stay where you are. We may be needing you soon."

Edging away from Jim Swanson, Dr. Belle asked wistfully, "Couldn't I do this experiment with Mr. Perkin instead?"

"No," Fay roared, while Alvin ducked.

"But from the scientific angle, Dr. Amelia, don't you be-

lieve . . . ? Very well . . . still, in my opinion . . ." Dr. Belle
returned to the indicated spot with the air of a Spartan.

Now, as her Goliath-sized escort looked toward Fay plead-
ingly, she shook her head. "Sorry, Jim. But as I said before, I
expect everyone here to give complete co-operation. So stay
paired as you are."

He nodded meekly.

"All right, girls. Put on your respective lipsticks." Then,
when this had been done, "One . . . two . . . three . . . go."
She clapped her hands briskly.

Remembering what happened next, I am more than ever
amazed by full-strength Giddy Moment. Because once I approached Dr. Surr draggingly, and looked into his eyes, we
came together with a wham. And there we stayed until Alvin
yanked us apart, almost breaking both my arms.

Although I was unable to watch experiment B, it must have
been interesting. As Alvin said later, Jim kept charging at
white-coated, piano-legged Dr. Belle, while she dodged, leaped,
screamed and pummeled viciously. And it was not until she
removed the mixture from her lips that everything was nicely
calm again.

I haven't the energy now to describe the other tests which
Fay put us through in sequence. But I know that they proved
what she expected they would — all Giddy Moment stock
which had been stored two months or more showed loss of
strength. It made a woman wearing it irresistibly kissable still.
But she was *free to choose* whether she wished to encourage a
man's advances or whether she didn't.

"Good God, we can't have this," Alvin hollered when he
heard this verdict. "It will be the ruination of the male species.
Hasn't every sociologist warned that American women have too
much power already? Look at the proportion of capital in-
vestments they hold, and the way they outlive us."

"I agree." Dr. Surr's spottled nose twitched furiously.

"These days husbands mix baby formulas while their wives wear business suits to work. I say someone should put a stop to it."

"We females have fought hard for our rights," Dr. Belle declared, including the superintendent in her baleful look. "Who's going to keep us from adding to them?"

"Balderdash," Fay roared. "We have one issue and only one issue here — achieving our goal as scientists."

"It's not the first time storage has raised hob with us, Dr. Amelia," the superintendent said after nodding agreement. "Remember how Aphid-Milk Lotion curdled a couple of years back? You managed to get rid of that clinker fast, and you'll correct this one too. Now I've got to get back to the factory."

As Fay smiled fondly, Tony added his two cents' worth. "Luckily, Dr. Amelia, all of us here know our jobs. Like we used to do at Amyrillis, I've labeled each lot of Giddy Moment by date of manufacture. So in no time I can separate stock A cartons from stock B."

When both men had hurried off, the assistant chemists kept examining the metal tubes in their hands. "We'll lick this little difficulty, won't we, friends?" Fay asked them grimly.

"Hell's bells, you'd better," Alvin shouted. "It's one thing to stimulate good old-fashioned kissing. It's another to detroy balance between the sexes." Then, after debating and giving a shrewd glance, "Dr. Amelia . . . Dr. Fay Bernice Amelia . . . it's not like you to do things by halves. Not unless you've begun to slip badly."

Ah, but I was shocked by this underhanded maneuver. For shame, I thought. If you keep needling this way, dear, we'll be lost! Must I buck your pigheadedness *too?*

"That's enough from you, sir," Fay said, her eyes blazing. Then, turning toward her helpers, she repeated, "Can I rely on your co-operation?"

"Yes." They clicked their heels together. "Yes indeed."

Chapter 17

Friday, November 4, 1960 (continued)

TONIGHT I keep asking myself this question again and again: If we had demonstrated the full-strength Giddy Moment to Star-Drake buyers, what would have happened? Would we have walked out with an order for twenty gross and a promise for a January promotion? Or would Mr. Lathrop and Mrs. Stevens, in spite of inexperience, have canceled out as Amyrillis executives had several months ago?

Truly I cannot understand why Fay and Alvin haven't mulled over this thought too. But I realize that both of them have one quality in common — driving resolution to build personal success and fame.

In comparison, I suppose that my interest in our lipstick venture may be more complex. Originally I wished to do what I had never had the courage to try. Then I began to see that increased effort could add new blessings to women and men everywhere. Now today, for the first time, Alvin's needs have been piled on everything else, demanding my best judgment, skill and endurance. Ah, but this is a load to bear . . .

In all honesty I have asked myself if I carry a secret urge to be in the limelight. Surely eagerness for recognition lay behind my attempts at love stories and the submitting of recipes to the Tasty-Flour Contest. Also, since Fay has been such a strong influence, can I be growing more like her than I guess? Dear, oh dear, I would not wish this to be so.

My, but I was surprised that Alvin took our Giddy Moment findings so seriously today. Why was he so worried about sample B giving women an unfair advantage? Has this attitude any possible tie-in with building Trendex ratings? Instead, isn't it a purely masculine gesture of defense?

In addition, I fail to understand why Giddy Moment in its original strength ever delighted him as it did. Was he grateful because it helped to break down lifelong shyness? Was it his wry way of jeering at the gymnastics connected with kissing? Was he curious to see what would happen if Fay and I went into business together? Apart from his burning business ambition, was some pixie quality in him bent on mischief? Perhaps some day, when we are married, I may learn the answers.

Though Alvin is very dear to me, I am completely baffled by him. Also, I shall never approve of his attacking a person's weakness as he does. Look how he taunted Fay today about "slipping" and doing things "by halves." Dear Lord, does he know my soft spots so well too? And is he taking advantage of them?

I should never have gotten off on this track, since it makes my head twinge. I had hoped that I was no longer subject to these spells. Yet Dr. Baxter says that often, after a nasty tumble, they carry over for years. How reassuring it is to know that he is here close by, ready to come instantly if needed. How lovely, too, that he has received the honor mentioned this morning on Louise Larrabbee's program. Certainly Horace could benefit by copying his brother's modesty.

It seems odd that Jack Hick was the first and only person today to comment on my radio appearance. If he hadn't taken that fourth drink of bourbon, perhaps he wouldn't have brought up this subject, creating bedlam. But I am getting ahead of myself, I see. Yet shaken as I am from that incident, why wouldn't I give it priority?

Surely when our host made his appearance this evening, he

seemed to be in good spirits. Once he had called out, "Where's my loving wife — buried in test tubes as usual?" Fay came running of course. After he had kissed her, he said, "Tonight I decided to spoil you." Then, while she squealed with delight, he set an emerald circlet on her finger. "Signifies faith and hope . . . and fits exactly, doesn't it? I was praying it would."

"Thank you," she cried, hugging hard. Then, as Alvin and I came forward, "Surprise, surprise! Two old friends staying for cocktails."

"Fine," he said warmly. "Neighbors are always welcome."

On the surface everything seemed very affable, very sincere. Yet I could read in Fay's glance toward her husband an inevitable question: So emeralds are another salve to conscience are they, Mr. Ace-up-the-sleeve? Also, behind Jack's rousing hospitality I caught a sign of displeasure in a slow surge of color to his neck.

In spite of the game which the Hicks continued to play together, they seemed genuinely happy in each other. As Fay kissed her husband again she said, "I meant to be upstairs when you arrived, dear. Really I did."

"I know I can't compete with your work," he said, a little sadly. "Besides, I sympathize with your obsession for it, scientific temperament being what it is."

"Thank you," she said again. "Understanding like this means everything — everything." Then, flushing, "Good night! Listen to us, with guests here too."

There's deep devotion between these two, I told myself, though Fay doesn't like to admit it. Why must she emphasize the misunderstandings and dark moments of marriage always? Is it because she tends to be so dramatic? Surely there's truth in the maxim that once the door to a home is closed, no one can guess what goes on there.

Though I had never tasted Kentucky sour-mash bourbon,

the men insisted that I try it. "Don't throw in the sponge," Alvin teased, as I made a wretched grimace.

"Ugh, it's like castor oil, only worse."

"Line up your glass next to mine, then. This stuff is too precious to waste."

Whoever started this horrid cocktail habit? I wondered. What's the use of strong drink anyway? Nothing can compare with a nice tinkling glass of fresh lemonade, sugared to taste.

"Where's that career-girl sophistication?" Fay demanded. "Did it poop out as quickly as it came?"

"Maybelle's the wholesome Girl Guide type," Jack said, leaning over and clapping my knee fondly. "It's a dying species, I'm sorry to say . . . That's right, isn't it, Alvin?"

"Yes. I like to see women *stay* women."

If the bourbon hadn't been so strong, perhaps the men would have kept talking in this friendly fashion. But after downing his third drink, Jack began to flatter me. "You did well, honey, on that radio program today. Sounded like a real professional . . . Keep on this way and you'll give Alvin a run for his money!"

"Do you *really* think so?"

"Of course. Ho-ho-ho. Next time he has a week of enforced sickness, Continentwide can call you as a substitute."

"Stop," Fay warned. "No one appreciates your capers."

He paid no attention. "Ho-ho. Just remember, Maybelle, there's no antidote to profanity like a woman's chirruping voice, the more maternal the better. Also, in a pinch you can corral your Community Choral Group and Horace Baxter free of charge."

"I'm splitting my sides," Alvin said, after taking a long swallow from his glass. "What a joker."

"Also, honey, if your efforts should advance Arlington's chances for the Arcturus Award, so much the better."

"But you know, Jack," I said, blushing, "this morning I was all atremble."

"Don't swallow such miserable bait," Fay cried. Then, swinging toward her husband, "If anyone's atremble, John Calhoun Hick the Third, it should be you! Since you must make an issue of this matter, suppose you answer a couple of questions. How did you *dare* to send Miss Barberry to Station ZDQ without first discussing this matter with me? If an announcement about our baby was to be made, wasn't Alvin the person to make it? Have you forgotten that he is my close friend and neighbor?"

"*Perk Predicts* was off the air this week," Jack said innocently. "You know this yourself."

"Off the air because of your influence. That's so, isn't it?"

After looking toward Alvin, he said firmly, "Yes."

"I knew it. I knew it. You should be *ashamed* to resort to such behind-the-scene tactics."

"Stop bedeviling him," Alvin shouted, taking this far too seriously. "Jack's spoken like a man and I respect him for it. Besides, you happen to be his wife, don't you?"

Fay faced him furiously. "I happen to be somebody besides a wife, in case you've forgotten. I'm a chemist investing time, skill and money in a business which Amyrillis wants to smash to smithereens. You and your radio program are essential to our success, as Jack knows damn well."

"Now, now," I cautioned as she paused for breath. "Let the men handle this themselves."

"Yes, please do," Alvin said, frowning severely. "When we need your help here, we'll ask for it." There he was again, defending the male species against the female. Why had I been so blind to this quirk?

"Have it your way," Fay said, gripping her waist and rocking back and forth.

Jack had turned toward Alvin with new respect. "I see no

need to mention the names of influential friends who are offended by your program. By now you must know that we'll use every possible resource to control you and the topics you mention. At the moment you are off the air for a week. Next time, my friend, you'll find yourself dismissed permanently."

"Especially if I should make the mistake of mentioning Giddy Moment again. Eh?"

Jack looked grim as an iron statue. "Yes. Exactly."

Instead of looking disheartened, Alvin chuckled. "So now we have threats, don't we?"

"Call it whatever you please. It happens that we board members at Amyrillis have a sizable stake here. Obviously we must protect it."

"Well, as I said before, you've spoken like a man," Alvin said smilingly. "And everything's fair in love and business."

"Everything isn't fair," Fay exploded, tossing her curly black hair. "Jack, if you squeeze Giddy Moment from the market, you'll ruin us."

He gave her a look with triumph in it . . . but sorrow and pity were melded too.

Oh dear, I told myself. We never, never should have started Amelia-Dent Enterprises. So far, it's brought nothing but heartaches.

"Fay, you may wish to consider another angle." Jack's tone was unusually gentle. "Some wet-behind-the-ears buyer may decide to buy Giddy Moment and put it on sale in his store. But he'll never be able to advertise it. I've made sure of this through a conference with Horace Baxter. Don't forget that he's a power at Transworld Press still. One flick of the finger will silence newspapers across forty-eight states."

"Oh no, Jack, no . . . no . . . You couldn't. You wouldn't do this, would you? After the effort, the months of sacrifice we've spent . . . No . . . no . . . no." Then she was burying her face in her hands and weeping. "Dear Lord, here I have a new scientific discovery which can sweep the world, one that has tried, pained and challenged me almost out of my mind. Oh no . . . no . . . no . . . no . . ." She's playing this scene masterfully, I thought.

As she continued to sob and rock back and forth, Jack cleared his throat again and again. Then, as she clutched her waistline, he leaped toward her bellowing, "Oh, God forgive us! How could we be so selfish and unthinking? Fay! Fay, darling! Control yourself and think of our baby. We're such idiots."

"And now you insult me," she cried, her tiny white face screwed up like a child's. "First you give a body blow. Then you . . . then you . . . Oh, I can't stand it. I can't! I can't!"

Now Alvin made what I believe was a most stupid, unfeeling gesture. Having tried futilely to get Fay's and Jack's attention, he began to whistle "Rock-a-bye, baby."

"Don't," I warned, ready to slap him. "How can you be so heartless? A little storm passes in time."

"What the hell . . . we've got to stop this hassle," he muttered as the Hicks quieted down in a flash. "I'm no midwife . . . and at this rate we're going to need one any minute."

"Yes, we've been selfish and foolish tonight," Fay told Jack when she was able to speak.

"I've talked too much, dear, and I know it. Forgive me for being a jackass."

"I'm glad you did talk." Stretching her arms about his neck, she drew him close. As she went on with effort, she seemed to portray womankind battling a miserable ache. "This way . . . dear . . . we know exactly . . . where we stand . . . don't we?" Then she fell into a faint.

Come off it, Fay, I thought to myself. Must you wind up with this grand super-duper climax? Then, as she lay pale and limp, I thought, But she's not play-acting after all. How could I have imagined that she was? Dopey me!

Next I remember rushing to call the doctor while Jack groaned, "Fay, Fay, why did we let this happen? Oh, God!"

Well, dear journal, it is almost midnight by now, but I must continue here, regardless. Truly this has been a day with upsets beyond number. But, as always, it has brought a scattering of blessings too.

How fortunate that Fay's collapse tonight has proved to be a warning, as the doctor says, rather than the start of a tragic miscarriage. If she were going to lose her baby, I suppose that she would have done so before its sixth month. Nevertheless, now she must stay in bed until the end of January. As I see it, this is a development which all of us should try to welcome.

In addition to being sales manageress of Amelia-Dent Enterprises, I am forced to assume control of every phase of it. Yes, this is the situation as of this minute. With no interference, we shall continue the manufacture of Giddy Moment.

Of course I plan to make shipment against our Star-Drake order with *reduced-potency* stock. Thus what we deliver will be exactly like the sample demonstrated to Mr. Lathrop today.

Frequently in the past Fay has said that those who hinder sound action should be kept ignorant. It is a comfort to remember this philosophy. Because my normal impulse would be to take her and Alvin into my confidence immediately. Yet perhaps the time comes in everyone's life when he must pick up his burden, struggling with it alone. What does this matter, though, now that Fay and her baby are safe?

As we made our way back from the Hicks' tonight, Alvin was unusually silent. But he came alive with a bang once he discovered a fresh pile-up of crates on his porch and sidewalk. "Hell in a basket," he howled, heedless of neighbors, "now this nonsense starts again."

But after he reached Grace Thorpe on the phone, she calmed him promptly. In addition to sending a truck here tomorrow, she plans to send several to the Hicks'. How kind she is to begin the transfer of Giddy Moment stock without charging special rates for Saturday work. "That's the least I can do," she said, "now Steve's reinstated me as his assistant."

Now at last I come to the most unexpected news of all. Nina and Larry plan to be married the day after Christmas. Yes, they made their announcement while they were enjoying their usual late-evening snack.

Certainly they seem too young to be taking this step. But since Larry's parents have given their approval already, what was I to do?

At first, I'll admit, I tried to persuade our lovebirds to wait until June. But Nina declared, "No, Mother. It wouldn't make sense. When are you going to let me live my own life? Must I fight continually for freedom and independence?"

In family crises such as this, Joe dear, I miss you more than I can describe. Nina and you were so tremendously close always, so very much alike. Perhaps you could have made her understand that her last year at high school should be full of girlish fun — cheer-leading, basketball games, gymnasium tumbling and dances. At her age, didn't I amuse myself this way, never regretting it?

Yet when I brought up these points tonight, she teased, "Please forget that Kate Greenaway era. Don't you realize that Larry and I know our own needs? Just look at us." Then she threw herself into his arms so violently that I shuddered.

For every reason I could not say no to this marriage. So starting tomorrow, we shall begin to look into trousseaus, guest lists, bridesmaid selection and December floral arrangements.

Again and again in the past, I have built air castles about dear Nina's wedding. Even when she was a toddler, I loved to imagine her as a bride in glistening white, stepping toward the altar and happiness ahead. But tonight I realized that these reveries never once took into account emotional drives and such. Ah, but it isn't easy for me to admit this.

Also, I find it hard to confess that I have purely selfish reasons for wishing to postpone this wedding. Truly it seems like the very last straw, added to my other responsibilities. Yet as Nina's mother, I know that she rightly must come first.

Fortunately I keep remembering that all of us are meant to live at full capacity. Also I have learned that happiness comes as an unexpected extra dividend to courageous action.

Who would have guessed that each day is more challenging than the one before . . . or that Alvin and I would find joy together? Oh, it is hard to believe that our futures are one and the same! Good night, my dearest boy. I love you. I love you. I love you!

Part Four

Chapter 18

EXCERPTS from the *Perk Predicts* program, Station ZDQ, New York, New York, Thursday, January 12, 1961.

"*Good morning, friends and listeners across America. Here is Alvin Perkin wishing you and your family the best of the best.*

"*Today Giddy Moment, the lipstick with the irresistibly-kissable-you guarantee, goes on sale for the first time in history. At the moment distribution is being confined to the Arlington, Long Island, unit of Star-Drake and Company. In the future, as supply increases, a far wider market is anticipated. Meantime, you folks across forty-eight states who have swamped us with inquiries, please continue to be patient.*

"*After Star-Drake opens its chromium-plated doors this morning, there will be a stampede of customers. Also, you may be sure that every top executive in the cosmetic and toiletries industry will be personally present in Arlington, observing developments there.*

"*Less than three minutes ago, the esteemed chairman of a leading company was seen rolling eastward across the Triborough Bridge. Whether he intends to negotiate for manufacturing rights to Giddy Moment remains a red-circled question. But he is known to be increasingly impressed by this lipstick as a mid-twentieth-century scientific phenomenon.*

"*The initials of the gentleman in question are B as in Buster, H as in happy. I regret that I am not at liberty to reveal his name as yet. However, Perk Predicts that Mr. H. will buy up*

Giddy Moment promptly, offering it side by side with beauty aids bearing his famous label. If this decision should be made, it will countermand one by his next officer in line, bringing about his immediate resignation.

"But now, my friends, let us consider Giddy Moment from a far more significant aspect. Once this marvel item is put into the hands (or perhaps I should say onto the lips) of the general public, a new force will be unleashed. Then indeed we must ask ourselves as individuals and as American citizens, 'Are we ready to cope with this tremendous power? Can we use it as we should, in building a better world? Will we achieve greater communion between the sexes and, in turn, a more compassionate humanity?' Finally, ladies and gentlemen, what will this beauty aid, eons ahead of its time, mean to you and yours?

"Now here are two last-minute news flashes. Mrs. John Calhoun Hick the Third (she is the internationally famous chemist known as Dr. Fay B. Amelia) has just given birth to a son at Rollingreen Hospital. Though the baby was a month premature, he and his mother are said to be doing well.

"Secondly, as we prophesied again and again, Arlington, Long Island, will receive the much-coveted Arcturus Award tomorrow. Presentation to Mayor Horace Baxter will be made at the Town Hall. Afterwards guests of honor, including New York State's distinguished governor and both senators, will convene at Star-Drake's Civic Assembly Rooms for a noontime banquet.

"If and when there are new developments to report, I promise that you will hear them first as always on this program."

Dent Journal . . .

Thursday, January 12, 1961

TRULY, dear journal, we are in the midst of success at last. Although today has been exciting, tomorrow should set us on a more even keel. Or so I hope.

Without boasting, I must say that my talents have grown amazingly in past weeks. Who would have guessed, after Fay's collapse, that I could learn to supervise others, handle the mechanics of Giddy Moment sales, factory operation, work hand in glove with Star-Drake's buying staff and the Thorpe Warehouse, with all details interlocked and running smoothly?

Fortunately Anna Baxter has proved to be my right hand as well as a skilled demonstrator. As a consequence, our supply of diluted stock is almost depleted. Thus new shipments tomorrow must carry full-strength potency.

This is no problem compared with the one of supply itself in relation to demand. Surely before going to sleep tonight, I must ponder how we can step up production both in our factory and packaging units.

Before discussing business more deeply, I must catch up on Dent family news. Yet giving this priority requires real effort as always.

First, Nina and Larry returned from their Bermuda honeymoon a week ago. By now they are resettled in their high school and college routines, with Larry planning to spend week ends here. How good it will seem to hear a man's voice resounding from room to room again.

Of course it is nice to see our young people brown as coconuts and so much in love. Also, I am glad that they are pleased with their apartment over the garage. "Mother, you shouldn't have gone to such trouble," Nina cried, observing fresh paint, wallpaper, bedspreads and curtains there. "But thanks loads, anyway."

Better still, Nina has expressed warm satisfaction with her wedding. I am sure, though, that she is as relieved as I am to have it behind us. During one period, it seemed that we would never succeed in getting our bride outfitted and ready. Oh those trials — selecting flannel pajamas, athletic-type underwear, ruby-red towels and shoes in that difficult quadruple-A size!

Though she was calm throughout our preparations, many of her ideas conflicted with mine. Especially in her insistence upon the "practical" rather than the "pretty."

I have been particularly gratified by our neighbors' reactions to the wedding. "It was the most beautiful church ceremony in years," they've said. "I've never seen a more self-contained bride or one whose mother looked more like her sister."

I would not bring up this sister angle now, if it hadn't been stressed so often. Yet I will admit this — I have never worn a more flattering gown than that little oyster-white lace with its sheathlike skirt, tight sleeves and provocative bosom.

As I remember Larry standing pale as death in his morning coat, I can't help smiling. At the close of the ceremony, when he kissed Nina, he seemed to forget himself completely. I believe that he might be lost in that embrace still if his best man hadn't muttered, "You're in church, kids." My, but we older folks tittered in spite of ourselves.

I regret that the reception at the Golf Club was spoiled by many unmannerly young guests. Though I took pains to ignore their noisy exhilaration, Horace Baxter could not. "If these were my sons and daughters, Maybelle," he clacked, "I'd march them straight home."

As a rule I cannot agree with our mayor's little speeches. But this time, indeed I did.

Horace also wasn't pleased when his daughter appeared with Paul Lathrop in tow. Yet I was happy to welcome this fine young man, invited or not. Long ago I accepted the fact that Anna is an unconventional one, fighting everything which is Baxterish. Besides, since she and Paul have been inseparable, why shouldn't she bring him if she wished?

Every mother, I suppose, twinges as her child starts off on her honeymoon. Certainly it was this way with me when Nina appeared in her nubbly gray suit and Persian coat under a bombardment of rice. I felt enormously sad that she and I had never been more congenial. It seemed that this early marriage indicated that I had fallen short somehow. Though goodness knows I have tried, in this past year especially, to please her intellectually and spiritually.

If Fay had been a mother before now, she might have understood my obligations. Instead, confined to bed week after week, she has resented my hours spent away from Giddy Moment and herself. Yet the fact that she has kept herself engaged in perfecting a new infant pharmaceutical formula has saved the day. Otherwise we might have lost patience with each other.

Though these past two months have been hectic, I have never felt happier or more full of pep. As Alvin said again last night, "Gad, girl, where do you get your bounce?"

Much as I appreciate a compliment now and again, I wish that my darling's disposition were better. Several weeks ago he developed an incessant twitch at the corner of his mouth. Also, instead of enjoying my chitchat, he has begun to scold, "For Pete's sake, woman, get to the point, will you?" or "Try to answer in one word, Maybelle, yes or no."

Often I am ready to weep over his sharpness. Then, of course, he gets angry. "Now don't start tears. You know I loathe them."

Does he really love me? I wonder. Or is he playing a game still, as Fay insists?

Underneath his flashes of temper, I sense genuine fear. Surely Alvin has been caught like a fox in a trap. In order to increase his Trendex rating and to land a better job in turn, he has had to steel himself to breaking a Continentwide edict.

Yes, in a desperate gamble, he knew he must give an opening blast to our Giddy Moment sales promotion this morning.

Evidently he expected resulting listener interest to compensate for the dangers involved. However, as we have seen, the balance swung the other way, bringing program cancellation.

Though Alvin has known for several weeks that Star-Drake would begin today with reduced-potency lipsticks, he has accepted this situation stoically. I suppose he figured that supply would be diminished promptly, as it has been. Also, he may have anticipated other developments which I cannot foresee.

Could it be that he expects Continentwide to reverse its position within the next twenty-four hours? What a paradox, if he should be rehired through the very outside influence which ousted him. Imagine his joy if he should be urged to give the biggest and best blast to Giddy Moment yet!

All this may be idle dreaming. Yet it would be like Alvin to count on such contingencies coming in sequence. Further, he has rare intuition when it comes to people, complex business situations and his own precious career.

Though as I say, I was able to take Alvin into my confidence on Giddy Moment a while ago, I did not dare to do the same with Fay. She had made her position as a chemist so clear that I knew she would fight my decision. I confess that it was wrong to deceive my friend and partner in this way. But what else could I do, with her health what it has been?

In any case, now that Fay has delivered the baby, she seems to have dismissed Giddy Moment from her mind. At the moment she is such a strange mixture of new qualities — beaming with motherhood, hepped up by her new infant-pharmaceutical formula, knitting a tiny blue sweater in spare moments and showing the first signs of becoming a housewife. At one point tonight didn't she ask what soap flakes are preferable for safe washing of woolens? Ah, but it's a pleasure to see this transformation!

In contrast, what has happened to me? Increasingly, Nina and I tend to eat delicatessen food served helter-skelter. Day after day I leave my bed unmade, my nightclothes hanging over a chair. I time my actions by the clock, carry a notebook and pencil always, snap fingers as I speak, dart here, run there, keeping my mind on a hundred details at once. Yes, Fay and I seem to be changing personalities and places, if we haven't done so already.

I wouldn't know whether this situation is good or bad. But I am aware that Jack senses at last what is happening to his wife . . . or rather, what *seems* to be happening. Obviously, too, he welcomes it.

Incidentally, since November, he has continued to be a prince and a gentleman. Day and night he has allowed machinery to keep thrashing in his cellar, though it jolts his nerves and robs him of sleep. Of course he could have put an immediate stop to this by reporting a building-code infraction to the mayor. Also, he might have wrecked our Giddy Moment promotion by using influence on Stanley Drake during golf sessions.

I realize that Jack would have been within his rights in taking these steps. Yet for Fay's sake he has kept silent, accepting home difficulties and Bernard Huggin's bedevilment. "Nobody needs to tell me that I'm a poor benighted buzzard," he says, "but so far I seem to have survived."

If he is still engaged in fighting Alvin secretly, I've seen no signs of it. In any case, they seem to have learned to respect each other as men committed to business success and a fine taste in bourbon.

Beyond everything else tonight, I realize that Fay and I should be everlastingly grateful to Jack. Without his sacrifice and patience, we never could have launched Giddy Moment successfully. But oh, we have exacted a heavy price from him in making the demands we did! Why must the bitter always be mixed with the sweet?

It is said that the bigger men are, the harder they fall. Surely this has been so with the two whom I love and respect beyond all others.

How hard it is to stand by helplessly in the midst of the crash.

Chapter 19

Dent Journal . . .

Thursday, January 12, 1961 (continued)

MY exhilaration in the success of Giddy Moment may be dampened tonight by concern for Alvin and Jack. Yet it is a fact that both men are healthy and unusually able in their respective fields. Neither of them ever makes a move without weighing its inevitable effect on the future. So they may be able to stand up under business reversals and loss of face.

In seeking comfort now, for I confess that I am seeking it, there are other compensations which cannot be ignored. Top among these is the honor lying ahead for Arlington tomorrow.

Imagine the town where I was born and where I have lived always being selected for the Arcturus Award. What a celebration we shall have here, with parades, banquets, speeches, fire sirens blowing and mercy knows what-all. Instead of continuing to push the sale of Giddy Moment at Star-Drake within a few hours, how I would love to share in this fanfare.

Looking back at today's events, I am able to see them with surprising objectivity. In some ways it is as though I were reviewing a series of colored photographs, each of them dominated by a person named Maybelle. Oh, it is hard to believe that this energetic woman in her sleek, fashion-right clothes is good old me.

This morning, in spite of the need to be at Drake's fifteen minutes before store opening, I was able to squeeze in a visit with Jack. Once he phoned his happy news from the hospital, I dressed, breakfasted and kissed Nina good-by in a rush. After making the trip in our new white Cadillac, which is a dead ringer of the Hicks', I danced into the coffee shop.

Jack was there as he had promised he would be, looking gray and old. After setting down his cup, he lurched to his feet, a mountain of a man in his brown suit, contrasting with the orderlies and nurses close by.

"Congratulations, Daddy!" I cried.

"Fay deserves the huzzas." A smile cracked through his tight-set jaw. "You should see that boy of ours. What a pair of lungs."

"I can't wait to see him and Fay tonight."

"Lord, I hope she'll look more fit than she does now. You'd think science would develop a better way to bear children. When I remember what she's been through these past hours . . ."

"Oh, she'll be herself in no time."

"The doctor has said so too." But as Jack mopped his forehead, he didn't seem to be convinced. "While Fay was in the delivery room, I thought I'd go crazy. Every selfishness and stupidity in my life kept parading back and forth. When I recall that clumsy Amyrillis conference months ago — when I count our endless arguments since — Believe me, it's a heavy load on my conscience."

"You have no reason to criticize yourself," I soothed.

"Hell, I wish I could see it that way . . . Do you know why this baby came three weeks early? Damn it, I've got to get this off my chest. Last night Fay and I got into another of those rows on Giddy Moment. I told her that if she didn't stop that cussed machinery in the cellar, I'd report it to Horace Baxter. Then, of course, she burst into tears, jumped out of bed and . . . and . . ."

"Stop, Jack. You're dead tired and you know it."

"So what? I should have been able to stand up under the pressures at home and in my office. Maybe I could have been more patient with Fay if Bernard hadn't gotten under my skin. But there's no justification for excuses here."

"I know it's been agony to watch a brilliant man slip mentally," I said, bending toward him. "Your chairman's been enough to drive anyone daffy."

"Don't I know it? The worst has been his increasing conviction that Amyrillis should have bought up Giddy Moment months ago. Also, he's failed to understand why I didn't clamp down on Fay, dismantling her laboratory."

"Ho, what a dreamer!"

"Dreamer is right." Pausing, he took a long swallow of coffee. "Also, when he heard last week that she has completed a radically *new* chemical formula again, he hit the ceiling. 'Even if Giddy Moment weren't an issue here,' he said, 'we can't allow *another* of Dr. Amelia's discoveries to get away from us. If it has the sales potential of all her previous products, think of the gold mine we'd be missing.'"

Aha, I thought, almost squealing with delight. If Bernard or Jack guessed that Fay's brain wave is an ointment for infant skin, they'd dismiss it in a flash. Thank goodness I've learned to keep my mouth shut.

"Don't be surprised," Jack continued, "to see Bernard act impulsively within the next few hours. As I say, he's sick with dread over this situation." Then, with mockery in his voice, "Still, I'm betting that once Giddy Moment is offered to the public today, he may wake up at last."

Looking across at him, I thought, So he still believes that our promotion will be a flop. Well, once Alvin gives his *Perk*

Predicts plug any minute, President Hick will sing a different tune.

Now the radio overhead boomed with a familiar rat-tat-tat. "Good morning, friends and listeners across America . . . Today Giddy Moment, the lipstick with the irresistibly-kissable-you guarantee, goes on sale for the first time in history."

My, but I felt a sense of tremendous satisfaction.

"Less than three minutes ago, the esteemed chairman of a leading company was seen rolling eastward . . . The initials of the gentleman in question are B as in Buster, H as in happy . . ."

"Where did that loud-mouthed comedian get this drivel?" Jack roared, purple with displeasure. "He could be sued for everything, including his undershorts." Then, looking heavenward, "Oh God, Bernard would come rushing out to Arlington now, wouldn't he?"

Oh, but I longed to stay where I was, listening to Alvin and watching Jack. But I knew I must leave for Star-Drake's immediately. "Sorry, Jack," I said, sliding off my stool. "I'm a business woman these days, you know, and first things must come first. Don't forget I'll meet you at your house after dinner tonight. Then we'll plan to have our visit here with Fay."

"All right," he said, rising automatically, with his head thrust out like a bull's.

As I hurried out through the doorway, Alvin's staccato followed. "*Perk Predicts* that Mr. H. will buy up Giddy Moment promptly. . . . If this decision should be made, it will countermand one by his next officer in line, bringing about his immediate resignation."

Oh no, I thought. Dear Lord, do you really plan to let this happen? Of course it would be nice to sell our rights to Giddy Moment at a handsome profit. But Jack's spent thirty hard years working up to the presidency of his company. Aside from his pride in accomplishment, he has a wife and baby son to support. So please, please take pity on him.

It was not until I reached the car that I began to think about Alvin and his courage this morning. Dear oh dear, in fulfilling his agreement with Fay and me, he had cooked his goose with Continentwide. It seemed like a heavy price to pay. But unlike Jack, he was a reckless gambler at heart and in a tricky type of business too. I can't feel sorry, I told myself. Alvin thrives on shenanigans — he always will.

The next scene I remember was my arrival in Star-Drake's cosmetic department. The air there smelled springlike with its garden-sweet hyacinth fragrance. For just a moment it stirred up nostalgia for Alvin, but there was no time for this now.

From the corner of my eye I saw Madge Reilly flicking a dustcloth over her Amyrillis jars and bottles. Miss Early-Bird-Ready-for-Business, I thought. She's getting ready to welcome Mr. B as in Buster, H as in happy, once he gets here. And if our lipstick does as well as I expect, she'll push him into purchasing rights to it.

After turning a corner, I found Anna Baxter giving the last touches to a superb Giddy Moment display. How fetching she seemed behind the pyramiding tiny boxes, each more virginal than the next. "Good morning, dear," I said, waving both arms. "Everything looks lovely."

"Thank you, Mrs. Dent." Then, to my surprise, she began to cry. "I have the nicest news. You'll never, never guess." She stretched out her left hand with its blazing, square-cut diamond.

"Me oh my, what's this?"

"Paul gave it to me on our way to work. But we can't tell anyone yet. Did you ever see anything more beautiful?"

Then, of course, I was hugging her and weeping too. "I feel as though you're my own daughter," I gulped. "I've known you and your family for so many years, and Paul is such a lamb."

As we were wiping our eyes, the buyer appeared with Mrs. Stevens beside him. Anna might be upset today, but her fiancé's mind was firmly on business. "That was a fine plug on *Perk Predicts*," he said, after checking our layout expertly. "I bet we'll have a mob scene which will build up to a tornado tomorrow."

"We'd better have it," Mrs. Stevens said darkly. "We've never had higher sales volume to make."

This comment, thank goodness, shook Anna back into shape. "I know what this promotion means to Paul," she said, flicking open her salesbook. "We mustn't let him down."

Before I could answer, the store bell rang. Next we heard a horde of women rolling toward us like surf. "Giddy Moment. I want Giddy Moment."

What a hectic, wearing day it was! Store policemen came with stanchions. Customers were arranged in lines as in the old days of cut-price cigarettes. Consequently everything was orderly, with women being hustled off after making their purchases in turn.

Meantime I was able to identify in the background men who must have been leaders in the cosmetic industry. I would not know why they seemed to carry a stamp all their own, these "ones" dedicated to making American womanhood more beautiful. Yet it seemed easy to identify them, with their high, intelligent brows, trim barbering, custom-made shirts and boutonnieres.

In contrast, Bernard Huggin seemed dried up and funereal in his black Chesterfield and derby. In spite of his age and dignity, he kept prancing like a fire horse. There was no mistaking the pronounced V between the brows, the glaze of eyes and flaring nostrils. He stood out especially vividly there, with his arm interlocked with Madge's as he listened and nodded agreement. Ah, he'll begin dickering for rights to

Giddy Moment soon, I told myself. Alvin's prediction was one hundred per cent right.

But any reminder of Alvin distressed me. Surely he might have been interested enough to pay us a visit before now. Also, after parting company with Continentwide, didn't he need to gather comfort from my presence? Searching for him futilely hour after hour, I was ready to shake him.

At last, an hour before store closing, I saw him, half hidden in the crowd. There he was, as debonair as usual, with that pixie grin on his face. Yet there was the oddest expression in his eyes: amused, sad, triumphant, beaten, relieved, resolute . . . Was I imagining this? Or were emotions contrary to each other fighting through his mind and heart? Oh dear, why did he continue to be such a puzzle? He's impossible, I thought. But just the same, I love him.

When I looked up a minute later, he was gone. Yes, he had disappeared completely. And after glancing into the mirror I knew why — my hair, so beautifully coiffured this morning, looked like a haystack; my face was red, with a large dirty smear across one cheek. No wonder he'd rushed off from such a mess.

Then I noticed Paul Lathrop shoving his way through the crowd toward Anna Baxter. They both looked tired and rumpled too, but they didn't seem to care. Of course I was happy for their love, their youth and the radiance they brought to each other. They'll be able to live through anything and everything together, I thought.

Examining myself again, I had to groan. Indeed my face showed its thirty-six years, the strain of today, of the past year and the long era of Papa's and Joe's dominance. Ah, I'd hoped to change for the better by dabbling in business. Instead I remained Maybelle Dent, plain Jane housewife and widow with a mist of tears in her eyes.

"Pay attention, miss," a customer demanded, thrusting two lipsticks forward. "You're here to serve me, aren't you?"

Yes, I thought dismally, hurrying into action, I'm here to serve you and everybody else everywhere. But then, somehow I felt buoyed up. You could be spending your time in worse ways, some inner voice seemed to say as I whizzed through this transaction, the next and the next.

Five-thirty came at last, with all of us saleswomen lame and exhausted. Yet there was no chance for Anna or me to admit weariness to each other. After totaling the dollar volume brought in by Giddy Moment, we grinned with satisfaction. Ah, but we were an unusually capable team!

Soon Madge Reilly let us know that we had outsold Amyrillis, killing its lipstick demand completely. Brooding over her reduced sales total, she said vindictively, "We'll correct this situation sooner than you guess. No upstart's going to cut into the finest beauty line in America."

Stretching out both hands, I gripped hers warmly. "I hope that Mr. B as in Buster, H as in happy comes through now as he should."

A second later, I bit my tongue. In the flush of success I'd forgotten what an Amyrillis–Amelia-Dent merger would mean to Jack. Oh dear . . .

Once I was outside heading toward the Cadillac, my thoughts returned to Alvin. Could he be waiting here somewhere? Might he pop up unexpectedly with a bloodcurdling shout: "Hi, honey, surprise! Surprise!" But of course these were idle fancies.

When I drew into my driveway, there was no sign of a light next door. "Damn!" I cried, jumping out of the car and kicking it. Why, oh why can't I stop thinking . . . hoping . . . praying . . . ?

What was the good of luxuries beyond number, of a career, of achievement with Giddy Moment? Here I was at an all-time peak in life, yet sick at heart.

Oh, Alvin, Alvin. At last I understand the reason for your

loving ways. Yes, I realize that they built courage and persistence as nothing else could. But dear, how could you take
advantage of me? Was this fair or right? Then, as needles of
light continued to pierce my mind, I thought, Maybe you lost
your job at Continentwide today, but your radio career is far
from finished. Aren't you still counting on establishing yourself at Liberty, with me as a foil?

At last I heard Pluto yelping at the front door and Nina
calling, "Hi, Mother. Dinner's ready. I'm starved, aren't you?"

Tonight, as we ate, I was aware of how close she and I have
become in past weeks. In spite of being mother and daughter,
we were able to accept each other as friends. Several times we
caught ourselves using the very same expressions, such as "Grin
and bear it" and "Since we have only one life, let's make the
most of it." Maybe, as Nina said, such statements are pure
corn. Still, pronounced by two voices melding as one, they
seemed particularly pleasing to us both.

As we finished dessert, she reached over and gave me the
warmest hug. Though Pluto was barking from the pantry, we
ignored him as she said, "You know, Mother, tonight I've
seen sides of you I never guessed were there."

"Exactly what your father said after reading Granny Dent's
journal," I cried without thinking.

"That was his favorite pitch wasn't it — a family record with
daily entries and such?"

"He hoped I'd follow in his mother's footsteps."

"I know. In some ways, I don't believe it was a kindness."

Looking at my daughter with her serious brown eyes and
smoothly combed hair, it was hard to believe that she was Mrs.
Lawrence Drake. How she had loved to curl into Joe's lap,
sniffing his pipe tobacco and urging him to tell "an interesting
story, Daddy, one that makes us sit up and *think*."

Why had she insisted on growing up too fast, seeking the
challenging always instead of the gay or the amusing? Why,

even in kindergarten days, had she insisted on leading me rather than letting me guide her?

"If I'm ever going to read your journal, it may as well be tomorrow," she was saying now. "While I'm waiting for Larry, I may as well keep busy."

Then, indeed, I knew I was in for it. Especially when she added, "Don't try to talk me out of this. I itch to know you better. Really I do."

It isn't easy to recall this conversation or to face the inevitable consequences of it. If I were rewriting entries covering the past year, I would give far less space to Giddy Moment, Fay and Alvin. Oh dear, why didn't I keep at least one or two incidents to myself? But as Fay says, "There's no sense in crying over spilt milk, fresh or sour."

It was kind of Nina to insist on washing the dishes so that I could hurry to the Hicks' and then on to the hospital. Again, this gesture indicated our growing congeniality. Of course, though, she may be preparing unconsciously for her own home and family some day.

Tonight, once I arrived at Jack's, he cried, "Come in. Come in." Holding himself like a soldier, he said in anything but a warlike tone, "Gad, I thought you'd never get here. It's been lonely as hell."

Instead of following him into the living room, I heard myself say, "As soon as I've checked the laboratory and factory, I'll be along."

"Mrs. Hustle-bustle," he grumped as I hastened toward the cellar.

"Fay's influence," I couldn't help quipping back.

Making my way into the laboratory, I paused to sniff a bubbling test tube. What this gesture indicated I would not know, but it seemed to come naturally. Then, as Dr. Belle and Dr. Surr looked up from their work, I caroled, "Good evening. How are tricks?"

Soon we were walking into the factory, where a crowd of workers swarmed busily. Ah, it was good to see everything functioning smoothly under Jim Swanson's supervision. No wonder I glowed with pride and satisfaction. In spite of Fay's incapacity and the rush of business today, operation was just as it should be.

Now, as Grace Thorpe and Tony approached, we discussed the Giddy Moment dwindling stock situation. "As of tomorrow," they said, "we are forced to ship lipsticks carrying label A. But customers should be even more pleased, shouldn't they, with full-strength potency?"

What was I to say? Finally I answered, "Beginning now, friends, our problem isn't shipping. It's manufacturing enough supply to meet demand."

"More and more Mrs. Dent reminds me of Dr. Amelia," Grace said respectfully. "Doesn't she, everyone?"

After nodding, the superintendent scowled toward his machinery. "We've got to find ourselves additional space pronto. Mrs. Thorpe recommends leasing a building out the Boulevard a ways."

"Very good, Jim. Begin negotiations there immediately."

When this matter had been settled nicely, I reminded our staff to "keep punching and some day we'll be wearing diamonds." Then, when we had shaken hands all around, I waved a last good-by. "Guard our livelihood well, girls and boys."

"Well, Madame Executive," Jack asked as I came into the living room, "is everything shipshape?"

"Certainly. One hundred per cent."

"Would you like a highball," he asked, fighting back amusement. Then, as I shook my head, "Well, I'm going to have one — double strength."

Once he had taken a long gulp from his glass, he began to unburden himself — about how he had worked his way through college by stoking furnaces; the thrill of starting as an office worker at Amyrillis; the desperation following the crack-up of his first marriage. "One morning, I found I was head over heels in love with Fay. Damn, but I fought it, knowing how strong-minded each of us is. Still, I couldn't resist her basic sweetness, courage and charm . . . *Now*, God knows, I couldn't live without her."

"We all know it, Jack."

"Fay's gotten her way always." His voice had become hoarse. "And by golly, she's going to get it again. Maybe you know already that Bernard's due at the hospital within an hour."

"What?"

"I tried to persuade him to wait a few days before buying rights to Giddy Moment. But after visiting Star-Drake and observing developments there, he won't listen. As a matter of fact, I heard him promise Madge Reilly . . ."

"Ah, I knew it. I knew it."

"Consequently Bernard plans to offer a contract to you and Fay tonight — a package deal tying up her brand-new formula too."

"Are you serious?"

"Yes. You're about to make yourself a mint of money. So sing. Shout. Revel in your success." He raised both arms in a gesture reminiscent of a world championship boxing bout. There was sportsmanship and respect in his tone, but I sensed that he was teasing somehow too. Could some unexpected reversal still lie ahead for Fay and me?

"Would our signing make you resign from Amyrillis?" Ah, but this was the important question, dwarfing all others.

"Of course."

"Then we won't sign. We can't."

"Fay will write her name so fast it will make you dizzy."

"Regardless, I won't. You Hicks and your future mean more to me than a few dollars."

"Eh?"

"Money is only money. But friends . . ."

"Ho. Should sentiment interfere with business?"

"Haven't you let it interfere again and again for the past six months?"

"Well . . . in a way . . . yes. But I repeat, Maybelle, nothing will keep Fay from closing that deal tonight. When my darling wins, she wins with a vengeance. I know . . . because I'm built the exact same way."

True enough, I had to admit.

"You're hoping that motherhood has changed her, but I promise you that it hasn't and it won't. What were Fay's first words when she returned to consciousness today? Something about making sure she'd brought notes on her newest formula and a sample of the stuff too along to the hospital. She wouldn't rest until she actually *saw* them there on the bedside table . . . Further," he added, while I continued to blink, "I have learned to expect steel and tenacity in my loving wife. What's more, in my future plans I'm counting on it. So don't try to talk her out of this decision."

"But, Jack . . ."

"Sorry. That's it!" Then, after glancing at his watch, "Up and off to the epitome of your business career." Wasn't there an airy, teasing quality in his tone again? But why?

Once we were in his car rolling along the Boulevard, he whistled "Row, row, row your boat" repeatedly. Something is cooking here, I thought, as his exuberance increased. Otherwise he'd be doing a rendition of "Grieg's Funeral March," wouldn't he?

Soon we were in the hospital absorbing its good ether and Lysol smell. Mm-m-mm, how I would have loved to be a nurse or a Gray Lady, if my menfolk had permitted it. "You outdid yourself, Jack," I said, while we stood at the nursery window, squinting toward little Johnny. "Truly, he's perfect."

"Thanks," he said, flushing.

After walking a few yards more, we came to an open door banked with flowers. Next I was flying toward Fay with arms outstretched.

How dainty she looked in her lacy white jacket with her eyes and cheeks extraordinarily bright. Yet what strength she had too, sitting up against the pillows already and scrawling some hieroglyphics on a sheet of paper. Yes, Jack had been right. First and last she was a chemist still.

"Hi, Maybelle!" she cried, kissing me. Then, catching sight of Jack, "Darling, don't ever, *ever* go away again. I've missed you dreadfully."

After removing her notes, he set them near a jar on the bed table.

"Just my way of keeping amused," she said apologetically. "Oh, but it's beautifully quiet here. Maybelle, have you seen our son? Isn't he sweet?"

"He's adorable."

"Aren't his eyes and chin exactly like Jack's?"

"It's hard to tell yet, isn't it?"

"Not for a mother." Her yellow-green eyes flashed under their lashes. "But do you know Johnny was born with a skin rash? However, he's responding to my treatment miraculously." She winked toward the little jar close by.

As Jack looked baffled, I had to smile. Ah, it was fun for Fay and me to have a little secret like this, as women should.

Now I realized that she hadn't mentioned Giddy Moment, not once. Just as a cook in baking a new cake dismisses the previous one from her mind, Fay's new laboratory project had superseded the old. Such is life, I told myself. Here today and gone tomorrow.

"You know Bernard should be here any minute, dear, don't you?" Jack asked.

"Yes. Miss Barberry called." She waved toward a bower of orchids. "He's paved the way for his visit nicely, hasn't he?"

"Why wouldn't he?" His voice was low-pitched and calm. "He was knocked end over end by your success at Star-Drake today."

"I knew he would be," she said gaily. "He's bringing a contract for us to sign, isn't he?"

"Yes, dear." His calmness was even clearer than before. "You win."

"Of course." Her tone soared like a trumpet note, though her face was inscrutable under its tangle of black curls. Then, turning to me, "As partner with full and equal rights, are you ready to sell Giddy Moment to Amyrillis?"

My, but this had developed suddenly. "Well," I stalled, "how about you?"

Ignoring this question, she said, "Remember, you have a financial stake here as well as the time and effort you've spent. You'd be nuts not to jump at this chance to make a fat profit."

"Yes, Maybelle, you have every reason to think of yourself," Jack added, almost too enthusiastically.

"All right. Thinking of myself, I refuse to sign the contract. I've told Jack why."

"Darling, you're a saint," Fay cried, reaching up and hugging me. "This settles it.

"Settles what?" Jack asked, his jaw sagging.

"We're going to say no to Bernard tonight."

Rubbing his eyes, he demanded, "Are you two girls mad?"

"We happen to like being your competitors," Fay giggled. "Also we're not eager to see you out of a job."

"But I want you to sign those papers," he said bluntly. "Since Bernard is eager to buy Giddy Moment and your new formula too, go ahead! Unload them both promptly. Then maybe we can start a normal family life as we should."

"You act as though you *want* to resign from Amyrillis. What's gotten into you, dear?"

"Some good old-fashioned horse sense," he said, pounding his fist into his palm, "at long, long last." Then, beaming, "Incidentally, what's this *new* formula anyway? Since it's been such a cussed come-on . . ."

"It's a honey," Fay said, as footsteps approached in the hallway. "Wait till you hear . . ."

"Halloo-o-oo, good to see you folks," Mr. Huggin called out from the threshold. "Fay, don't tell me you're sitting up already." How grandfatherly he seemed stepping toward her, the eyes hazy behind their pince-nez, the features scholarly and finely chiseled.

Once he had kissed her and shaken hands with Jack and me, we settled ourselves in a circle. "Daughters are fine," he said, fingering a cigar and tucking it back into his pocket, "but there's splendor in a son."

What a contrast this speech seemed to the dancing, derby-hatted person I had seen earlier today. Did he know himself what he was going to do or say next?

"You girls put on a nice little lipstick promotion," he continued, eying us with approval. "I tell you this even if Jack won't." He gave his president a bleak look.

"My opinion of Giddy Moment hasn't changed, sir. It never will."

"I know." The chairman's eyes glinted unpleasantly. "Until tonight, we've been forced to accept such short-sightedness." Then, smiling toward Fay, "My dear, I realize that we let you down very badly six months ago. This was a grievous mistake."

"That's behind us," she sighed. "Besides, I've been so obsessed with a new formula . . ."

"That's another reason why I'm here talking with you."

"Is it?" she asked, with wonderful languor.

"Yes indeed. I'm ready to make a package deal purchase

on both formulas. In fact I've brought along a contract for signature." Reaching into his pocket, he brought out some papers. "See if these terms aren't very generous."

Jack sat nodding his approval.

"I see no complications," Fay said, after catching this signal and reading fine print in a flash. "If you insist, it may be possible to offer Giddy Moment side by side with Amyrillis products as of tomorrow morning." Then, turning to me, "Maybelle, one clause here would tie in your services, manufacturing and selling, while demand builds toward a height. Is this agreeable?"

"Well," I stammered, flattered to the skies. "Well, yes."

"Good." Mr. Huggin cleared his throat. "Incidentally, young Paul Lathrop will be fitting into this picture too. A half-hour ago, I managed to get his signature on a separate contract, setting him up as Jack's assistant. Once Paul winds up obligations at Star-Drake, he'll begin his new responsibilities."

"Gad," Jack groaned, pink in the face. "This too?"

"Paul's changed since you knew him," I said vehemently. "And he's engaged to marry the loveliest girl."

"He's good material," Fay agreed. "With proper guidance in the future, he's sure to zoom to success."

"I never make a mistake in picking top men," Mr. Huggin said happily. "That's so, isn't it, son?"

"Your record's *been* excellent, sir."

Ah, Paul will be lucky to work with Jack, I told myself. Then, as the disagreeable truth hit, No, this won't work out. It can't. Why have our hands been forced here? Poor Jack.

"Here's my pen," Mr. Huggin said, thrusting it toward Fay. "Sign on the top line, please, with Mrs. Dent directly below."

I hope we never regret this step, I thought a moment later, laboring with my most beautiful backhand script.

"Girls, let's plan to discuss details in a week or so." The

chairman rocked with pleasure. "Also, son, I hope this conversation has opened your mind as it should."

"Sorry, sir. As I told you before, this means my resignation. Now."

"Think it over tonight." Then, including Fay in a fond glance, "Over the years I've learned to depend on you both."

Jack had jumped to his feet. "It's no use. I'm through at Amyrillis."

"All right. But I promise you'll rue the day. Jobs like yours aren't easy to find, my boy."

After fighting to control herself, Fay wailed, "Jack, Jack, don't let this transaction wreck everything. Why did you talk us into it? Think of your future."

"Exactly." Squaring his shoulders, he turned and marched off.

"Stubbornness without limits brings ruination," the chairman wheezed, tucking the papers back into his pockets. Then, sailing off into another subject, "Incidentally, my dear, what's the second item in this package deal, a new facial cream?"

"Facial cream? It's anything but. My new formula is a beauty preparation dedicated to the buttocks."

"Buttocks?" His face was apoplectic.

"Yes, sir. There's a huge market waiting for Dydee-Eeze."

"Dydee-Eeze, you say? Oh dear God."

"Sir, can you name an ointment eliminating baby skin rash within *two minutes?*"

"Babies? Rash? What has this to do with Amyrillis?"

"Everything. Please ponder the possibilities of infant pharmaceuticals. Think of the booming birth rate."

"The devil with birth rates. Our market, as you know, has confined itself to products building female beauty. Would a . . . er . . . cream for the buttocks add to our stature, our reputation with top fashion stores from here to Los Angeles?" He buried his face in his hands.

"There you go again, sir," she chided. "Every time I come up with a winner, you throw cold water on it."

"Saints in heaven, Fay, one of these days you'll give me a stroke."

"One of these days," she corrected gaily, "you'll thank me from the bottom of your heart."

"Will I, my dear?" he asked, trying to smile. "Surely I hope so."

Later, when he was standing in the doorway, he remembered me at last. "Good-by, Mrs. Dent . . . er . . . I wonder . . . would you know where I might reach Alvin Perkin?" Then, as I shook my head, "It's possible that someone at Continentwide may be trying to contact him tonight. Yes, it's very possible . . . since Amyrillis owns Giddy Moment and could benefit from further news flashes, ha-ha-ha." After blowing a kiss, he smiled gently. "Thanks for the co-operation, girls. I appreciate it."

Well, it is midnight by now. Why did I never learn to write in an easy scrawl like Fay's? My, how painfully cramped I feel from head to toe.

Winding up, I realize that I should be thankful for all that we have achieved. Yet this is difficult, with Jack hurt as he has been, and with no sign of a light still, next door.

Dear Alvin. Alvin dear, have pleasant dreams wherever you are. What are business reversals or Trendex ratings compared to love, companionship and *us*? Here's to a bigger, better and more serene tomorrow!

Chapter 20

Dent Journal . . .

Friday, January 13, 1961

HAVING written the above date, I realize that it is an extremely unlucky one. Others in the future may try to avoid Friday the thirteenth, black cats, ladders and sidewalk cracks, but not me. Because now more than ever I believe that we forge our own destinies through our decisions and actions. Or, as Alvin might say, quoting a favorite philosopher, "We are the outcome of what we do and what we eat."

But why bring up the word "eat" *tonight*, reminding me that none of us had our usual late-evening snack? Tomorrow, somehow, I must get a few goodies together. Yes, cross my heart, this is a promise!

Regardless, dear journal, let us get back to the subject at hand. Surely my making entries here on *two successive nights* is not a matter of chance. Rather, it must be the consequence of accumulated steam again finding release. It is satisfying to see that old lazy patterns can be broken through a combination of circumstances, isn't it?

Anyhow, this *second* day of our Giddy Moment promotion has forced me to laugh, cry, rub my eyes with wonder and shock. It has tossed me end over end like a child caught in mountainous surf. Yet throughout this drama, I have felt exhilaration building steadily. Truly I am glad to have lived at capacity with absolutely no sense of fear.

I might feel less keyed up than I do if Pluto, the dope, hadn't wakened me at dawn. Evidently he had heard cats screeching or had experienced a horrid nightmare. In any case, once he began to bark, I hurried him to the kitchen so that Nina might sleep.

After I had started to drink a second cup of coffee, I heard a tap-tap at the window. As Pluto went into a fit of yelping, I discovered Alvin Perkin there, smiling broadly.

Oh, but I was in a tizzy of embarrassment, with my face unwashed and my hair in curlers. Resisting the urge to dive under the table, I sat frozen.

"Let me come in," he mouthed, pointing toward the door.

"We're not ready for visitors," I scolded, obeying instructions. "Just look at me."

Instead of commenting on my appearance, he took a long appreciative sniff. "Fresh coffee. Mm-m-mm." Stepping forward, he was no dreamboat himself, needing a shave and in a rumpled state.

"I'm afraid Emily Post wouldn't approve," I said, glancing at my negligee.

"A pox on Emily. I need to talk to you."

Soon he was settled, with elbows resting on our red checked tablecloth. From all appearances we might have been married for years.

"Good," he cried, after taking a gulp from his cup. "Say, how about a slice of your famous oatmeal bread?"

"Sorry. With Giddy Moment and all, I haven't fussed with baking."

His disappointment was pitiful. "O.K. I'll settle for toast with some of that special cherry jam."

"Oh dear, we finished the last jar a week ago."

"No woman should let her domestic talents go to blazes, damn it. Well, maybe there's more coffee here at least."

Who says that the way to a man's heart isn't through his

stomach? I wondered. But oh dear, I'm not making much progress lately. And I've never looked more sloppy or ugly.

After I had filled his cup, Alvin said suddenly, "I'm here to celebrate really. Listen to this, Maybelle. Fifteen minutes ago I was reinstated by Continentwide."

"They phoned already?"

"You bet. Pleaded for me to forgive previous hotheaded action. So tomorrow . . . *Perk Predicts* will return to the air as usual."

I couldn't help gloating. "So Bernard got busy once he bought out Giddy Moment."

"Sure. Contacted my bosses immediately, promising the sky in advertising appropriations. He urged rushing through a follow-up plug today, but shortage of time made this impossible."

"If anything interesting occurs at Star-Drake, I'll report it to you."

"I'm sure you will . . . How soon will full-strength Giddy Moment stock go on sale?"

"About noontime, I believe."

"I'll come by to see the excitement."

"Do, dear. And this time don't rush right in and out again."

"This time I won't," he agreed, his lightish blue eyes shining. "Especially if you put on the show I expect."

"You're thinking only of yourself and your program," I scolded. Then, after he nodded wryly, "Go away. *Go away.* I can't bear you."

"Let me finish my coffee at least. Lord, when you explode this way with no warning, you're like Fay."

"Go away," I repeated.

"Perhaps you'd feel better if I explained my absence last night, eh?" Then, as I tried to keep my expression impassive, "Bill and I made the rounds in Greenwich Village — had a stupendous time."

"Who's Bill?" My, it was a relief to hear that he had been on a bachelor party.

"He's the engineer handling all mechanics of *Perk Predicts* transmission. We were celebrating our hunch that I'd be back on the air promptly. And, well . . ."

Now what was he trying to tell me?

"It's a little complicated maybe. But you remember how suddenly I was cut off months ago, after that lapse into profanity? Both Bill and I were boiling sore over the situation, so . . ."

"So what?" I shook with irritation.

"So if a situation like this should arise again . . . well . . . instead of obeying executive instructions . . ." He was chuckling too hard to continue.

"Please, Alvin . . ."

"Well, Bill has promised to be a little deaf, stupid and bungling. He's got a crazy darn sense of humor anyway."

"Lord, I wouldn't want to be in the radio business."

"It's not so bad," he laughed as he got to his feet. "Cheerio and thanks for breakfast. I'll see you later — about noontime, to be exact." He hurried off without once looking behind him.

Cold self-centered man. If he had any affection, he certainly hadn't shown it.

Now Nina appeared, dressed in school clothes and laden with books. "Where's my breakfast, Mother?" Then, observing the unwashed dishes, "Don't tell me Alvin was here."

"He was. And look at me."

"For Pete's sake, why did you entertain him in curlers?" Then, as I bit my lip, "No matter. But this household is deteriorating sadly lately."

While she was fussing with her notebook, I prepared fruit juice, eggs and toast. "Enjoy these as energy-builders, dear."

"O.K.," she cried, attacking her plate with gusto. "Say,

you're planning to fix steak for Larry's dinner tonight, aren't you, with plenty of onions? I'm dead sick of delicatessen food, honestly."

By the time she had finished and was hurrying into her coat, we heard the wail of fire sirens. "Someone must be in severe trouble," I said, almost jumping out of my mules.

"No. They must be starting to celebrate the Arcturus Award," she said, reaching for her books. "How juvenile." Then, exuberantly, "Wow, I hope school is dismissed early. Then I can do *exactly as I please.*"

There she was again, a grown woman one minute and a teen-ager the next. "Good luck," I cried, following at her heels. "Keep that wool scarf tightly about your throat. There's no need to ask for sniffles."

Pausing in the vestibule, she couldn't have been more annoyed. "Mother, I'm eighteen years old and married, though you never like to admit it." Then, trying to sweeten this remark, "Take care of yourself and be good."

After I had given the kitchen a lick and a polish, I hustled up to my bedroom. I'd better begin to think of my duties at Star-Drake today, I thought. Probably Madge Reilly spent the night there, supervising the move of Amyrillis stock. With her line and Giddy Moment intermingled, we're sure to be busier than ever before.

While I showered, dressed and took pains to make my bed, the fire sirens grew deafening. This is a proud moment for us Arlingtonites, I told myself. Newspapers, radio and TV are sure to make us famous within the next twenty-four hours. Horace Baxter will see to that.

Yet, in my pleasure, I couldn't help wishing that I had been a more hard-working, conscientious citizen. I had given many hours to activities such as Community Chest, Child Guidance and the Choral Group. But what were these compared to the Baxter family's incessant dedication? Or to the civic interest and generosity demonstrated by Larry's father, president of Star-Drake?

My respect for Stanley Drake rose as I entered his store a few minutes later. What expense and effort he had spent here on the main floor! Each column now carried a waving blue streamer with its gold enscrolled message: *Congratulations, Arlington, on the Arcturus Award.*

All walls were hidden by a huge photographic panorama emphasizing our town's innumerable organizations: Girl Scouts, Boy Scouts, Rotary, Chamber of Commerce, Health and Visiting-Nurse Service. In a balcony on the left, the American Legion band, in brilliant uniform, was already testing its wind and percussion instruments. Dum de dum . . . dee dum dee.

How I wished that Alvin could see this, could be describing it this minute on his program. What a build-up he would give to the noontime festivities ahead too, listing innumerable celebrities with pithy comments on each, repeating high points of the invocations, speeches and distinguished musical repertoire. Never mind, tomorrow his thunder would be doubly strong — a credit to him, to Continentwide and to fellow citizens.

Approaching the cosmetic department with its booths of Giddy Moment, I tingled with happiness. What warmth, what familiarity and satisfaction it carried after yesterday's success. Now again we'd serve the public with humility, with talent, offering our supreme best.

As expected, Amyrillis products had been moved next to our space, handsome jars and bottles pyramiding in the midst of Giddy Moment. While Madge Reilly and Anna emptied a last truck of Aphid-Milk Lotion, the buying staff stood conferring close by. My, once Mr. Huggin got his contracts signed, he'd moved fast.

"Now, Miss Baxter, I want no additional counter displays,"

Madge was saying firmly. "We won't have room for them once customers come." Ah, but she was enjoying increased responsibility and her queen-bee role.

It was easy to see that Anna welcomed instructions. Also that her mind kept fluttering from her work. Again and again she kept stealing a glance at Paul Lathrop from under her long lashes. Setting some jars into place, she smiled toward her ring. At this rate she wouldn't last long in a business career.

"Good morning, Mrs. Dent," Madge hollered, catching sight of me. "It's lucky I didn't count on your back and arms this morning. We had enough confusions anyways." Her Irish grin was anything but flattering.

"Hello," Anna said, her eyes glowing a welcome from under the honey-colored coiffure. "Congratulations on selling out to Amyrillis." Then, with a joyous glance toward the buyer, "Isn't Paul's new job going to be divine?"

"Smartest move Mr. Huggin ever made!" Madge cried. "Though it took more than a little persuasion." Reaching for a tube of Giddy Moment, she held it fondly. "Believe me, we'll haul in a mint today." Unrolling the lipstick, she smeared it on her mouth.

"I wouldn't . . . not just yet," I warned.

"Ho . . . one of the first lessons we teach demonstrators is to model our products effectively."

"But I'm still in charge here."

"Are you?" Her tone was ugly. "One phone call will settle this pronto . . . and you know it."

Don't waste breath arguing, I told myself. With another customer jam-up today, what man can get close?

"Anna, try some of this lipstick too," Miss Reilly said. "It feels delightful." Though she had begun to throb, her voice sailed out in a strong contralto.

After a questioning look toward me, Miss Baxter shrugged her shoulders and obeyed.

"Now, Mrs. Dent, don't be a pantywaist," Madge insisted, thrusting a tube into my face. "I tell you it's scrumptious . . . rea-aa-al-ll-ly." The last of her words were lost in the clang of store opening.

The next hours, as I remember them, were like the 1938 hurricane all over again. What confusion, what a downpour of flaying arms, voices, anger, violence and wind. Meantime, we three women kept working in unison like machines, getting additional clerks, cashiers, store policemen, more counter space, innumerable truckloads of new stock.

Now and again I noticed that Anna and Madge were as ebullient as they were efficient.I mean even on the stage, they couldn't have portrayed beautiful-womanhood-surviving-a-storm more gloriously. While customers dived toward them screaming, "Miss, miss, I was next, miss," they smiled unfailingly. Also, whenever they observed a man in the distance, they seemed to struggle to catch his eye. Then, as he went on his way behind the tidal wave of women, they'd ogle the next overcoated passer-by.

I accepted all this stoically until we were forced to begin selling full-strength Giddy Moment. Yet again, I realized that no unexpected drama would develop. No man could come within thirty yards of us still. And in this mob, what customer would pause to apply her purchase to her lips?

Just as I was nicely reassured, I saw Madge glance at herself in the mirror. After reaching for the nearest lipstick, she applied it in a flash. You're a severe trial today, I thought.

Having beautified herself, she nudged Anna. "Freshen your face, honey. It won't hurt this crowd to wait a minute."

Ah me, both of them were wearing the real McCoy by now. What next?

During the following hour, everything went along as it should. We're cozy as a bug in a rug, I thought. Idle worries are a waste of time and energy.

Now a thundering roll of drums overhead was highlighted by trumpet blasts. Next Stanley Drake's voice rang through the loudspeaker system. "Ladies and gentlemen, your attention, please . . .

"Our distinguished governor, senators and other guests are about to arrive here in celebration of the Arcturus Award. Therefore it is necessary to clear the main aisle immediately for their entrance. We ask your co-operation in complying with instructions from our store policemen."

"Murder, this would happen at our noontime peak," Madge squawked, as customers were shooed off like sheep. "Damn. Whoever expected a wedding aisle to be formed here right under our chins. When I report this nonsense to Bernard Huggin, he'll explode."

Lawks, I thought, observing row upon row of women we had served recently. You'd think they were lined up for a St. Patrick's Day parade. With time on their hands and important men approaching, they're sure to start primping like mad.

"Who says we're not ha-cha saleswomen, honey?" Madge asked Anna. "I've counted fifty dames in the pile-up there, putting Giddy Moment on their lips."

"Oh, Fay, Fay, Fay," I groaned. "You should be here now. I need your quick brain."

As the band burst into a rip-roaring medley of "God Bless America," the column of dignitaries came marching forward. Of course our mayor and the governor led the way in their morning clothes, attention and posture committed to the ceremony at hand. (Joe dear, if you were alive, you'd be here too, I thought, adding stature to Arlington's and the Dent family's reputation. Then, with a little wince, I thought, And I'd be home where I know I belong.)

If the senators and other guests had followed the same eyes-front routine, all might have gone well. Instead, confronted with a huddle of goggle-eyed females on either side, they couldn't resist smiling toward them gallantly. A moment before, they had been goose-stepping along in rhythm. Now they wavered, yelped, capered, made kissing gestures and tossed their Homburgs into the air.

At heart men remain little boys, I thought. Dressed in their best clothes or not, the imp comes cavorting out every time.

Meanwhile, far worse bedlam was taking place behind the roped-off area. Customers threw up their arms, shouting and wrestling with each other. Next, stylishly outfitted matrons came bounding over the stanchions or wriggling out from under at amazing speed.

Those who had not been smitten by the appearance of the men stood swaying where they were, all of them bearing signs of damage — swelling eyes, battered noses, scratched cheeks. Yet this sisterhood carried an air of martyrdom too in their glazed expressions and smiles of astonishment.

Somehow the contrast between these "onlookers" and the milling "doers" reminded me of the relay races Nina and her chums played when they were Brownies. While some members of the team waited patiently, others jumped through a sequence of hurdles, wriggled through a carton, did a back-somersault or spun about in a double circle. As the game progressed, screams, shouts and excitement rose to a deafening crescendo.

Veering from this thought, but rooted in my tracks, I found myself quipping, Which women are the ones wearing Giddy Moment today? Single them out and count them, friends. Then, wagging my finger, No. No. No, Maybelle. This is no time for levity. In fact, you'd better start running for your life.

Overhead the music had continued to boom. Now, instead of a neat pairing off into couples, each morning-coated man became surrounded by a buzzing hive of women. Again and again shrill voices rose and fell. "Get away. I got him first" — "Now it's my turn, selfish." Oh, but I felt sorry for the male prizes as they were clutched, shaken and almost killed with endearments.

As store policemen and men executives rushed to the rescue, they received the same treatment. As they'd approach with head thrown back, intent on action, they succumbed one by one. The more I watched, the more I was sure that my eyes would burst from my head.

Mercifully, the mayor had been standing until now with his back toward this drama. Having discovered Anna in the arms of a senator, he screamed, "God in Heaven, child, have you gone crazy?" Then, turning in a semicircle, he cried, "Help here, somebody!"

"Ah, ducky doodle," a mink-hatted dowager squealed, catching his eye and consuming him like an avalanche. "Where have you been all my life?"

"Sorry, Horace," I whispered. "As Joe's old friend, you deserve better than this."

Now Mrs. Stevens, the assistant buyer, approached with hair on end and cheeks livid. "Mrs. Dent! Mrs. Dent! Mrs. Dent! *What* is going on here? Paul Lathrop started off for some help but got entangled with a dozen women. There's not an able-bodied man about anywhere. They're all . . . all . . ."

"I know," I said helplessly.

"We've got to call the police. Imagine something like this happening after all my years at Star-Drake."

"Not the police," I moaned. Then, looking about desperately, "Oh, Alvin, Alvin, where are you?"

Then, beautiful moment, I saw him approaching. There he was in an old horse blanket of a coat, his eyes eager and twice their usual size. But a second later he became surrounded by a cluster of women.

"No, ladies, no," I cried, rushing to the rescue. "Remember your manners, please." Then, to Alvin, "Shut your eyes tight, dear, and put your hand in mine."

But this strategy did not succeed too well. Consequently, until the first group of policemen arrived, Alvin and I continued to struggle as best we could. "Beware," I said at one point. "This poor soul has trench mouth."

"No, ladies . . . leprosy!" he yelled, remembering to keep his eyes screwed together and thus blessedly rational still. "It's virulent . . . contagious . . . So lay off, girls."

"Who cares, Red? You're cute."

"Lay off, I say. Lay off. Maybelle, Maybelle, for Pete's sake get me out of here."

At last a phalanx of blue-uniformed men came marching toward us with billy-sticks in hand. Ah, but they personified the best in towering, clean-cut masculinity. American men have a carriage and strength which is the best in the entire world, I thought. Then, as the group was mowed down and devoured by a horde of women, *Here goes Nassau County's finest down the drain. My, but Giddy Moment deserves credit. Against it, billy-sticks and law and order don't stand a ghost of a chance, do they?*

Within the next half-hour, precinct after precinct had to be called, until Star-Drake's main floor was literally blue with policemen. As sirens kept screaming from the Boulevard and whistles kept blowing, the sound of male voices close by grew to thunderous volume. "Begorra, this dame's a double-handful . . . Come on, sister, stop clawing. You're under arrest for assault and battery."

I could catch only fragments like this, since I kept fighting to protect Alvin. Perhaps this situation was good, though, because it kept my attention glued on one objective, with no sensation of panic or timidity. Ah, but I felt warm with the glow of being needed, just as a mother does when she shields her child from danger, physical maiming or possible death.

Darling Alvin, if an inch of your skin is scratched, I thought,

I'll never, never forgive myself. Now more than ever I know I love you, love you.

While I was repeating this speech to myself for the twentieth time, two enormous police officers appeared. "Come along, ma'am," they said, each grabbing an arm. "And no fuss neither. You're number one girl responsible for this riot, ain't you?"

"Greetings and thank fortune," I cried, with tears of relief. "But gentlemen, please protect Mr. Perkin first. He's had a frightful time."

By now, of course, Alvin had opened his eyes. Though he looked a little harried and sheepish, his amusement was very clear. "Has the typhoon passed? Good."

"The typhoon's just beginning," one of the officers said, nodding toward Star-Drake's front entrance. "First with a ride in the patrol wagon. Then with a session at headquarters. Come along, ma'am." He tugged my arm.

"But I can't leave Alvin," I cried. "He needs me."

"Does he now? Ho . . . there's the laugh of the week. Like a bang on the boobkus he needs you."

"Excuse me," I said in my best manner. "You're extremely rude, my good man. And I don't care for it."

"Don't you, eh? Well, princess, that's going to cause me real lack of sleep. Right now, though, suppose you cut out the lip and march along to headquarters."

"Very well," I said, delivering a look which suggested that he should wash with better care about the tongue, ears and nose. "I shall be delighted to comply. But I would like Mr. Perkin to come with me." Then, when this request was met bleakly, "Besides, both he and I know Captain Timothy O'Rourke as a good Arlington friend and neighbor."

"Do you so, princess? That's interesting. Yeah . . . real . . ." Then, catching himself and growing more respectful, "O.K. Instead of the patrol routine today, we'll use my car.

A-number-one service and nothing but the best for friends of the captain. That's me."

"Thank you, my good man."

"I don't know," Alvin said, with a grin which seemed unbearable. "The paddy-wagon might be nicer in a pinch. It's at least a week since you rode in one, Maybelle, isn't it?"

"Stop, you dope," I whispered.

"So you're an old offender, sister, eh?" the officer asked, clamping my arm tighter as he yanked me forward. "And this accounts for close acquaintance with the captain? Well, we'll see that you and your gentleman friend here get special treatment." He bowed gallantly. "No shenanigans, now, either of you . . . or by gum, you'll regret it."

Once we had settled ourselves in his ultramarine-colored car, we sailed down the Boulevard with sirens wailing. "How does this trip compare with previous ones, Maybelle?" Alvin asked loudly, taking my hand and squeezing it. Then, when I was too upset to answer, "Does this roadway seem rockier than usual?"

"Clown," I hissed.

"Old offender," the officer muttered, keeping a wary eye on me.

"Now, of course," Alvin continued, "there'll be the problem again of caring for your brood of children . . . seeing they're fed and aired properly. But since the eldest is eleven, she can handle the baby . . ."

"Comedian . . ."

"Whether little Doreen can cope with his rickets is something else again," he added, looking lugubrious. "But we can be sure that she'll *try*."

The officer began to show concern.

"Oh dear," I cried, slapping at Alvin. "Why are you this way? You try me terribly."

"Do I?"

"Where's your husband, ma'am?" Having ignored this interchange, our man's tone was gentle. "Maybe we can phone him from headquarters."

"I'm afraid we can't. You see I'm a widow."

"Left with all those children to raise by yourself? Why didn't you say so before? Tell me, why would a fine woman with a grand fine family get into this hocus-pocus?"

"I'll tell you why," Alvin said quickly. "Mrs. Dent needed to buy milk, bread and bowls of Pablum beyond number. Officer, what would you do if eight little faces welcomed you home night after night, crying, 'I'm hungry, Daddy dear. I'm hungry'?"

"I wouldn't start no Star-Drake riot, I promise you."

"But are you convinced that this woman did start a riot? Can't you *see* that she's good, upstanding, dutiful? I've been joking, of course, about previous visits to headquarters."

As the officer turned toward me, I couldn't help smiling.

"You're O.K., I guess," he said after deliberation. "Remind me of my Mrs. in a way, though she's plumper and darker-complected, maybe." By now we had swung into a circular driveway before a broad brick building. "I'll deliver you and let the captain carry on from here." Then, patting my knee, "Good luck, ma'am. And get home fast to those kiddies. Believe me, no eleven-year-old should try to handle rickets herself, takes a *mother*."

"Thanks, Officer —"

"Murphy, ma'am."

"Thanks, Officer Murphy."

"And good luck again, ma'am."

Once Alvin and I were in the police station, we stood with hands entwined. "Easy, Maybelle," he whispered. "We're doing fine so far, aren't we?"

"I'm not sure, loaded with eight children and rickets, thanks to you."

"Once you feed baby some Pablum, he'll *thrive*," Alvin quipped. "Or so I tell my listeners, day after day."

"Darn you and your listeners!"

After Captain O'Rourke had come forward and greeted us, he exclaimed, "Mrs. Dent, you're the last person I expected to find here. At this rate every blueblood in the county . . ."

Though it was embarrassing to be where I was, it was interesting too. I mean, I had never guessed that "headquarters" would be painted olive green, with endless clanging doors, steel bars, a big impressive-looking circular booth and the formality of an inquisition. Handsome men in uniform kept tramping back and forth, while countless women kept squealing, "Please, Officer, get me out *quickly*. And promise not to breathe a word to my husband."

"Pomp and ceremony," Alvin said, observing all this with no sympathy. I could see that he was thinking in terms of tomorrow's radio program, with little attention to me.

You're heartless, I thought. But anyhow, it's good to have you here. Oh, Alvin, Alvin . . .

Finally, after a long interrogative session, Captain O'Rourke asked, "Mrs. Dent, have you any statement to make?"

"Yes indeed. You may write it in your book if you wish." Ah, but I couldn't help swaying with delight at his interest. "I don't regret failures . . . not as long as I have the faith and the courage to do *whatever* is required. This way and *only* this way can a man or woman *really find himself*."

"That's nice," he said kindly. "But I don't get it."

"Don't you? Then perhaps we should put it this way. Regardless of reverses, I've done my very, very best."

"Well that's great, isn't it?" he asked, winking at Alvin and scratching his head. "Tell me . . . are you subject to dizzy spells sometimes?"

Reaching for my hands again, Alvin held them in both of his. There was a new brooding, protective light in his eyes. It was as though he was calming a confused child and despairing for it too. Ah me, why had my statement affected him this way?

"Any dizzy spells?" the captain repeated.

"Not lately . . . though Dr. Baxter says . . ."

He sighed with relief. "So you've been under a doctor's care, have you?"

"Oh yes."

"Under the circumstances, get out of here fast." Then, turning to Alvin, "You'll make sure she gets home safely, will you?"

"Sure."

It is well that Captain O'Rourke misfigured the situation as he did. Yet it is a fact that since Fay took to her bed last November, I haven't had a single dizzy spell. No . . . not one.

Still, I suppose it might be natural for a police officer to question the sincerity of one's convictions, especially when they were expressed under the circumstances today.

But I was less amazed by the captain's reactions than I was by Alvin's. Who would have thought that he would show such concern — urging me to watch my nerves, to forget recent happenings, to try to regain serenity and strength. (Aren't those the exact same words which he delivered to his mother during her last days? And isn't this ridiculous, when I feel better, happier and more sure of myself than ever before?)

Again, tonight, Alvin's solitude was pathetically clear in our get-together with Nina and Larry. At the time, we had just finished discussing recent developments among the Hicks — the fact that Fay and the baby are in excellent health; that Jack has become chairman of Amyrillis now the Giddy Moment boomerang has forced Mr. Huggin's resignation. Finally, I said from my place on the sofa, "Thank goodness Jack *won* after all. Fay must feel this way too. Toward the end of the battle she showed she had learned her lesson. So live our chums happily forever after."

"Maybe so," Nina said, "but they phoned their news at an inconvenient time. After this trying day, wouldn't you expect more consideration?"

"But dear . . . Fay and Jack know that I love them."

"Suppose they do, Mother. Does this help your position and mine at the moment?" Then, bitterly, "The joke of Arlington, that's us."

"Cut it out," Larry said, while Alvin nodded approval, "Haven't we given your mother a hard enough time already?"

"But why did she keep all her activities so secret?"

"Remember that everyone is entitled to interests of her own," I said resolutely.

"Ho . . . I repeat, we're a laughingstock. And we'll be more of one tomorrow, once Alvin gets to his microphone. That's correct, isn't it, Mr. Perk Predicts?"

He flushed.

"You do plan to broadcast our disgrace through forty-eight states, don't you?"

Ah, but I sat torn for Nina and for him.

"It's a marvelous story, I'll admit, sir. Maybelle Dent, Arlington housewife, proves that idle hands get into mischief unfailingly. After opening a twentieth-century Pandora's box, she casts its evils upon the world."

"I didn't. I didn't. I was trying to bring everyone more happiness."

She waved for silence. "So back to our story, friends." Her voice aped Alvin's so closely that I winced. "In slamming the box shut, Mrs. Dent imprisoned one unique bit of goodness — hope. Yes, ladies and gentlemen, h-o-p-e, hope. Listen tomorrow as usual to the *Trials of Maybelle*. Will she hold her head high in the midst of adversity? Or will the last feeble ray of spirit be extinguished?"

Alvin was trembling with anger. "Stop, Nina. You've been your mother's key trial for years — you're smart enough to know it." After taking a long breath, he lowered his voice. "I came here tonight to tell you something. Now you've spoken your piece, perhaps you'll listen to mine."

"O.K.," she said, after glancing at Larry.

"I'll admit that I planned to feature Giddy Moment on my program tomorrow . . . and to mention your mother's name. But after what she's been through today, I find I can't."

"Praise the Lord."

"No, Alvin, no!" I cried, jumping to my feet. "Your future depends on Giddy Moment. You've spent a year working toward tomorrow's big world-shaking blast. If you fail to deliver it, you'll never forgive yourself or me."

"Talk your head off, but I won't weaken."

"You'd better not weaken," Nina warned. "I know how you've been bulldozing my mother. Today when I read her journal it was very clear."

Now indeed my heart hit bottom.

"She's innocent and easily led, isn't she, expecting the best always? Until she met you and Fay, no one was ever more protected."

"That's right," he said overloudly. "I won't deny it."

"Also she hit her head on the ice a year ago, didn't she? If you imagine she's been right since then, I'll tell you she hasn't been. Can't you see the change yourself?"

"That's enough, Nina," I interrupted. "I've been fine for months."

"Have you?" Her eyes darkened. "Oh dear. Forgive me, Mother . . . but well . . . look . . . Why did you take Alvin's advances so seriously? Every line written these past months rings with love for him."

"Shush," Larry said. "Now you've gone too far."

"I love Alvin," I sighed. "Yes, I do."

"I know. I know. That's exactly what I'll never forgive."
Then, facing him, "Bah . . . a justice-of-the-peace ceremony
. . . a honeymoon in Spain. Sir, you should be tarred and
feathered."

"Should I?" He gave the oddest smile. "Might raise hob with
my supersensitive skin . . . It so happens that I prefer Spain
to Bermuda — much less plebeian." Then, reaching into his
pocket, "That's why I keep a couple of plane tickets handy."

Next I was in his arms with my head buried against his
chest.

But of course this didn't settle our problems, because I knew
he must proceed with his Giddy Moment blast tomorrow.
After arguing and getting nowhere, I asked myself, If Fay were
in this situation, what tack would she take? She'd look for an
Achilles heel, wouldn't she, and hit it dead center? All right,
Maybelle, review facts carefully. Use the good head you've developed lately.

Then, quick as a flash, I heard myself saying, "All of us here
feel strongly about freedom of speech, don't we?"

The hush that followed was beyond all expectation. Making
the most of it, I raised my voice. "What will happen to this
country if a man like Horace Baxter sets himself up as a censor?
All of us know that no newspapers will carry any mention of
Giddy Moment tomorrow. Now please answer this question.
Shall we sit here protecting our own petty interests, with vital
civil rights at stake?"

As Alvin gave me a look of astonishment mixed with admiration, Nina cried, "My oh my, Mother. Where did you get such
knowledge?"

"From listening to your social-study reports, dear. You've
taught me more than you guessed."

"No one can argue with freedom," Larry said with dignity,
"but we can with license. Have you considered the embarrassment this will cause us?"

"Whatever stir Alvin makes tomorrow will blow over in time. Besides, it won't hurt people to laugh."

"Laugh?" Nina winced.

"Are you sure that this will affect us so deeply?"

"Of course."

Ah, but my stubbornness surprised me as I asked, "Did you condemn me as you read my journal?"

"No. I felt sorry for you."

This was the very last answer I had expected.

"Stop this chatter," Alvin said, patting my hand. "I can always find a radio job."

"No. No. Nothing but the biggest and best will ever satisfy you. We both know it."

"You're unreasonable, Mother," Nina cried, stamping her foot. "If Alvin dares to mention your name and Giddy Moment on *Perk Predicts* tomorrow, I'll . . . I'll insist on publication of your journal."

"I wouldn't like that, dear. All diaries are extremely private."

"But you're a respectable woman. We want the world to know it."

"Through publication of my journal? . . . Oh, you can't be serious." Yet I could see a newsstand teeming with periodicals and streamers shouting my name: *Read Maybelle Dent's own true-life story complete in this issue.* Next I pictured a bookstore window heaped with volumes carrying my signature . . . If printing and circulating this chronicle would ensure Alvin's future, did I have any right to say no?

"I *am* serious," she insisted. "Besides, what you wrote seemed very interesting."

Alvin had heard more than enough. "For Pete's sake, you two, come to the point," he commanded. "If I'm going to do justice to this story tomorrow, I've got to get busy with the script." Throwing back his head in radio announcer fashion, he rat-tat-tatted, "Our press and our citizenry may be throttled by self-elected do-gooders. Regardless, *Perk Predicts* . . ."

"I've been weighing that censorship angle," Larry said solemnly. "The four of us could perform an important service if we took a stand together."

"Huzzas," Alvin mocked. Then, turning to Nina and me, "How about it, girls?"

"Yes." Our voices soared out together.

"Oh, you dolls."